Totally Bound Publishing books by Karin Baine

Single Books
It Could've Been a Wonderful Life

IT COULD'VE BEEN A WONDERFUL LIFE

KARIN BAINE

It Could've Been a Wonderful Life
ISBN # 978-1-83943-928-5
©Copyright Karin Baine 2020
Cover Art by Louisa Maggio ©Copyright November 2020
Interior text design by Claire Siemaszkiewicz
Totally Bound Publishing

IT COULD'VE BEEN A WONDERFUL LIFE

Dedication

For George, my Guardian Angel xx

Chapter One

"No man is a failure who has friends."

Annie Marlowe's sneeze shot through her entire body as the parting words from Guardian Angel Clarence blazed across the screen.

"Pff-ft. What does that say about me, eh, George Bailey?" Annie asked her tufty-haired, toffee-coloured guinea pig named after her favourite movie character. He was the only one she had to talk to, and even that was a one-way conversation, since his defective squeak made him sound like a chewed dog toy.

He snuffled his little nose at the bars of his cage, looking for food, when he heard her opening the box of leftover pastries that Sam, her landlord, had brought her. There were some advantages to living above a coffee shop, even if moving there from her family home of over thirty years had felt like a step back at the time.

Fletchers Café was nestled on the corner of a row of shops that otherwise looked only fit for demolition. Faded advertising signs, cracked windows and graffiti-covered shutters told the story of the crisis-hit local economy. In contrast, the French-style bistro was an oasis of luxury for those busy office workers and people who wanted to catch up over a coffee that didn't come from a jar. Fletchers was a beacon of hope for future retail development and regeneration of the area.

Even Annie found some comfort there. The aroma of fresh bread and cakes baking in the oven reminded her of her mother, before that bastard cancer had got hold of her. Reliving those memories of her baking up a storm in the kitchen on a Sunday afternoon was as close as she could get to her mother now that she was gone forever.

Sam also kept her fed during the times she couldn't afford to go grocery shopping...*like now.*

"I should just paint a giant L for 'loser' on my forehead," she muttered as she took a bite of a *pain au chocolat.* The buttery layers melted with the chocolate filling on her tongue, every nibble dispensing a trail of flaky crumbs down her front.

George Bailey gave an asthmatic wheeze in agreement before giving a little popcorn kick and scooting sawdust over her bedroom floor. Annie didn't bother to sweep it up. There'd be a bigger pile to clean up by morning and it wasn't as though she was expecting any visitors.

She tossed another used tissue onto the growing collection littering the floor along with her clothes. The hard-worn beige carpet was almost completely covered with her mess, but it gave her a sense of ownership in a place she didn't yet think of as home. The magnolia décor was functional, but there was nothing exciting about it—kind of like her life at present. She needed to put her own stamp on the place. If she had the money or motivation, she'd redecorate—preferably with something far removed from her mother's predilection towards floral prints. Her festive spirit being in short supply this year, she hadn't even managed to put up her Christmas decorations.

Sitting there in her fleecy, gingerbread-man onesie, stuffing herself and bawling along to *It's a Wonderful Life*, she was the poster girl for loneliness.

She sneezed again and sprayed her pyjamas with a fine mist of chocolate saliva and crumbs. *Nice.*

"And you wonder why you can't keep a man? You're so classy." She yanked another tissue from the box on her nightstand. *Great.* Not only had she been dumped and was grieving for her mother, now she had a cold to contend with too.

Annie collapsed back onto the bed as tears threatened once more. She pulled the crocheted blue-and-pink blanket she'd kept from her mother's bed around her like a woolly cocoon. Her throat was burning with a sorrow she couldn't seem to shake off.

In a nutshell, her life was shit. Watching a film highlighting the value of friends and family when she had neither hadn't been the best idea, especially at a time when her mood was already dragging itself by the fingertips across the floor. It merely served as a reminder of how much she'd lost and how little she'd really accomplished with her own life.

Weary of the fight, she closed her eyes. With any luck, her blocked sinuses would suffocate her in her sleep and put her out of this misery.

* * * *

The December sky was so black that it was difficult to see the rain until the car headlights illuminated the kamikaze rain drops attempting to dodge discovery and soaking everything in their path.

"Don't you think you should slow down?" Flame flipped down the visor mirror on the passenger side of the Lamborghini and painted another coat of scarlet gloss across her lips.

David Reece cast a sideways glance at his date, who was now taking pouting selfies. It had been fun to date the darling of the tabloids for a minute, but there really wasn't anything behind that stage-managed façade. He didn't even know her real name, for goodness' sake. It was doubtful she did either, with her every move scripted for the cameras.

"We want to make an entrance, don't we? I thought that's what this was all about—grabbing headlines."

"Is that really all you think there is between us?" The concern he detected in her voice suggested that she might actually care about him. *Impossible.* No one did.

"Would it matter? I thought we were both only in this for the publicity? You get to pretend you've tamed the playboy millionaire and I get to boost my toy shop empire when customers believe they'll run into their idol shopping for stuffed animals." He wasn't in this charade of a relationship for anything else. Well, the sex had been good…when they'd had it.

"I need this, David."

The soft, unconfident voice sounded so unlike her. *Does she really think we're still in a relationship?* Since his divorce three years before, he hadn't been in the market for another long-term commitment. He was happy with his bachelor life. It was much less painful than being married to someone who'd loved his money more than him.

"Flame, this was only ever supposed to have been a bit of fun, and it was in the beginning, before we knew the press were interested. Now everything is a business transaction. There's no spontaneity, no intimacy anymore. We don't even see each other now, outside of these high-profile functions." These days, their simple want of each other's company had been traded for photo ops and press exposure. Suddenly it was no longer enough to keep him satisfied.

"Are you saying you want to end this?" She tightened her lips into a jammy red line as she primped her atomic red curls around her bare, perma-tanned shoulders. David couldn't help but wonder what she'd looked like pre-celebrity, before she'd succumbed to changing her appearance to suit society's version of beauty.

"I mean, I hadn't planned to — at least, not tonight — but yeah. It's been a fun ride, but I think it's run its course." Now the novelty of the relationship with Flame had worn off, like every other one he'd had since his divorce, and it was time to get out, especially if she was beginning to take it seriously.

"I thought we were both benefitting from this arrangement."

"We were, but we can't keep faking this forever. We'll meet other people…then things will get messy." Or worse, she'd expect some sort of commitment from him.

"I can't believe you're actually doing this when we're on our way to my movie premiere." Flame took several deep breaths, her pneumatic breasts rising perilously from the red velvet sweetheart line of her dress. One wrong move and there'd be a serious wardrobe malfunction hitting the front pages the next day. That would be an incident to devastate her, he was sure.

"There's no point in getting upset about it. I'm not going to do anything to spoil your big night."

"Except dump me."

"You can dump me, if you'd prefer. We can make a show of it. A public break-up would get you the headlines you want." The sympathy vote had worked in his favour when a cheating wife had brought record numbers of shoppers to his stores. Although, the reality of that particular betrayal had been painful at the time and too raw for him to enjoy the profits of his despair. He'd learned his lessons since then, though. These days he didn't let anyone get close enough to do that kind of damage again, and he appreciated the value of pre-nups. Now he made sure to take care of number one.

"You really don't know me at all, do you?"

"What do you mean?" David didn't have to turn his head to know those ice-blue eyes were trained on him, laden with disappointment.

"I'll bet you don't know anything about my career, never mind my personal circumstances."

"I know you did some reality dating show, and, er…had a pop career after that. To be fair, Flame, we never did go in for a lot of talking."

She sighed and gave him a wobbly smile. "I guess not. I want you to know I'm not just some fame-hungry wannabe. I don't care about any of that. This is just a job like any other to me. I'm simply waiting for that big payday so I can leave all this behind."

This was a brief glimpse of the real Flame. It was a shame she'd been hidden for so long. She was right. He didn't know the woman beside him at all.

"Then what?"

"I go back to my real life, as plain old Beverley Smith. By that time, I hope to have enough money to buy a place for me and my daughter."

David swerved the car as she dropped that bombshell on him. "You have a daughter?'

Flame nodded. "Selena, and before you ask, no, the dad isn't on the scene. We've been living with my mum."

"You did all this to give your daughter a better life." David reiterated what she'd told him, trying to come to terms with the fact that he'd been dating a single mum. If he'd known that from the beginning, he'd have run a mile.

"I'm with you because I like you, David. Don't worry. I'd never expect, or want, you to play daddy to my daughter. You're far too selfish." Her laugh cut him deep, only because he knew it was true. He was no role model for a child and not any more reliable than his own parents.

"That takes me back to my original point. I don't think we have a future together."

"Okay, but can we talk about it later? Let me get this premiere over with first."

Stunned by the revelations tonight, he agreed to put the big talk on hold until they had time and privacy for a proper conversation.

"The rain's getting heavier out there." Flame sounded far away as he pondered over these past months together and the reasons behind them, none of which were particularly flattering.

His other shiny red status symbol picked up speed as he pushed down on the accelerator, keen to get tonight's charade over with as soon as possible.

The city lights streaked by until he felt as though he were flying. Then he was.

"Look out!"

Flame's shout came too late. The car skidded across the greasy road, leaving him powerless as they hurtled towards the steel barriers edging the hard shoulder.

The windscreen shattered around him and the deployed air bag buffeted his body.

The last sound he heard was the ticking of the engine punctuating the eerie silence. Then the world around him descended into blackness.

* * * *

It took a while for David's eyes to adjust. When he first opened them, he'd feared he'd gone blind. Then he remembered the sound of the tyres screeching as he'd tried to regain control of the car and the pungent smell of burning rubber. They'd crashed. The lights had been smashed when they'd hit the barrier.

He didn't know how they'd got out, but at least he didn't appear to be hurt. Unless he was suffering from delayed shock, he couldn't feel any pain. There was no sign of Flame to see if the same could be said for her.

There was some rustling nearby and he remembered they were down in a ditch at the side of the motorway. *Oh God.* He'd read that people were never more than a few feet away from rats in the city, and he couldn't handle vermin being around him. He had to get out of there.

"Hello?" There had to be someone out there, hopefully with a torch so he could see where he was going.

"W-who's there?" A shaky female voice sounded in the shadows a second before he heard the flick of a switch and a bright light blinded him.

"It's David. Who am I talking to? Where the hell am I?" He lifted his hand to shield his eyes from the light and squinted at the source of the voice, which certainly didn't sound like Flame.

There was a high-pitched squeal and some shuffling from what he now could see was a bed. *I'm in someone's bedroom? How the hell did I end up here?* It wasn't anywhere he recognised. This was smaller than his en suite bathroom, for goodness' sake. The clothes and rubbish strewn over the floor made it look like more of a squat compared to the five-star opulence of the residences he usually frequented.

"If it's drug money you're after, I don't have any. The café's not mine. There's nothing worth stealing here."

"I can see that." A glance around the room told him there was nothing of value there—unless one counted the old TV-DVD combo perched on a cheap white melamine chest of drawers or the cage in the corner where some furry creature was trying to gnaw its way through the bars. When he compared it to his bedroom—or even one of his spare rooms—he felt as though he should be donating something to this charitable cause.

"Keep away from me or I'll phone the police." The puffy-eyed, red-nosed creature with mad bed hair gradually rose from its pit. David held his hands up in surrender, afraid to spook her any more than he already had. Besides, it was one thing courting publicity for his own benefit, but if the press got wind of him breaking and entering some random house, his business would suffer along with his reputation.

"Pardon me for the inconvenience, madam. I don't know what I'm doing here either. I'll leave now. There's no need to get the police involved." He backed up and reached for the door handle. Instead of it turning in his hand, he seemed to miss his mark altogether.

Strange. Perhaps the accident had somehow affected his hand-to-eye co-ordination. He tried again. To his horror, he watched his fingers swipe through the metal handle as though it was nothing more than a figment of his imagination.

"Get out!"

He turned back to see the squat-dweller lob a box of tissues at his head. With no time to duck out of the way, he closed his eyes and braced himself for the inevitable hit. Except the anticipated pointy-edged box stabbing him in the eyeball was replaced with that strange whooshing sensation again. The box slammed into the door and slid to the floor as though he wasn't standing there at all. There was another scream, followed by a string of projectiles launched in his direction. A book, an alarm clock and a phone—which he knew she'd come to regret—hit the wooden panelling behind him in quick succession before creating a small pile of bewilderment on the threadbare carpet.

Another shriek.

"Please, will you stop that incessant screaming? You're giving me a headache."

Strictly speaking, he couldn't feel anything—not even his heart pounding in his chest or his pulse throbbing in his veins, which he would've expected in such strange circumstances.

Nothing. It was disconcerting, to say the least.

Still, the high-pitched squealing was getting on his nerves, and he'd prefer she stopped so he could think straight and figure out what was going on.

"W-what are you?" Not *who*, he noted but *what*, which was an odd term to use when he was obviously a man—a rich, handsome, successful man who'd never been thrown out of a woman's bedroom in his life.

She hugged the knees of her ridiculous nightwear tighter, although there was no need for her to be afraid. He had no intention of going anywhere near her and he'd be out of there as soon as he worked out how. There was a chance he'd catch something if he stayed much longer.

"I'm afraid I have no more clue than you do as to how, or why, I'm here, and I certainly no desire to stay a second longer but, as you can see, I appear to be having a problem with that." His efforts to open the door again produced the same futile result. He even tried putting his foot through it, to no avail. Every attempt at physical contact resulted in him swinging at thin air.

"A little help might get rid of me quicker." If sarcasm could unlock doors, the whole world would be open to him right now.

The wary warden of his current prison cell climbed slowly from the bed and padded towards him. She stopped just short of the door, waiting for him to stand aside, away from her, before she opened it.

Hallelujah!

The prison gate swung open, enabling him to follow his liberator out through the flat towards the front door, the rest of which was no more glamorous than the main bedroom. Plain painted walls were devoid of any pictures or art, and the whole apartment was so small that it was claustrophobic.

He had no clue what was waiting for him outside, but it had to be better than being locked in this bizarre new territory, frightening in its austerity, with a strange woman—a very strange woman, who was breathing her own sigh of relief as she opened the front door for her uninvited guest to leave.

Except David hit some sort of invisible wall every time he tried to step outside the apartment.

"What on earth?" He lost the very last thread of his patience as he tried and failed to shoulder-charge his way through the invisi-shield.

The worst bit was that whenever his new friend tried to shove him out, she fell right through him and landed in a heap on the landing, looking up at him with complete bewilderment. He couldn't even help her up and had to watch her gather what little there was left of her fleecy dignity and get to her feet.

"What the fuck?" She echoed his bewilderment with more colourful language than he'd have preferred, but with exactly the same pitch of horror and desire to break out of this nightmare as he had.

They stood staring at each other, wide-eyed and open-mouthed, until she slowly extended a finger and attempted to prod him. Instead of skin touching skin, her digit gradually disappeared into his arm. She withdrew her hand, only to jab it again into his other arm.

"Will you please stop poking me? I'm not some sort of sideshow at the circus." He didn't know what he was in his current state.

"Can you feel it?" She did it again, her forehead furrowed with concentrated effort.

"No, but it's not very nice having a complete stranger prod me as though I'm some sort of unidentified object."

"Technically, that's exactly what you are, and, for your information, it's not very nice having a complete stranger turn up in your flat who you can't get rid of, either." She folded her arms and tilted her chin into the air. At least she was no longer looking at him as a threat—more of a household pest, now that they knew he had no physical presence. It was a fact which wasn't as comforting to him as it seemed to be to her.

"Good point, but apparently we're both stuck with me being here until we figure this thing out." He followed her back inside the apartment with a heavy heart.

"Right. We need to think of a logical explanation." She paced the small living room, hands on her hips, clearly trying to accept this was actually happening. Then she rolled up her sleeve and pinched the skin of her forearm between her thumb and finger.

"I'm still here. It's real, I'm afraid." He smiled and waved to prove he wasn't the product of her imagination she hoped he was.

"Okay. Okay. What's the last thing you remember?" Stroppy, ploddy lady stopped walking around in circles long enough to question him.

That image of the windscreen wipers and the blurred city lights popped into his head.

"I was driving... It was dark...raining. I think I crashed." That dizzying sensation had his head spinning again, only this time it came with the significance of the memory.

The woman slapped her hand over her mouth. "Oh God, I think you might be dead!"

Chapter Two

"I can't be dead. I don't feel dead. There must be some other *logical* explanation." The ghost in the tux with the silver spoon lodged in his gob — David, so he'd said — was clearly in denial.

Stage one of death was probably acceptance. Perhaps that was why he was still there.

Annie was happier to have him in the living room, which was slightly tidier than her bedroom. To be fair, she hadn't felt the need to be that house-proud with the few visitors she had. Certainly, she hadn't had a man in her bedroom since Jim, her ex-boyfriend. And that was a long time before she'd even moved here.

With such a small living space, she hadn't been able to keep much furniture from home and she couldn't afford to keep it in storage. She'd ended up giving most of it to charity shops who were able to collect it from the house, saving her the removal fee too. A second-hand sofa, an old TV and a coffee table weren't much of a legacy, but they were the last connection she had to her old life. That was more than David had at the moment.

"Did you see the light? You should've walked towards the light instead of coming here." He must've taken a wrong turn somewhere, because no one could've mistaken this hovel for heaven. *Hell, maybe.*

"There were no bright lights, heavenly angels or dead family members beckoning me. I'm not dead, I told you. I'm too rich, too pretty and too young to be a corpse."

"And blatantly too modest," she muttered. It was typical of her luck to get haunted by a cocky, upper-class prat, because clearly, she hadn't been punished enough lately.

"Why would I be here with you if I'm a spirit? Tell me that."

He had her there. There was something familiar about him, but she was sure she would've remembered seeing someone this smokin' hot before. Tall enough to look down his nose at her, with short, dark, tousled, just-out-of-bed hair — which conjured up way too many erotic images to her mind — and eyes the colour of melted chocolate, framed with long lashes that most women would kill for, he was sex on legs, especially with just enough facial hair to give that edge. His dark features combined with his tanned skin gave him a Mediterranean look that didn't match his cut-glass English accent. It was just a shame he was doused in enough *eau-de-arrogant-arse* to repel a woman with all her senses intact. *And dead.*

"I've seen enough movies to know that if you're still here, it's because you have unfinished business, Patrick Swayze. You need closure in this life so you can move on, and apparently I'm the one to help you find it." She gestured towards the sky, but for all she knew, there could be little black demons waiting to drag him off to the netherworld.

"I don't want to move on! I'm only thirty-five, for goodness' sake." He collapsed onto her sofa and rested his head in his hands as the enormity of the situation seemed to hit him.

Annie would've said he was hyperventilating if there had been any sign of him breathing at all.

As far as she was concerned, they'd established that he was dead, a ghost roaming her flat, even if he was having difficulty coming to terms with it. This wandering spirit might just require a nudge in the right direction, and once he remembered how exactly he'd met his end, the powers that be could whisk him off to wherever he was supposed to go.

There had to be some reason she'd apparently been chosen to help him complete whatever mission was required to send him on his merry way to meet his maker.

While he was having some sort of spectral breakdown, a ridiculous idea slowly formed that this incorporeal hunk currently sat — *hovered?* — on her sofa could be her Clarence, although he didn't look much like a guardian angel. He appeared more like a pin-up she would've had on her wall as a teenager before she'd realised that handsome, conceited men couldn't see past their own selfish needs. Besides, she doubted anyone in her life would even notice if she ceased to exist.

She grabbed her laptop and pushed the dirty cups aside to make space for it on the coffee table. The Internet was the fount of all knowledge. It wasn't solely for depressing herself by reading about other people's fantastic lives on social media.

"I'd really appreciate it if you didn't plaster my existential crisis all over the web, thank you. I'm not even sure you could take a selfie with me in my current form."

"Get over yourself. I'm not that kind of shallow attention-seeker." As if she would broadcast images of her wallowing in self-pity for the world to see.

"Obviously." He mocked her onesie comfort-blanket—which had never been meant for public viewing—with an arched eyebrow.

No doubt he preferred his women bleached, plucked and pumped full of additives like supermarket poultry. She was more the free-range, organic type— natural, with a few defects and a smear of dirt here and there.

After she tutted a protest at his less-than-gentlemanly assessment of her attire, she began her online investigation in the hope she could get rid of him as soon as possible.

"I'm going to see if there's an obituary for you. What's your surname?" It was a tad blunt, perhaps, but the quickest way to settle the argument.

"That's cheery."

"It's not supposed to be cheery. I'm being proactive and trying to find some proof either way. So, name?"

With a begrudged scowl he eventually offered, "David Reece."

"D…a…v…i…d… Is that Reece with an 's' or a 'c'?" She tapped the info on the keyboard, unsure exactly what she was hoping to gain from it. *A biography of his tragically short but likely eventful life? A page dedicated to his memory on RichArseholes.com? Photographic proof of his headstone?*

"C."

The name sounded vaguely familiar, but it could be a common-enough name. On sight, she'd have figured him as more of a Theodore Montague or something equally pretentious fitting his ego and outfit. Who wore the full dickie-bow ensemble around here anyway, if they weren't in an aftershave ad or being paid by the hour to entertain rich, lonely women?

Even at this distance, she could see that the silky quality of his suit and the way it was tailored perfectly to his long, lean body said it had been custom-made for him. Everything about him screamed high class—a world away from her life.

"I'm Annie, by the way. Annie Marlowe." She supposed she should make a proper introduction now that they'd established he wasn't a burglar.

Thankfully she didn't have to scroll down too far in the top mentions to find news of the crash.

Pop Princess Flame Involved in Car Crash on Way to Film Premiere, the headlines screamed, with mention of David Reece, owner of Reece Toys Superstores, in the small print below.

Wait. What?

Annie clicked on the link as the name finally registered. Reece Toys was the centre of hell, her retail nightmare of long, underpaid hours and combative customers. David was her absent boss, making her life unbearable from his ivory tower. They didn't recognise one another because he had never spent any time on the ground floor of his business empire. The beard was new too. He'd been clean-shaven in any photographs she'd seen of him. To be honest, she was usually so disgusted by the mere mention of his name that she didn't tend to dwell on those stories of him living the life of Riley at her expense.

Her misdirected rage made her attack the keys with more ferocity, any sympathy she may have had for him fading fast with every *tappety-tap* of her fingers over the keyboard. Although it didn't give her any satisfaction that he was most likely deceased, as some other faceless millionaire would no doubt take over the company and run the staff into the ground. People like her were disposable, to be hired and fired at will, because there was always another poor sod struggling to pay the bills who was willing to take the place of the fallen.

"Well? Put me out of my misery."

Only if you put me out of mine, she wanted to protest, but he was obviously past the point of caring about the demands or concerns of his employees. *If he ever has.*

She cleared her throat and tried to set aside her uncharitable thoughts. After all, it wasn't good manners to diss the recently departed.

"Apparently you were on your way to a glitzy film premiere with Flame. That would explain the getup." He might've blended in perfectly with the other clotheshorses on the red carpet, but he was a tad overdressed for Internet surfing in her flat. She couldn't picture him sitting there in his jim-jams either. *A pair of perfectly fitting silk boxers, maybe…*

She shook the image from her head. Clearly it had been too long since she'd had a man there, dead *or* alive.

"That's right. We were going to see her film debut." He jumped to his feet, his brown eyes bright with the spark of recognition. That twinkle would dim soon enough when he remembered what had brought him here—and it wasn't so he could give her an exclusive review of Flame's performance.

"Tonight? That doesn't explain why you ended up here. The flat is nowhere near the cinema, so I don't know why this should have been your first port of call."

David shrugged, unable to explain either. "What about Flame? Was she hurt? Is she okay?"

His concern was touching, even if it did pique a moment of irrational jealousy. It did nothing for her confidence sitting there, a snotty, puffy-eyed mess in manmade fibres, looking at photos of the glamorous popstrel who probably didn't get out of bed for less than six figures. She'd be lucky to get six quid in her current state.

"*The red-haired songstress of the moment, Flame, was involved in a serious accident on the way to the London premiere of her new movie...*yadda, yadda, yadda... *although not seriously hurt, her current partner, David Reece, sustained serious head injuries.*"

At that point she decided it kinder to stop reading aloud, should the graphic details of his demise become too upsetting for him to bear.

There was some speculation that he'd been speeding, which he didn't need to hear either. There was no point spending eternity blaming himself for the crash when they couldn't turn back the clock.

Then she saw a sentence that she had to reread four times before it sank in.

"*Mr. Reece is said to be on life support in the private St. George's Hospital, London.*"

Annie lifted her head to peer at him over the top of the screen. "You're still alive."

"But... But...how? Why?" His dark eyebrows knitted together into a frown. None of this made sense to her either.

"Perhaps the impact of the crash was so severe that it forced your soul out of your body? It could be as easy as reuniting you with your physical self." What happened after that might not have a happy ending, but that would be in the hands of the gods and hopefully no longer her problem.

"And how are we going to do that when I can't leave your apartment?" He threw his hands up in the air and glared at her as though she should have all the answers — as if assisting disembodied spirits to the afterlife was an everyday occurrence for her. If it was, she would've dressed for the occasion and charged premium rates to supplement her income.

"Well, I don't know. You didn't come with an instruction manual, did you?" Okay, she might not have had a high-speed crash or be currently hovering between life and death, but she was tired, over-emotional and equally as ratty as he appeared.

"You're going to have to go down there and see what's happening."

"Me? Go to the hospital? It's one o'clock in the morning. I can't simply swan into a swanky private clinic as if I've any right to be there alongside your glamorous girlfriend."

"All right then. I guess I'm spending the night here." Her uninvited house guest put his shiny shoes up on the sofa and stretched out, making himself at home. The contrasting image of her boss in his designer tux sprawled out on her ancient floral sofa was too surreal for her to handle, not to mention entirely bereft of manners.

"Um, hello? I know my house and my belongings may not be as fancy as you're used to, but I'd appreciate a little respect. Shoes off the sofa, please." It was his fault she couldn't afford anything half decent, with his zero-hours contracts and minimum wage. Now he thought he could wipe his feet on her furniture? *Hell no.*

"You know I'm not actually touching anything here, right? Besides, I think you could do with investing in something new." He drew her attention to the holes in the arm of the chair, which she was already aware of, along with the broken springs making the couch sag in the middle.

"I'm sorry if my flat isn't up to your high standards. Let me upgrade you to our penthouse suite. Oh wait, this is the only room we have available right now, so I'm afraid you'll have to like it or lump it." She could only imagine the kind of swanky place he lived in, built on the backs of minions like her. The only reason she wasn't casting up his failings as a boss and a basic human being was because she was trying to be kind in his hour of need.

Much more of this and she'd show him her bank statements. Now that really would make him ashamed of himself and the meagre possessions she had here.

"I'm sorry if I offended you. It wasn't a criticism, merely an observation. I am grateful for your help thus far, but I'd appreciate it if I could impose on you further by asking you to attend the hospital on my behalf?" He was sitting up now, giving her his full charm offensive with an air of sincerity that she wasn't sure she quite believed.

"Hmm. I'll go get changed into something less comfortable and see what I can do." What choice did she have, other than lying in bed awake wondering if he'd still be here come morning?

"Thank you. I won't forget your kindness." Yeah, she was pretty sure he was taking the piss now.

Annie left the bedroom door open so she could see if he went snooping around the rest of the flat with his nose turned up.

"I'm afraid I don't possess the expensive haute couture I imagine visitors wear to weep at the hospital bedsides of the rich and famous, even at this hour," she shouted as she poked through the pile of clothes lying in the corner of her bedroom, realising she had very little to wear out at all. The few clean items she had were a crumpled mess, yet to be ironed. The upside to not having a social life was not having to worry about her appearance outside of working hours, dressing for comfort above all else.

Which was fine until some strange man materialised in the dead of night expecting her to venture out in public to perform some sort of voodoo magic on his behalf.

"Anything would be better than your current attire. No offence." His cutting reply elicited a one-fingered gesture from her that he couldn't see.

"I guess you're going to have to do." In the end she settled for her uniform of non-descript black skirt and white polyester blouse teamed with a pair of heels more suitable for this outing than an eight-hour shift on the shop floor. It was the only half-decent outfit she had, even though she loathed the sight of it and what it represented.

She ran a brush through her hair and gave an obligatory swipe of the mascara wand and berry-stain lipstick to attempt a semi-presentable appearance before she stepped back into the living room. At the last minute, she realised she was wearing her name badge and unpinned it to save herself from the humiliation of showing her working-class status at the hospital.

"Very presentable."

It was as close to approval as she could expect from him.

Unless this visit produced a solution to their current problem, she might never have her flat to herself again. A shiver played havoc across her skin and prompted her to reach for her black wool coat with the furry hood.

The last thing she needed was for her mission of mercy to end in a bout of pneumonia for her and land an identical fate to her friend here—doomed to wander this flat for eternity in her work uniform.

"I'm so glad I meet with your approval," she sniffed, trying hard to ignore any pleasure she might have found in the compliment from her nearly dead admirer.

"What am I supposed to do while I'm waiting for you to do whatever alchemy it takes to get me back where I belong?"

"I'll do what I do for George Bailey when I'm out and I don't want him to feel lonely. I'll leave the radio on. You two can rave away into the small hours."

"You're too kind. I'm sure your pet rat and I will be comforted by the sounds of disco music in your absence."

"He's a guinea pig, not a rat." She tutted, insulted on George Bailey's behalf.

David walked to the door behind her, not that she could hear his footsteps, and she daren't look to see if he was somehow gliding across the floor. That would really freak her out.

Although, since he was door-opening-and-closing challenged, it would be down to her to ensure the flat was locked securely. In this neighbourhood, not even a watch-guinea-pig and a transparent James Bond would put off potential burglars.

As she reached for the door, she realised something out of the ordinary—more extraordinary than the night's already-weird events. "Your foot!"

"I have two actually. I seemed to have managed to keep all my parts intact in spirit, if not in body."

They were so locked into the battle of who was more pissed off about him being there that he couldn't see she'd swapped sarcasm for surprise. She would've slapped him if there was a chance he would feel it or she would've gained any satisfaction in the sensation in causing him pain.

"No. Look." She pointed at the foot which appeared to be half in and half out of the doorway.

David slowly slid his foot farther and farther into the hall until it was abundantly clear that there was no longer any obstacle in his way.

"Okaa-ay, now I'm really confused." Despite his apparent reservations, he managed to step out into the cramped hallway beside her.

"Logic hasn't played a huge part in tonight's proceedings, but I don't care what's brought this about—only that it means I'm off the hook. The hospital's that way. Good luck with your missing body parts." She didn't hang around for goodbyes. With any luck, she'd wake up in a few hours and think this had all been a dream, a portent that she needed to do something significant with her life or run the risk of being haunted by arrogant ghosts for the rest of her days.

She let herself back into the flat and slammed the door shut, her body sagging against it as she let out a sigh, relieved that this weirdness was at an end.

"Sorry. I don't think you've seen the back of me yet." David's voice as he materialised in front of her again made her yelp in fright.

"Why would you do that to me? Are you trying to give me a bloody heart attack?" She clutched at her chest, where her heart was pounding violently in response to his sudden reappearance.

"I didn't do it on purpose. It just sort of happened when you went back inside." He shrugged an apology and she reminded herself that none of this could be any more fun for him than it was for her, not knowing if he would live or die and frustrated by his thwarted attempts to leave and find out that he couldn't.

"Talk me through what happened. You must have done something. All I did was close the door."

"There's nothing to tell. One minute I'm out there, the next back in here. Just like that." He had all the guile of a five-year-old at a magic show, and rather than scolding him further, Annie was inclined to laugh. Innocence wasn't the first thing she would instantly attribute to this cocky so-and-so.

"Okay, okay. I believe you, but obviously something happened to bring you back in here with me." Once again, she opened the door and walked out. It was beginning to feel like a tedious game of hide-and-seek.

David followed her without any problems.

"So far so good," he muttered.

Annie crossed her fingers as they made their way down the narrow flight of stairs to the main exit. Since he didn't seem to have managed the walking-through-doors stage of his limbo life, she unlocked it for him.

"After you." She stood back and left the path clear, but that invisible shield was back and annoyingly preventing him from leaving. "Oh, for fuck's sake."

"Must you continually use that vulgar language?" He scrunched up his nose and Annie was tempted to call him every foul thing she could come up with, just to make him clutch his pearls in utter horror.

She fluttered her eyelashes at him. "Yes, I must. It saves me from doing time for murder most days." Swearing was her release and the only legal alternative to throat-punching idiots who insisted on riling her.

"Well, it's not very becoming."

"I. Don't. Care." She needed some fresh air. It was becoming too stifling, being locked in with her boss and their growing exasperation at the situation they'd found themselves in.

With a push, which sent the heavy metal door flying into the outer brick wall of the café, she tried to free herself of the nightmare out on the pavement.

"Boo." A voice she'd already grown tired of hearing sounded in her ear, quickly followed by the appearance of the grinning man she couldn't seem to shake off.

Trial and error had brought her to one terrifying, mystifying conclusion. Like it or not, David Reece was anchored to her until they completed whatever heavenly task had been assigned to them for him to ascend, or descend, to the next level of this strange astral game someone was playing with them.

Chapter Three

Annie had no choice but to fire up her old brick-red Ford Ka if she expected to get to the clinic as soon as possible. She caught herself reaching across the passenger side to open the door a fraction of a second before David materialised in the seat beside her.

"I'm never going to get used to that," she shuddered. "Ghost or not, that sudden appearing and disappearing trick will never cease to creep me the hell out." Until he was successfully returned to his rightful place, far away from her, there was always going to be that sense he was hanging about in the atmosphere and she was never truly alone.

"I can't say I'm loving it myself. Hopefully, this is just a transitionary phase." David kept his gaze straight ahead, refusing to meet her eye, and she could tell he was trying to convince himself that there might still be a happy ending in store for him.

"Look on the bright side. At least you don't have to bother with a seatbelt." This time she could feel him glaring daggers at her, but she simply let off the handbrake and manoeuvred the car out of the small carpark at the rear of the building.

It was going to be a long evening if he couldn't have a sense of humour about their predicament. She had enough doom and gloom in her life without adding more, and she preferred to keep the tone light, despite the heavy subject.

"Do we have far to go? I don't even know where I am." For once, he focused on something other than his current physical state as they drove through the back streets of her town.

"Not far. You're still in London."

"Good."

There weren't many people about at that time of the morning. One man was out walking his dog, his face barely visible with his hat pulled down and his scarf pulled up to combat the cold. The dog was a beast of a thing, black with tan markings around the eyes and paws the size of dinner plates. As they crossed the road in front of the car, it looked more as though the dog was taking the guy for a walk. That was likely why he'd ventured out at this time, when there were fewer cars on the road.

A group of teenagers were hanging out on the corner of the street as she turned off at the traffic lights. The boys, in their uniform of skinny jeans and hoodies, were lounging against the wall, smoking and swigging from cans in an attempt to look cool. The girls crowded around them in their barely-there outfits were apparently impervious to the freezing night air. Annie shivered just looking at them, longing for her warm bed.

Another sneeze proved she would be better off at home rather than driving the streets in the dead of night.

When they were closer to the city centre, more signs of life appeared. The inky-black sky was now illuminated with glowing star-shaped lights. Every tree in sight was strung with blue fairy lights, creating a winter wonderland to entice shoppers to spend, spend, spend. Buses and taxis were busy ferrying passengers around the city and revellers still lined the footpaths. Some were wearing bright paper crowns, others glittered with silver-and-gold tinsel wrapped around their necks as makeshift scarves. All were failing to walk in a straight line. The sounds of their slurred Christmas carols filtered into the car.

"Someone's had a good night. They're probably just getting home from their Christmas work parties." Annie contemplated telling David the work connection they had through his flagship store in the city but thought better of it. It wasn't going to improve the situation for either of them by sharing her personal gripe with him now. It would merely add more tension to an already-awkward dynamic.

"Lucky them." David clearly didn't care about anyone else, and on this occasion, she'd let him away with it.

They fell into a silence that couldn't even be broken by the sounds of background music, since paying to fix a broken car radio had been at the bottom of her list of things to do. As she exhaled white wisps of breath into the car interior, she figured she could add having the heating looked at to that list. David obviously wasn't feeling the cold at all, so being in limbo had some benefits…

Thankfully, the hospital lights blazing up ahead stopped her from making that observation out loud and risking further Reece wrath.

"This is us," she said, pulling into the car park, her stomach beginning to turn over at the prospect of the task ahead.

The thought that the next few minutes could get them both back to normal saw her unbuckling her seatbelt and striding across the car park. It wasn't long before the hunky-man-shaped mist formed alongside her.

The sleek glass building looked more like a luxury hotel with the eight-foot-high Christmas trees tastefully decorated with red and gold baubles marking the wide double doors at the entrance. She half expected a bellhop dressed in matching colours, waiting to escort guests inside with their luggage.

Unfortunately, the path to the brightly lit foyer just beyond them was already blocked with waiting press, nixing the plan to sneak in and out as unobtrusively as possible.

"Don't they have anything better to do at this time of the morning?" There was a band of photographers smoking just at the side of the entrance. Most of the others had their hands wrapped around cups of coffee, trying to keep warm or stay awake.

"They all want to be first with the story. I wouldn't be surprised if at least one of them had tried to sneak in to get a photo of me with my brains hanging out."

"David! Don't even joke about that. We both know you don't have any brains." Clearly, he'd been thinking about what they might face in that hospital room, but she did her best to take his mind off it by making him laugh.

"Very funny. There's no room for a man's ego around you, Annie, is there?"

"Definitely not. If you're looking for someone to stroke it, you're with the wrong girl."

David grinned, apparently amused by her choice of words. "I didn't know that was an option."

Annie didn't know why she was blushing, but she didn't like it. Even in solid form, there would be no stroking any part of David Reece. Thank goodness she hadn't said that aloud or he'd be rolling on the floor by now. Double entendres were only going to make things harder. *Ugh.*

Once she regained her composure, she gave him her steeliest look. "It's not. Now, how are we going to get past all these people?"

Despite the chilly air, Annie could already feel the sweat beading on her top lip at the expectation of her having to blag her way through this throng, hot on the tail of a juicy story.

"Something tells me they're not here for either of us." David wasn't merely being humble. There wasn't even a second glance from the assembled masses, who were oblivious to the fact that this *nobody* was, in fact, a key player in tonight's drama as she dodged her way through the bodies. Still, it gave her a heads-up that David Reece's presence was very much visible only to her.

"Okay, that was easier than I thought. Now what?" she whispered out of the side of her mouth, trying not to arouse suspicion that she could be an escaped patient talking to people who weren't there.

Although there were several large men dressed in black with walkie-talkies in hand, who she assumed were security guards keeping out undesirables, the reception area was loaded with a number of suited types holding court.

"They're part of Flame's entourage. Don't worry. They're not likely to pay you any more attention than the media." David wasn't really helping to put her at ease, even with the confirmation that she was invisible to most people too.

"Receptionists are a different story. They're the real gatekeepers in places like this. I can't just walk up there and demand to see you." She hovered by the automatic doors, where the constant swish as people came and went drowned out her apparent one-way conversation.

"I'm sure Flame did." A wide smile spread across David's face and prompted Annie's stomach to do a few extra somersaults. She didn't need reminding of his glamorous girlfriend, who had definitely more right to appreciate that his sexy grin was in the building. Anyway, if she was so amazing, why hadn't he turned up at *her* place all cute and ghosty? This could all have been solved much more easily if Flame was in charge. These men would've parted like the red sea to let her pass instead of making Annie elbow her way to the front desk like some sort of interloper into the realm of the rich and famous.

"I'm here to see David Reece," she said after she'd marched up to the stony-faced madam controlling the world around her from her computer screen, noting it was the one area in the foyer without the Christmas cheer of shiny decorations. Although, the desk was surrounded by baskets of flowers, the scent of roses and lilies overpowering the usual antiseptic smell of a hospital. Annie wondered if they'd been sent by well-wishers for David already. Then again, this was the sort of place that probably had potpourri and rolled towels in the toilets. Their budget for floral aesthetics was likely more than her monthly rent.

"Isn't everyone?" The receptionist didn't even bother looking up from the monitor to witness Annie's supreme effort to go into warrior mode — her shoulders back, spine straight, chin high.

It was a painful pose to hold for any length of time and really deserved an appreciative audience. The bored dismissal was already chipping away at her new, confident persona and it was tempting to slink back into the shadows. David, however, wasn't used to such treatment. He stepped up beside her and Annie was sure that if he had the means to do it, he'd be rapping the desk or clicking his fingers in her face to direct her attention where it ought to be—although Annie doubted he ever had any trouble grabbing any woman's attention.

"Tell her you're my sister or my cousin. If you're family, as far as she's concerned, then she has to let you in." He was somewhat pissed off now. It was there in his clenched jaw and flared nostrils. This was obviously a man who wasn't used to being kept waiting.

"B-but..." It was one thing fronting up here as though she belonged, but quite another to outright lie to someone's face.

"Stand aside please. We're a hospital, not a sideshow." The woman peered at her over the top of her horn-rimmed glasses.

"Wow. She really missed her calling as a customer services representative. Those people skills are something else." David's appraisal of their new obstacle was accurate, but it distracted Annie's attention from her task at hand.

Unfortunately, the receptionist took her silence as an admission that she was nothing more than a rubbernecker here for the unfolding drama.

"I'm family," Annie blurted out, her voice shaking with nerves at the fib and fear she could lose her chance to reach David's bedside.

"Well, why didn't you say that?" An exasperated sigh greeted this breaking news, followed by frantic tapping on the keyboard and a renewed interest in Annie's presence.

"Cousin. We haven't seen each other in years." That was infinitely more believable than trying to pass herself off as his sister. She might get away with being a distant relative from the undesirable side of the family before trying to persuade snippy strangers that she and David were cut from the same designer cloth.

"You're the first family member to arrive. I thought there'd be more of you here, given all the publicity..." Miss Congeniality suddenly decided to become chatty and Annie suspected it was because she was looking to gain admittance to the Reece realm herself at some point.

"You mean he's on his own?" The thought of him lying back there with no one to comfort him brought a lump to Annie's throat. She knew how it felt to be truly alone and wouldn't wish it on anyone. Sure, she knew he wasn't in that room – he was here with her – but it was sad if she was the only person here for him, and even that was under duress.

"That *Flame*, or whatever you call her, is here, but it's good to see he has someone who *actually* cares." Jobsworth Jill let her humanity shine through for a split second, but it only served to make Annie even sadder to find that there were two of them pretending they were here for his benefit. It didn't take a genius to work out that a grieving starlet might provide the perfect photo op for the media scrum outside and guarantee front page headlines.

The heartfelt moment passed as her unlikely new ally rolled across the floor in her swivel chair, away from the desk and Annie. "He's in ICU. Fourth floor. Take the lift."

"Thank you." The relief that she could finally let go of this charade and get where she needed to be was overwhelming, so much so that Annie wanted to hug her for the information, but that really would've aroused suspicion—and possibly a restraining order.

It was only when they'd walked away that she dared to look at David again. He'd been awfully quiet since hearing his family was AWOL, and seeing the pain etched on his brow told her exactly how hurtful that news had been.

As they stepped into the lift, David saw the same pity reflected in Annie as he'd seen in the receptionist, although her warm brown eyes were infinitely more comforting.

"Hey, don't be sad on my account. Flame and I have an understanding. It was never any great love affair."

"Still, you'd think she'd show some compassion after what you've been through together. Your first thought was for her welfare when you found out what had happened."

"She has other things going on in her life that are more important than me. Besides, we'd had a bit of a disagreement in the car. She's probably not feeling very charitable towards me." He tried to brush off Flame's apparent disinterest, but it still hurt that he had no one here in his hour of need.

"I take it you and your family don't get along either?" Annie broached the part of his life that he'd done his best to erase from his consciousness. There was no escaping the subject now that they were trapped in a small steel box climbing towards his hospital room.

"Nothing a lot of time and distance didn't solve." That was all she was getting. At the end of the day, she was a stranger, and it wasn't unheard of for any offhand comments he made to people to be sold to the press. These days, it seemed anyone was prepared to give their soul—or his personal details—in exchange for a fat cheque. Although his strained relationship with his parents would be the least newsworthy story of the night.

"That explains why they're not here." Annie nodded in understanding. Their absence at the bedside of their seriously ill son should've said all there was to know about their dynamic.

"I haven't seen them in years." Most children, no matter what age, just wanted their parents' love and attention—something that had never happened for him.

Fortunately, as he and Annie made their way to ICU, the crowd assembled at the end of the corridor made for a suitable distraction.

"Flame, I presume?" Annie whispered as they spotted the unnatural blaze of red hair at the centre of the melee in the distance.

The nurses' station was a blur of blue scrubs, with staff retrieving files and seeking information on their patients, but she dodged further interrogation surrounding her appearance on the ward, instead taking it upon herself to find out which room David was in.

"My poor baby...he...he..." Flame's loud sobs echoed down the hallway.

"Note how there isn't any sign of a single tear. She doesn't do much without an audience or a cash incentive, but her dramatics should keep everyone too busy to notice you." It was only now, in the midst of such emotional turmoil, that he could see how mercenary those traits were in a person—and how unattractive—even if she was doing it to benefit someone else.

He thought he'd learned his lesson after the divorce by not getting emotionally involved with anyone else, but his taste in women hadn't changed. Flame wasn't any better for him than his ex-wife had been, and vice-versa. Everything about their so-called relationship was toxic, enabling the worst to come out in each of them.

Deep down, he would rather have had a woman he loved, who truly loved him, waiting there for him to wake up so they could go home together. Nothing else would matter if he had that. He'd simply been protecting his heart, because he thought it would never happen for him in this lifetime. It didn't make him any happier knowing he'd been right.

He peeked into the tinsel-surrounded windows of the private rooms until he found what they were looking for. "Quick, Annie, in here."

"He was going to propose to me tonight." Flame's wailings could still be heard ringing down the corridor. It was a good performance, regardless of the blatant lie, and he had to admit that he kind of admired her opportunism. The tragedy of a fiancé-to-be made for much better publicity than a casual acquaintance, but he hoped Annie hadn't heard.

For some reason that he didn't dare examine too closely, he didn't want Annie to think he had plans to spend the rest of his life with someone like Flame. Marriage wasn't on his agenda, and certainly not when he was halfway to being dead. It wasn't like a green card. He couldn't get married in the hope it would keep him in the country — or save him from dying.

"You would've thought they'd have had someone keeping an eye on you after all the fuss downstairs." Annie had snuck into the room, so they were now at his bedside staring down at the battered body lying there.

It was odd to see himself, nothing more than a shell, being kept alive by hospital machinery. It was a genuine out-of-body experience, but they had no time for him to dwell on his mortality if they were ever to bring this nightmare to an end.

"I don't suppose there's any point if they can't do anything for me. They're waiting for me to wake up." He gave a bitter laugh at the irony. There was no one who wanted that more than him, but so far it simply hadn't been in his power to *make* it happen.

He watched the rise and fall of his chest, wondering if the man lying there had achieved everything he'd wanted. If he flat-lined now, could he honestly say his life had been significant and he'd lived it to the fullest? The answer to that was an unequivocal no, and it was a sobering thought.

Sure, he had money and ran his own company, but that didn't carry any weight in the grand scheme of things. This room was a prime example. Compared to Annie's flat, it was the height of luxury. There was a huge flat-screen TV on the wall, several comfy sofas dotted around, and even the windows were draped with red velvet curtains and swags. It would cost a fortune to stay here, and for what? He couldn't use any of this stuff. It was all for show and, ultimately, a waste of money. All that mattered was the equipment keeping him alive.

He'd been entirely selfish in his life, and it had left him here, alone. If he died now, he wasn't leaving anyone he cared about behind and there was certainly no one to mourn his loss. He had no family of his own to carry on his name, and he hadn't donated huge sums of money towards any deserving cause to enrich anyone else's life. When he was gone, they'd simply redistribute his wealth to the other selfish bastards he worked alongside, who only cared about their own bank balances, not where the money came from.

If he got a second chance at life, it probably meant he had some serious changes to make.

Since Annie was the one he'd been drawn to in the dying embers of his existence, it stood to reason she might be the one with all the answers.

Chapter Four

"I know this has to be weird for you. I mean, it's freaking me out seeing two of you here. Not to give you a bigger head than you've already got, but I've kinda got used to seeing that handsome face of yours. I don't like this other version." Annie was trying to keep the tone light, but she wouldn't have recognised him since he was so swollen. The visible parts of him, not hidden by tubes and wires or crisp white hospital sheets, were covered in a dark rainbow of purple-and-black bruises and deep red lacerations.

"God knows what damage there is on the inside." David was too lost in his own thoughts to even jump on the compliment she'd paid him, and she would've hugged him if it had been possible.

"Are you sure there's no one I can call for you?" She felt for him, mostly because of how reflective this was of her own circumstances. It hurt knowing that when it came to the end of her own life, there would be no one sitting at the end of the bed mourning her loss either.

He shook his head. "I'm afraid it's just you and me."

With that thought in mind, she made the decision to be a little kinder to David, in case she was the last person he'd ever get to see or speak to — someone who had been a stranger to him only hours ago.

"So, what now?" He turned to her expectantly.

"Umm-m…hello? Returning a spirit to its body isn't something I do for fun on weekends. I hoped whatever mojo had brought you to me would've beamed you back into your body in a blaze of heavenly light or something equally fabulous by now."

"Bad luck. I'm still here." The wave and sarcasm ruled her earlier vow to be nicer to him null and void. This had to be disturbing enough for him without making him wonder why she'd started suddenly feeling sorry for him.

"Any suggestions about what I should do?"

"Plenty, but none are PG-rated or related to your current predicament." She smiled sweetly and batted her eyelashes at him.

He countered with an equally insincere smile. "Perhaps I should make some sort of contact?"

David reached out to touch the limp hand wired up to the IV stand by the bed. Nothing, except for that bizarre sight of his body parts disappearing as he tried.

He gave a frustrated growl and withdrew his hand again.

"We've got to figure this out. No offence, but if I'm expected to share my home, I'd rather to do it with someone contributing to the household bills, or, at the very least, someone capable of making me a cup of tea every so often." Living with a smart-arse ghost, spirit or whatever the hell he was would only drive her even more demented.

She began reciting what she could remember of the Lord's Prayer.

"What are you doing?"

"I'm praying. If there is a God, he's obviously got a very warped sense of humour. Perhaps this is his way of trying to get me back into the fold. It's not any more unbelievable that this could be divine intervention attempting to set us both back on a more righteous path than self-pity."

"Right. Good plan." He closed his eyes as she finished with an "Amen."

Popping one eye back open, he glanced at his unconscious self on the bed and swore.

"Perhaps an ex-girlfriend has put a curse on you? I've only known you for one night and I could easily imagine a coven of your exes stabbing David dolls and plotting revenge for whatever heinous crime you've committed against them."

"Thanks for that lovely character assassination, but can I remind you that you're the only one aware that I'm stuck here?"

"That we know of. Although I don't think I've done anything to deserve sharing this curse with you."

"For all I know, you could be in cahoots with Linda, my ex-wife, reporting back on my misfortune?"

That could have been the moment to confess that they did have a tenuous connection, but in doing so, she was afraid they'd no longer be on an even footing. If he knew she was a lowly employee, she wouldn't get away with any more of her snarky comments. That was her coping mechanism and the only thing keeping her sane in the face of this madness, but she couldn't afford to lose her job either.

"Trust me… If I was going to curse you to wander the Earth as the invisible man, I wouldn't have chosen myself as your conduit for the living. I'd have hooked you up with my ex-boyfriend and shown him a thing or two about karma." This wasn't any more fun for her than it was for him.

"Then help me out here." He ignored the mention of her ex and the associated drama, clearly not interested in her personal life or anything other than his own problems. She supposed in this instance he had the right to be a little self-absorbed—no pun intended. There was no telling how much time they had left here to try to figure this out before someone else came into the room or she was rumbled as a fake family member.

"Let me think." She pressed her fingers to her temples, trying to force her brain to come up with a solution. "One body, one soul. There must be some easy way to join them back together. Perhaps you need full body contact to sort of…merge."

David climbed on top of his body, going toe to toe, nose to nose and crotch to crotch.

"Well, this is awkward," he said, waiting for something to happen.

Annie let out a snort-laugh at the sight.

"What?"

"Nothing." She tried to stifle further laughter, but when he gave her the side-eye, she confessed what she'd found so funny. "I just thought this might be your ultimate fantasy come true. You, shagging yourself."

"Oh, ha-ha. I'm so glad my near-death experience is amusing you." He climbed off the bed in a huff. At least when she was winding him up it gave them less time to dwell on the failure of their mission.

The laughter ceased the second she heard the door handle move and a man and a woman walked into the room.

"Oh great. Here we go." It was apparent David knew the couple, but she couldn't very well ask him who they were, when she was the only other visitor in the room as far as they were concerned.

The slender woman, who Annie estimated to be in her fifties, oozed elegance and sophistication in her camel coat, even though she was wearing pearl silk pyjamas beneath it. Despite obviously just having woken up, there wasn't a honey-gold hair out of place in her sleek bob and the only thing spoiling her perfect complexion were her red-rimmed eyes.

"Are you David's wife?" she asked on entering.

"What? No." Annie snorted with incredulous laughter before she'd had time to think about her new identity or why she was supposed to be here.

"As if." It was David's turn to mock and Annie gave him her I-am-not-amused stare.

He wasn't exactly a catch in his present state either.

"The receptionist mentioned another family member. We just assumed... We haven't seen him in a long time." Her silver fox of a husband put his hands on her shoulders. With those familiar dark eyes and fine head of hair, he was the spitting image of David, only with more frosting. These had to be his parents. Clearly the Reece genes ensured a lifetime of good looks and swooning women.

"Let me get my tiny violin out," the voice from the corner jeered at the couple.

David constantly made Annie want to throw things at him. She had to watch with growing apprehension as he walked over to the pair of strangers gawping at her.

"Divorced, I believe."

David was circling them, looking them up and down like a shark sizing up its prey.

"Annie, meet mom and pops. These sorry specimens call themselves my parents." There was such vitriol in his words that she had to wonder what they'd done to deserve it, when they seemed so well put together and...nice.

"Oh, yes. I had heard something about that. Such a shame."

"Glad to see you're keeping track, Mother. As invested in your children as always." David did have a right to be put out if they hadn't offered their support during what would have been a difficult time for him, Annie supposed.

"I, I, er..." It occurred to her she still had to explain her relationship to their son and she couldn't get away with claiming to be a cousin of any description now. "I'm Annie, a friend of David's. The receptionist must've misunderstood."

"She did seem under pressure." Mrs. Reece nodded and accepted the half-truth so easily that Annie immediately felt guilty.

"I'm Nicholas and this is Melanie." Mr. Reece senior removed his black leather gloves to shake her hand as his wife moved to their son's bedside.

"Hi." Annie swallowed a sob as Melanie burst into floods of tears, despite knowing David was fine. Seeing other people cry was her kryptonite, and she reckoned she was some sort of empath when she tuned in to other's emotions so easily. Perhaps that had something to do with why she could see David and no one else could. She'd discuss that with him later and do some research into all that clairvoyant-medium nonsense she'd never believed in, even when her own mother had died.

"Oh, Nicholas, look at him. I would hardly have recognised my own son." She pulled out a handkerchief from her oversized cream leather handbag, which Annie just knew was worth more than her entire wardrobe.

"That's all superficial, Mel. The swelling will go down in time. Have the doctors said any more about his condition?" It was clear by Nicholas' gravelly sound that he had a lump in his throat too.

"They just want to know how long it'll take for me to kick the bucket." This was hard when their son was here and clearly not convinced about the sincerity of the visit.

"He... He seems to be holding his own," she offered, ignoring David, not knowing what it meant other than he was still annoying the hell out of her.

Melanie took bedridden David's hand, stroking him with a tenderness she couldn't imagine was put on solely for her benefit. "Are you down as his next of kin, Annie?"

"Here we go. I wondered how long it would take to get around to this subject." Spirit David threw his hands up and walked away as if he were a lawyer in the middle of a courtroom drama, making his final summation.

"No. I don't know who that would be. Flame, perhaps? She's his current squeeze." Annie wasn't enjoying being piggy in the middle of this argument.

"God, no. She might come in and finish the job herself if she thought there was something in it for her."

He really did have trust issues, and Annie wondered why he socialised with people he apparently could barely tolerate, never mind call a friend or a girlfriend. He'd do better surrounding himself with grounded people who wouldn't let him get so big-headed and far above his station — someone like her. An alternative would be to get himself a guinea pig that only expected kale and clean bedding from its human.

"Is that the redhead with the big—" Nicholas held out his hands to exaggerate the size of the chest he was thinking about, earning him a scolding from his wife. It was clear where David had inherited his tact from.

"Yes. She's around somewhere if you want to talk to her." Then Annie could be spared any more of this debacle.

"We might do that and see if she knows anything about his wishes."

"See? What did I tell you? They're only interested in knowing if I've left them anything in my will and getting their hands on my company. I'd heard things weren't going so well for them now that the arse has fallen out of the construction industry. My fortune would prop them up very nicely. Ha! I guess I didn't turn out to be so useless after all." David was becoming more and more animated and it was difficult to carry on a normal conversation with his parents when he was bouncing around in the background like a hyperactive kangaroo.

Although, she had to admit that the last bombshell did make her question their motive for being here and if she was the one being duped after all. "I should go and let you spend some time alone with your son."

She backed away towards the door.

"I wish we could've met under different circumstances, Annie. Why don't you give us your number, so we can keep in touch?" As Nicholas handed over his phone for her to enter her contact details, she didn't even have a chance to think of giving him false information. Besides, if they met up again, it would be awkward if she had.

"Really? You're giving them your number? Strap yourself in for a torrent of calls and texts trying to track down the PIN numbers for my bank accounts."

She was guessing David didn't have his parents on his contacts list.

"Okay, bye." Once she was out of the room and back in the lift, she was able to relax a little.

"Now what?"

She wasn't sure if there were CCTV cameras in there, but she was past caring if she looked nuts, talking to someone who wasn't there, when he was a constant pest buzzing in her ear.

"I have no bloody idea, David. I've driven you here as you asked, done everything I could to put you back where you belong and lied to your parents. I'm tired and I've got work in the morning. I'm going home to bed." It wasn't that she didn't have any sympathy for his predicament, but she didn't know what else they could do to fix it tonight.

"This hasn't been a picnic for me either, you know," he grumbled, as he had every right to do. Both of their lives had been thrown into utter turmoil without any warning. Although, to be fair, the crash sounded as though it might have been his fault, so she had more reason to be pissed off. At least she'd had the decency not to spread her personal misery around, but David had literally brought his to her front door.

"No, but I can't see what else we can do here without raising suspicion. If the receptionist or your parents realise I lied, they'll have me barred from the premises. Then we'll both be up shit creek. It's not as though I can tell anyone the truth without running the risk of getting locked up either. Who the hell in their right mind would believe this?"

"What am I supposed to do?" For the first time since he'd dropped into her life, David sounded unsure of himself, and they both knew he was at her mercy.

They were going to have to come up with some serious theories about what all this meant, and on the top of her list was the possibility that she was supposed to reunite him with his family so he could find peace.

"Well, we can't spend all night staring at your comatose body, so I guess you're coming home with me for the night." They didn't have a choice and it certainly wasn't as suggestive as it sounded. In any other circumstances, Annie knew neither of them would even consider that idea.

Although, now her wayward thoughts were drifting towards the idea of being bold enough to make that offer to a man like David Reece, and how hot one night with him could be if he was in a solid form, there of his own free will…and didn't speak.

* * * *

"Thank you," David said, breaking the depressing silence that had descended upon them in the car on the way back to Annie's flat.

"What for? We didn't achieve anything." She sounded as defeated as he felt.

"You tried. You did everything I asked of you. It has been a fraught night and we both expected you'd be coming back here alone. I just want you to know I appreciate your help." It wasn't as though anyone else appeared to be doing anything to bring him back to the land of the living, except perhaps those at the clinic being paid a hefty sum at his expense.

"You're welcome. That's not to say I won't stick some earphones in from now on and pretend I can't hear you." She gave him a half-smile, and the renewed banter was preferable to the previous defeatist atmosphere.

"Ah, but you know I'm here and that's enough for now. I don't know how I would've got through that without you tonight. I'm glad you were there." When he'd seen his injured body lying on that bed, he'd wanted to weep. He was realising money didn't mean a thing at the end of the day. It was having the people he loved and who loved him around. He'd had neither — only a stranger who'd been strong-armed into being there. Currently she meant more to him than the vast fortune sitting useless in his bank account.

"Me too." Annie reached her hand out as though she was going to take his, remembering at the last second that it wasn't possible. He longed for that touch, that simple human contact providing comfort in this time of uncertainty.

"I'm sorry you've been dragged into this whole nightmare along with me. Tomorrow, if I'm still playing the role of unwanted houseguest, we'll work on a new plan for my eviction." All he knew now was that he was glad he had Annie to talk to rather than wandering this limbo alone forever.

This virtual stranger had become his life raft and the last link he had to this earthly realm. For now, she was his world, whether she liked it or not.

Chapter Five

Annie yawned and padded into the bathroom, the white tiled floor cold under her bare feet. Her full bladder thanked her for swapping her onesie for the more practical navy nightdress, not that she was trying to impress David. It was the only one she had that wasn't covered in chocolate and didn't have cartoon animals plastered on it.

With no sign of him so far, she plonked herself down on the toilet seat to relieve herself. Eyes closed, she took advantage of the few seconds of respite before she had to get ready for work.

"Ahem." A cough immediately snapped her wide awake.

"Where the hell did you come from?" She pulled her nightie down over her knees to cover some of her modesty, but nothing could save her from the indignity of David seeing her having a wee.

"I have no idea. I just kind of...appeared." To his credit, he did turn his back on her to afford her the grace to finish without an audience.

"I don't suppose you could just stop appearing?" she asked, once she'd flushed, and focused on washing her hands because she couldn't bring herself to make eye contact with him.

"I'm sorry. I don't seem to have any control over it." She could hear the smirk in his voice and knew he wasn't sorry at all.

"So, I can't even have a pee in peace now? Great." How the hell was she supposed to live the rest of her life with him as her shadow? She'd go insane. If she hadn't already and this wasn't some elaborate hallucination she'd been having all along.

"Look... I don't know how the hell this works. I'm not doing this to purposely embarrass you."

"I know. It's just" — *annoying, awkward, humiliating* — "weird. There doesn't seem to be any rhyme or reason as to where and when you show up. I mean, I was able to go to bed without an escort last night. At least, I don't remember you hovering by my bed. I was pretty zonked out by then."

"The last thing I remember is you going to bed, and now this. I wasn't wandering the apartment waiting for you to wake up. It's as if I'm somehow attached to your consciousness, but like I said, I don't know how this works." He shrugged his shoulders, still facing the corner like a naughty schoolboy. She was tempted to let him stay there.

"I'm afraid I have to get ready for work. I wish I could pull a sickie, but unless I want to get sacked, fall behind on my rent and end up living on the street, I have to go the soul-sucking hell that is my job." Just wait until he found out he was the devil incarnate who was inflicting everlasting misery on her. It would be some payback for this indignity.

"If you hate it that much, why don't you leave? Life's too short to do something you obviously hate." While his back was still turned, Annie stripped off, jumped into the shower and pulled the door closed behind her.

"There speaks the man who's never had to work for minimum wage to keep his head above water. When you've spent most of your adult life as a carer to your sick mum, there aren't a lot of job opportunities available out there — or any financial support when she dies."

She switched on the hot water to drown out the bitterness she could hear in her own voice. Simply thinking about the injustice of everything she'd been dealing with alone since her mum had died and Jim had cheated on her brought tears to her eyes. At least she could hide her sorrow from view under the water — the way she'd trained herself to do ever since her mum had received her cancer diagnosis.

"I'm sorry. I didn't realise you'd lost your mother. For the record, though, I worked very hard to get where I am today." David began to materialise in the steam of the shower with Annie, making her scream.

"Eyes front, mister. I'm showering here. Okay, you pulled yourself up by your bootstraps. Good for you. I barely manage to get out of bed most days." She was trying — and failing — to cover any part of her body sufficiently with her flannel. "Now get the fuck out of my shower!"

After letting him cop an eyeful of her naked body, she knew it was going to be another one of those horrendous days.

* * * *

"It's like herding cattle down here." David was swept along in the tidal wave of commuters alongside Annie. Thankfully, he'd never had to endure the trial of the London Underground. The family had always had access to their own drivers, but he could vividly imagine the cloying heat and acrid smell of diesel and body odour in this claustrophobic tunnel of peasants.

"The joys of public transport," Annie muttered as she speed-walked down the left-hand side of the escalator through to the platform.

"You do have a car," he pointed out. "It's not as though you're completely at the mercy of the Tube. Given the choice, I know which one I'd rather take every morning."

She waited until they'd found a space along the edge of the platform before she answered. "I understand that the concept of a budget or traffic congestion is probably alien to you. I don't suppose you have to clock in and out on time or risk having your wages docked, but us lesser mortals don't have the luxury of jump jets or whatever you have to get you from A to B on time."

As the train arrived, he watched, aghast, at the game of sardines as the scrum of commuters fought for space on board as though it was the last transporter to reach civilisation.

The zombified expressions of city workers who looked like they were being shuttled towards death row was unsettling, especially those sporting Christmas jumpers. Despite the jolly, bright reindeers and snowmen on display, the unhappy faces of those wearing them said it was all for show. Christmas was the busiest time of the year in his shops, yet he hadn't given much thought to those schlepping to work every day like this and forced to provide the cheer most here obviously weren't feeling.

"Can't you ask for a raise or a travel allowance to make all this drudgery a little less gruelling?"

She gave him that look again, which said he had no clue what he was talking about as she clung to the overhead rail, jostled by the momentum of the underground train and her fellow passengers. He knew she wouldn't want to draw any attention to herself, so he answered for her. "Your boss must be a real piece of work."

That at least brought a smile to her face, which didn't go unnoticed by the guy standing closest to Annie, who apparently took it as an invitation to move closer until his armpit was eye-level with David. Thank goodness he didn't have smell-o-vision.

"Hey, chum, she's smiling at me. Back off." He wasn't sure he'd be as confrontational if the stockily built admirer in stained overalls could see and hear him, but the sentiment was there all the same. He wanted to claim the victory of making Annie smile when it was such a rare and beautiful sight. Okay, so she wasn't on the highly maintained level of the socialites he dated, but she was pretty in her own way. Now that she'd washed her hair, he could see the hint of copper through her dark brown locks that tumbled to her shoulders. Her pale skin was flawless, with no need for more than a hint of makeup, and he knew she had a body that shouldn't be kept hidden under shapeless clothes.

He was a red-blooded man, so of course he'd looked when he'd found himself in the shower with her. Water cascading over her the crest of her full breasts, caressing her body and winding its way in between her inner thighs... It was an image he couldn't seem to get out of his head. Only a few seconds in real time was now a memory frozen in his mind forever. She was a natural beauty — understated but still mesmerising. Until she was transported into the wider world, where there were so many other brightly coloured creatures attracting attention, that she went virtually unnoticed among them.

At least her uniform, which seemed to be the only proper clothes she possessed, showed off something of her curvy shape, although he was certain she wouldn't give a fig what any man thought about her appearance, especially him. Whoever had made her so defensive, so defeated and ground her self-confidence into the dirt, had really done a number on her. If she was right about the reason for him still being around, perhaps that was his *mission* — to help her enjoy her life to the fullest, just as he thought he had.

"What is it you do, anyway?" It occurred to David that he didn't know anything about Annie's line of work other than that it was soul-destroying and underpaid. That could've covered anything from cleaning toilets to teaching. Although, a skirt wouldn't have been practical for a cleaning job and he wasn't convinced she had the right temperament for teaching.

"Retail hell," she informed him with a saccharine smile, sweet enough to make him wary. She was being cagey, but he supposed he hadn't shown much interest in her personal life when he'd been so consumed by his thoughts of how to get his own back.

Now that no longer seemed like a possibility, he should get acquainted with the person he was dealing with beyond the brusque veneer. If he was supposed to guide her towards a more fulfilling path, he'd need to know more about her than that she had a vocally challenged rodent and wasn't what he would call a domestic goddess. She was a smart, savvy woman and he had enough contacts and business know-how to help her improve her lot. Money he could do if that was what she needed.

As they headed towards Covent Garden, he realised she must work somewhere in the markets. This area was tourist heaven. Decorated for the season, with over-sized reindeer guarding a present-stacked sleigh, the site was more popular than ever, despite the cold. People visited to take photos, to shop for gifts at the craft stalls and just to feel Christmassy in general. It was prime real estate and he knew from experience how much it cost to be part of this community.

The eclectic mix of goods offered was what drew so many here. From designer handbags to colourful knitted hats and gloves, there was something for everyone. He rarely bought anything himself. It was the bohemian buzz about the place, the energy, he came for. The sounds of happy chatter, cutlery clashing on plates in the café inside and someone singing carols to the customers enjoying breakfast added to the enticing atmosphere, but Annie didn't stop. Not even the chalk signs advertising mulled cider and wine tempted her. David could almost smell the cloves and cinnamon. How he wished he could taste the warmth of the season and be part of this — or even buy one for Annie in return for her kindness. But he couldn't do any of that.

Instead, all he could do was follow as she carried on around the corner, past St. Paul's church.

Annie stopped in a shop doorway.

"Welcome to hell," she said, and gestured to the red sign above the shop door with the name emblazoned in bright yellow lettering.

Reece's Toys.

David realised that if he was here to atone for his sins, he was totally screwed.

Annie popped on the festive reindeer antlers they supplied to staff at this time of year, and it made him feel worse that her miserable existence and empty purse was his fault. Indirectly, of course—he would never knowingly have devalued her worth or anyone else's. Now he understood why she resented him so much, and it wasn't simply down to his untimely appearance. What he didn't know was why she hadn't said she knew him. If it was to create maximum feel-like-shit impact, she'd succeeded.

He'd never been more ashamed of who he was.

Annie didn't get the wave of euphoria she'd been expecting with the great reveal. The look of shame on David's face was replaced with a pained expression that she'd chosen to uncover their connection in this manner. Instead of jubilation at extracting revenge, her stomach plummeted as though she'd betrayed him in some way.

"Why didn't you tell me? We might've been able to figure this out sooner if you'd just told me I was a despicable boss and I should change my ways—you know, like Jacob Marley did with Ebenezer Scrooge. I wouldn't have needed the sight of my lonely, un-mourned demise to convince me. The state of you and your flat would've done the job." He was lashing out like a wounded animal caught in a trap, but every word of it was true, even down to the insult.

"Charming."

"I'm serious, Annie. It wasn't fair for you to spring this on me. I feel bad enough as it is."

"Okay. Maybe I didn't go about this the right way, but there didn't seem to be a good time to tell you I was one of your employees."

"I don't understand why you despise me so much. Surely Reece's Toys provided you with employment at a time you've said yourself was very difficult."

"I never had the chance of a university education or working my way up the corporate ladder, because I spent my adult life caring for Mum. That apparently doesn't amount to much in the real world. The only other work experience I had was part-time shop jobs after school to earn a few quid for essentials, not something I expected to spend the rest of my life doing. Your business employs people on zero-hours contracts. That means we have no idea what hours we'll be working from month to month. There's no financial stability and I can't predict whether or not I'll be able to pay my bills with no guaranteed wage coming in. I can't retrain without taking time out, so I'm trapped." Maybe, just maybe, she'd taken some of that frustration out on David, who represented everything she'd never had—money, success and a life of his own. Okay, that last one was looking a bit sketchy right now, but she was sure that up until the accident, he'd done more in his life than scan barcodes and wallow in self-pity.

"I had no idea. I'm sorry."

Terri, her manager, appeared on the other side of the glass door and brought the conversation to an end. Annie had to quash the rising anger at what David's business practices meant to her personally as she unlocked the door to let Annie in.

"You're late," Terri snarled, with that wasp-sucking-bulldog expression she used so often that her thick make-up had settled into those lines around her pursed lips.

"There's fifteen minutes before we actually open." Annie suspected it wouldn't matter what time she arrived. Terri would always find fault with her.

Perhaps it was Annie's age which upset her, or her single status, when both made her a viable candidate for promotion and thereby threatened Terri's position. With no dependents, Annie could be called in at a moment's notice, and these days, that was all that mattered for employers.

Terri needn't have worried. Annie had no aspirations of being lumbered with keyholder duties and complaints for an extra fifty pence an hour — or whatever the going rate for a soul was these days. It was bad enough that she was designated cover for most of the holidays because, *'It's not as if you have any family to go home to.'* Sensitivity was not one of Terri's strong points, along with compassion or general kindness to others.

"Some of us were here an hour ago," she pointed out as she powered up the cash register.

Annie didn't waste any energy arguing the fact that she didn't get paid for starting early or the extra time that was spent locking up at the end of the day. Terri was the sort of woman one could never win an argument with, and it really wasn't worth the hassle of getting into one with her. Instead, she walked on across the floor and past the shelves laden with games and toys that seemed soulless without the jubilant interaction of excitable children. She left the brightly lit shop and stepped off the busy carpet onto the concrete floor of the stock room. The grey breezeblock walls made it feel even more like a prison, and the chill was already pervading her bones, but she hoped for a moment of respite before the working day began in earnest — or maybe not.

"Is she always that pleasant?" David asked, mouth agape.

"You hired her." Annie hung her coat and bag on the back of a plastic chair and tried to psych herself up to spend the day with a forced smile on her face when all she wanted to do was sleep.

She was one of those people who'd imagined working in a toy shop, especially at this time of the year, would be fun. Surely it would be a dream come true, having all those pixie-faced children peering through the windows as she played Christmas fairy. It was bound to take away the loneliness of not having her own mother around. *Wrong.*

The reality was a lot of heavy lifting and dealing with irate parents who'd left it too late to bag the sell-out toy of the year. There were some pluses, she'd admit, such as locating the perfect present for a stressed customer on their way to a child's birthday party or spending time with the kids who treated the shop like a giant playroom. It was the management, long hours — if any at all — and being treated like a second-class citizen that made all her days merge into one long drudge.

"A little bit of power tends to go to people's heads," she said, wondering if David had been an asshole before becoming king of his own empire. He seemed to be the type, with or without money.

"I hope that's not a dig at me. Terri is not my fault." He was lounging against the stock shelves, arms folded, casting a critical eye over the corner of the room designated as the staff area. "Does no one ever clean this place?"

"It's the housekeeper's day off."

"I'm serious." He walked over to inspect the dish-laden sink and the wonky table with the remnants of someone's lunch encrusted on the surface. "God knows what strange new colonies of micro-organisms are developing as we speak."

Great. He's a clean freak too. Given a chance, he'd probably don a white glove and trail a judgemental finger along the surfaces. Although one wouldn't have to search that hard for dust. The air was thick with it. Annie coughed. *Okay, he has a point.*

"First off, it's not in our contract. Secondly, we hardly get the breaks we're entitled to, so we have to eat and run. Finally, and most importantly of all, I do clean out here. It's everyone else who are pigs."

She rinsed out the cups and cleaned all the surfaces with disinfectant, hoping he hadn't been judging her apartment the same way. It was disgusting in here, but her place wasn't much better compared to whatever MTV crib he inhabited. Mr. Reece wouldn't sully his own hands with the housework either, and if she had his money, she'd employ a whole team of cleaners to keep her house spick-and-span.

"I swear I had no idea about any of this. I'll do whatever I can to improve conditions for you all."

"How can you? Not to highlight the obvious, but you're not any use to anyone in your current state. There's no point in making promises you can't keep. I've learned the hard way not to believe everything a man promises me—things like marriage, babies... fidelity." This past year had made her cynical and she wasn't prepared to live any more of her life based on a lie told to keep her sweet.

"Annie, I'm not your ex. I don't want to hurt you, and when I can, I'll take the necessary steps to make things right with you."

She wanted to believe him, but she wouldn't hold her breath.

"Are you taking your break early?" Terri yelled with more than a pinch of sarcasm as she hammered on the door.

"Just coming." Annie stuck two fingers up at the closed door. "I can't do this with you now, David. I won't have time to talk when this place is crazy busy. I don't know what you're going to do, but please don't make me start arguing with you in the middle of the shop floor. I won't be able to hear you anyway with those Christmas tunes we have playing on a loop since last month. I still hear them in my sleep, you know."

"Take your phone and pretend you're on a call. I need to know what else is going on here so I can fix it."

"No phones on the shop floor. Company policy." He could watch and learn for himself. She wasn't going to do everything for him. If he was right and the working conditions of his staff was the issue he needed to deal with to gain his wings or the gold star on his arse or whatever else it took to get him out of her life, he had to open his eyes to it, not take her word alone.

Until then, she simply had to get on with the hand she'd been dealt, one which made her jealous of a dead man who still had a purpose in life when she was yet to find hers.

Chapter Six

Being stuck in limbo was only made more excruciating by spending it in one of his own shops. Not only did this shift feel like an eternity for David, since he was unable to keep himself busy like Annie, but also because he'd discovered so many things he wished he could fix and couldn't.

"You know there's a board who do the hiring and firing for me. They're supposed to be overseeing the chain of stores and staff whilst I'm doing all the deals in the background. Otherwise I'd be on top of people like Terri abusing their position. Well, not literally, but you know what I mean." After another encounter with the increasingly unpleasant Terri, who was blaming Annie for some missing stock, he needed her to understand he wasn't personally responsible for her appointment.

He hadn't known her very long, but even he realised she wasn't the type of person who would steal from anyone or enable others to do so. It was a ridiculous accusation, but it appeared Annie didn't have anyone on her side to refute the charge—neither could she defend herself in the vehement way he knew her to be capable of when she was so afraid of losing her job and her only income.

Annie sighed. "I guess it's easy to lose sight of the human element in business when it's presented to you as a list of figures and statistics. Unfortunately, that blinkered approach, which isn't unheard of at the top level of business, especially retail, is partially responsible for the high turnover of staff at ground level." She wasn't wrong. It hadn't taken long for him to realise his failings as an employer, once he'd been forced to take a step back and see his business practices from a different angle.

"I'm sorry, Annie. If it's any comfort, she can't take this any further when she doesn't have any proof."

"Of course she doesn't. What the hell would I want with an electronic toy dog?"

It was on the tip of his tongue to say she could sell it, but one look at her thunderous expression and he knew to swallow the comment back. Terri was the one in the wrong here, accusing a staff member of theft with absolutely no just cause.

"She's trying to cover her own back. Someone likely walked out of the door past her when she was too busy talking on her phone and swigging out of that silver hip flask in her pocket to notice." David wasn't going to forget anything going on here in a hurry.

Annie gave a smirk. "I'm not the only one who sees her doing that, then?"

"All noted for future reference." He tapped his finger at his temple to let her know he'd filed that away to confront Terri with if and when he was able to.

"Annie, there are customers waiting." The woman herself appeared, ignoring the queue to requisition the only employee who was busy replenishing stock on the shelves.

She rolled her eyes at David and he knew that was the end of the conversation for now, even if the matter wasn't resolved in his mind. He'd get justice for Annie in some shape or form, because this woman was making her life more miserable than it already was.

Due to being rushed off her feet serving customers and answering the phone, Annie hardly spoke to him for the rest of the day. David wasn't used to being ignored, and even last night he'd had her to talk to. Today proved how much he was relying on her, and he wished he could do something for her in turn. It didn't make any sense to be shown the ways in which he'd failed as an employer when he wasn't in a position to do anything about it at present.

He might not have had to work in similar conditions with snide managers belittling him at every turn, but his parents' suspicions that he'd never amount to anything had prompted his Herculean effort to prove them wrong. It didn't mean he was proud of running this kind of workplace environment.

With a lot to ponder and burdened by guilt, he kept out of her way as much as possible, even though she was his anchor to the world.

"We have the very thing just down this aisle." Annie whisked past him with a customer in tow and he instinctively stepped back. Even though he wasn't physically in her road, he didn't need the reminder that he wasn't a solid form every time someone walked through him. Being the invisible man wasn't as much fun as he'd imagined when he was a kid. If this was how working for him felt to his employees—being ignored and forgotten about—it was little wonder Annie was so disillusioned with life.

"You're a miracle worker. Thank you very much." Another satisfied customer made her way over to the till where sour-faced Terri was standing, filing her talons, and who would no doubt ring the sale in as her own.

Annie must've walked miles ferrying customers and stocking the length and breadth of the store.

There were a few junior members of staff who appeared at staggered intervals, but they seemed more interested in gossiping with each other in the blind areas of the store where they thought no one could see or hear.

"I can't wait until this shift is over. I'm dying." A young guy he guessed was about eighteen was slumped dramatically over a shelf just around the corner from where Annie was working.

"Hangover?" His heavily made-up female colleague with dyed-black hair winced in sympathy.

David didn't want to think of it as eavesdropping, more of an undercover boss thing, going incognito to find out what was really going on in his store.

"Yeah. I haven't even been to bed yet." Although the lad's crumpled uniform and generally unkempt appearance would attest to that boast, David got the sense this was more about trying to impress his pretty friend with his antics.

"Does that mean you're not going out with us tonight?" She did that pouty thing all men were a sucker for at any age.

"Hell no. That's the only reason I made it here at all today. I need the cash for drinking money."

David couldn't bear to hear any more. He could see what a false economy it was to take on young, inexperienced teenagers because they were cheaper than mature employees. They did little in the way of actual work and simply wanted to put in their time to earn money for going clubbing at the weekend. It was people like Annie, who actually cared about helping customers and keeping the store tidy, who were the real assets. Yet, when they were the ones doing all the work, it was inevitable that they'd get as fed up as she clearly was at the store.

The only chance he got to say any of this to Annie was during her lunch break, which ended up being closer to dinner time. Terri, naturally, had managed to get hers on time, after she'd sent a junior to fetch it for her.

David was bored out of his tree wandering the aisles, but he had come up with some bullet points for overdue changes. His suggestion that they get one of those white boards to work on their *missions* didn't go down well with Annie.

"This isn't bloody CSI, you know. A pen and paper will do just as well." She took a notebook from her bag, along with her tinfoil pack of ham sandwiches, banana, chocolate biscuit and orange juice. He couldn't remember the last time he'd even bothered to make himself a meal, never mind packed a lunch.

She divided the page into two sections with a swipe of a pen and labelled the columns, 'Annie' and 'David'. It was such a simple thing, yet seeing his name written down was confirmation he still existed—at least in Annie's eyes, if no one else's.

"Right. We need to approach this logically. What reasons could there possibly be for us to have been forced together? How can we help each other? I'll start with you…shit boss. Now, what do I need?"

"A life?" Clearly, he'd felt slighted at the words she'd written on the list.

"Look who's talking," she bit back. Neither of them was coming out of this looking good.

"We could start with the obvious things such as money, a decent flat, a relationship—all the things most people take for granted." David rattled off everything she was lacking with unsettling ease. He'd only known her for a matter of hours and he had her sussed. She was a nobody with nothing and no one in her life.

Annie scribbled down his suggestions, and she could see why it had bothered him to see it in print. It was depressing when one's life was reduced to a list of pros and cons. Though she doubted that she had any positive points, even if they added an extra column to save face.

"That's all well and good, but how are you going to help me with any of that? Besides, you had all of it and it hasn't made you any happier than I am, from what I can tell."

"I could advise you on business and financial matters. Retail aside, is there anything you've always wanted to do? Perhaps I'm here to guide you towards a new career."

"Nothing I can think of right now. I left school and started straight into caring for Mum. There wasn't a lot of room for daydreaming." She'd been made to grow up quickly when her peers were taking the time to find themselves, doing everything university life offered alongside further education. Parties, romances and travel had all passed her by, and though she'd never regretted spending that time with her mother, she realised she had nothing positive to focus her attention on now that her mum had gone. Perhaps that was why she'd been so down, so lost. She needed a distraction or a hobby to fill what time she had outside of work.

What can I add to my pro column at present? Keeper of small, defective rodents and major contributor to the world economy via my chocolate habit?

For all David's faults, he employed lots of people and potentially donated to many charities. At least he'd done something, was recognised for something in his life. Her only legacy would be a rented flat full of empty chocolate wrappers and her body, likely having been lying for weeks before anyone noticed, half-eaten by George Bailey.

"Have a think on it. As for relationships, well, you've got to get yourself out there."

"Out where? On the street?" She had visions of him setting her up on a street corner with a neon arrow pointing towards her screaming 'Desperate'.

"Out of the flat would be a start. Don't take this the wrong way, but if you made more of an effort, invested a small sum in a new wardrobe and some beauty treatments, you could be a real stunner."

Ouch. There was no other way to take that than, *'You're a mess. Sort yourself out.'*

"Gee, thanks. It's no wonder you couldn't find anyone else to take you in, making back-handed compliments like that."

"Hear me out. There's no need to be so defensive all the time. You're pretty and you've got a great body. All I'm saying is you should show it off more."

Annie immediately wanted to curl up and die. "You looked?"

"Of course I did. I'm a man," he said without a trace of remorse. She, on the other hand, was regretting not having shaved any part of her body for some considerable time, since she hadn't expected anyone but George Bailey to see her naked.

"So, you're saying if I put it on a plate, I'll snag myself a guy and give my life some meaning? That doesn't sound shallow at all." Since her last relationship, she hadn't been in a hurry for another one. In fact, she'd been so not bothered about how she looked that she could've been accused of purposely appearing as though she'd been dragged through a jumble sale backwards to steer clear of any men. Clearly, that hadn't worked.

"I don't mean... It's not that... Don't you ever just get horny?" David got straight to the point, making Annie's eyebrows almost disappear into her hair with surprise.

"I can't say that's, uh, ever been a priority for me." Sure, sex was an important part of a relationship and she was no virgin, but she could take it or leave it—not that she had a choice these days.

"Then you're not doing it right," he muttered.

Shivers danced up and down her spine and she shifted uncomfortably in the plastic chair. The way he said it made her think he *definitely* did it right, and she wondered about what it would be like with him. Somehow, she knew a night in bed with David would change her mind on the subject, when even the thought of it was awakening parts of her that she'd shut down after her ex. Perhaps she wouldn't end up a dried-up old maid after all.

"I'm not doing it at all, and that's the way I'd prefer to keep things. I'm depressed enough without having another lying, cheating bastard in my life."

"Don't you miss it? Christ, I'm horny as hell and I can't do bugger all about it. Trust me. I've tried."

"Eww-w. Are you telling me you can still have a hard-on, even like this? Men are insatiable, obsessed with sex and their dicks. Even when they have a girlfriend at their beck and call, they aren't happy and have to have a bit on the side."

"I think you're confusing me with your ex. I'm not in the habit of cheating, thank you very much. In defence of my, er, arousal, I was standing in the shower with a naked woman. I'd have to actually be dead not to get turned on."

"Yuck. Yuck. Yuck. Don't say any more. New house rule... No more Peeping Tom shit and absolutely no touching your dick anywhere near me." She should've been grossed out at the thought—and under any other circumstances, she would've been—but she'd be lying if she said there wasn't a teeny, tiny part of her secretly pleased that she had the capability of turning him on with her naked body alone.

"I'll see if I can control myself." The twinkle in his eye suggested he was winding her up about the whole thing, but a needy part of her wanted to believe she mightn't be so repulsive in his eyes after all.

"Moving on, I think we should add unresolved family issues to your column."

"Now *that* is definitely one way to deflate my mood."

"I'm serious. We have to consider that a possibility." Families were full of secrets and lies, and she was sure the Reeces were no exception. She wanted to find out more about David and his relationship with his parents in case there was the slightest chance she could reunite them.

"You saw them, heard what they had to say on the subject of my possible demise. They're not interested in making amends, only money."

Annie wasn't entirely convinced it was that straightforward, so she wrote it down anyway. It wasn't as if he could stop her doing some investigating.

"Hmm-m, well, it's going on the list. What about relationships for you too? Perhaps there's a wife and kids waiting for you out there somewhere." She tapped her pen on the pad, anxious to show that she wasn't the only one with a dismal love life. Flame wasn't wifey material, and perhaps he needed pointing in a different direction if he was supposed to have settled down by now.

"Ugh. Divorced from the last woman I thought I'd spend the rest of my life with, along with half of my fortune. Next."

Oh yeah, she'd forgotten about that. It had made the headlines at the time and his following drunken shenanigans had made him the name he was today. She wasn't sure she'd want to be known for falling out of clubs every night with a different conquest on her arm rather than her business empire, but that was how people got famous these days. Maybe when this was over, she'd sell her story. That would deadbolt the lock and secure her room at the funny farm.

The stockroom door swung open, a cold blast of air making her surroundings more desolate than ever. Terri was propping the door open and tapping her watch. She'd gone a whole minute over her allotted time.

"Coming now." She tossed her rubbish in the bin and filed away their pity notes for later, when they didn't have the 'fun police' breathing down their necks.

With Terri on her—*third?*—break, Annie was allowed to take up residence behind the till. At least she got to stand in the one spot for a while, though David did see her kick off her shoes and wiggle her stockinged feet. He had a few things to add to his own personal list of things to sort out once he was back in his rightful place at the head of the company.

1. *Take a personal interest in my employees and revise contracts regarding their working hours.* Annie had lectured him on the moral and financial implications of zero-hours contracts.
2. *Get rid of people like Terri, who are bad for morale.*
3. *Improve working conditions with small improvements like redecorating, fitting out proper staff rooms and providing seating.*

He had a front-row seat to see how she interacted with customers and, though she wouldn't admit it, helping people was in her nature. It pained him to say it, but she was wasted there. David had been on the receiving end of her kindness, hidden behind her outer spiky shell, and it was a shame it went unnoticed and unrewarded by others. It had taken him reaching death's door to realise she existed, and now she had his full attention, he'd make sure she got all the recognition she deserved...somehow.

"Hey, Annie, how's it going?" A smartly dressed man carrying boxes walked into the shop and straight over to the counter. He seemed familiar, but David couldn't quite place him. At least he was acknowledging her, which was more than most people around there did.

"Hi, Kevin. Busy, as usual." Annie was leaning over the counter, returning the friendly smile. *Is she actually flirting?* She hadn't done anything other than greet the guy, but her body language and the way she kept fixing her hair said she was interested in him. It was the most animated David had seen her in anyone's company bar his, but what they shared was the opposite of flirting.

"Too busy to make me a cuppa?" Pretty boy Kev, who David instinctively knew was being followed by a cloud of cheap cologne, dared to wink at her. He waited for the fireworks to start. She wasn't the type to fall for this schtick and dissolve into a puddle of simpering hormones.

"Never."

Apparently, she was.

"Cameron, can you take over at the till so I can see to Kevin here?" Annie called over one of the younger staff members and the hungover teen slouched over unenthusiastically. Both Kevin and David watched Annie walk towards the stock room, hypnotised by the sway of her hips in that figure-hugging skirt. David swore he heard Kev sigh and wondered if Annie knew she had an admirer, or was this typical banter between the two? She didn't strike him as the sort to engage in that sort of flirtatious behaviour unless there was meaning behind it, and she certainly wouldn't have responded well to him taking that approach with her. He'd have been more liable to get a knee in the balls if he'd expected her to be at his beck and call.

A whistling Kev carried his mystery packages over to a display stand of board games and proceeded to unpack a load of promotional stickers and posters for what must be his company's latest product to hit the shelves. David remembered now that he was one of the sales reps who toured their retail distributors, making sure their brand was visible to customers in the lead-up to Christmas.

Annie returned carrying a mug with a chocolate biscuit on the side. "Here you go. Don't let Terri see."

Now she was winking and making things more uncomfortable for him, wondering if this happened every time Kev came into the shop.

"It can be our little secret." Kev tapped his finger at the side of his nose as he winked back.

"Eww-w. This is like watching one of those wildlife documentaries with horny creatures engaging in some weird courtship ritual. Any second now he's going to show you his colourful plumage."

Annie was getting good at pretending she couldn't hear him, but it was clear she hadn't been entirely truthful about her views on sex and relationships. He could see she was interested in this particular man. From the few comments she'd made about a cheating ex, it was clear she'd been hurt too and was wary of repeating past mistakes. David knew what it was to go through that, but a person had to get back out there or end up spending nights alone, crying and talking to people who weren't really there.

As long as Kev wasn't one of those randy salesmen who had flings all around the country, then they should go for it. They were both adults, attracted to one another and had work in common. That was more than David could say about most of his recent hook-ups. Dating, he could do. It was relationships he had a problem with. If Annie needed a helping hand to nudge her into the arms of hunky Kev, he'd be there for her. Neither of them had any choice in that, but in this case, David would enjoy being close and playing Cupid for once. At least he'd be helping her in some small way, in return for everything she'd been doing for him.

"He likes you, you know." David took it upon himself to obliterate any doubts she might have about the matter when she was back serving at the counter.

"Hmm-m?" She bagged up the various stocking fillers her harassed customer had purchased and handed them over. "Thanks for shopping at Reece's Toys. Have a nice day."

"Kev. He fancies you." David carried on, confident in his assumption, since he'd caught the rep staring at her every now and then when she wasn't looking.

"No, he doesn't. Don't be daft." Annie batted away the idea and gave the impression that she did it with any compliment tossed in her direction.

"Trust me. That guy is practically salivating over you." It was sweet in a sickening way, watching them turn into two shy teenagers every time they accidentally brushed past each other or caught each other's eye. And so was the girlish blush staining Annie's cheeks.

He'd forgotten about that first spark of recognised attraction and the dance around it until the parties finally gave into temptation. The people he'd surrounded himself with lately had no guile about them. They saw what they wanted and went for it with no worries that they could possibly be wrong in their assumptions.

When he'd got together with his now-ex-wife, there'd been no elaborate courtship. They'd homed in on each other and he'd let passion overtake any of those doubts apparently stopping Annie from acting on impulse.

"I'm back now. There's no need for you to hang around making the place look untidy. I'm sure there's plenty of work to do elsewhere. If not, I'm sure I can find you something to do." With Terri claiming her rightful place, Annie was relegated back onto the sales floor.

"No problem. I'll go finish the merchandising," she said through gritted teeth and set to facing-out stock on the shelves and generally making the shop contents look tidy.

At least it gave David a chance to chat when she was working without an audience.

"So, how often does he come in here?" He wanted to get an idea of the timescale of this budding romance with Kev.

Annie shrugged. "Every few months or so."

Shit. David had no intention of standing around twiddling his thumbs until studly Kev made another appearance.

"Why don't you ask him out?"

"What? No. I couldn't." Annie blustered on, rearranging boxes she'd already tidied two seconds earlier.

"Why not? You like him and he likes you." Hopefully, after one night of passion, David would no longer be playing gooseberry but be back where he belonged.

She shook her head and shot down the only lead he had into solving this mystery. "What if he said no — or it turned out to be a disaster? I couldn't face him again and it would make this place an even bigger nightmare."

She had a point. He'd learned some time ago not to get involved with co-workers. Linda had started out as his personal assistant, and he should have left their relationship in the office instead of crossing that line and mixing business with pleasure. However, this seemed the obvious solution to their predicament and it was a shame to not to at least explore the option. Inspiration suddenly struck, and this time around he was grateful for divine intervention.

"The Christmas party... Surely he goes to that?" Where was better for two people to get together than a drunken orgy of underpaid, overworked colleagues, where they could let their hair down and do something they'd possibly live to regret? Although he wouldn't be in attendance himself, he'd heard enough stories of what went on over the years to understand the nature of a work Christmas party.

"He might. I don't." She was further gone than he'd realised if she didn't even go to the obligatory work Christmas do. He would've thought it was a good chance for her to get out and socialise, but apparently, she didn't do that, regardless of if she had time off or not.

"Why on earth not? Free drink, free food and people making a show of themselves... What's not to like?" For normal people it sounded like the highlight of the year, especially if a person was single.

"You only pay ten percent of the cost and the first drink. Apart from that, I've no desire to mix with most of these people when they're sober, never mind listen to drunken renditions of Shakin' Stevens and Wham! or watch them vomit into their handbags."

"No, you'd rather sit crying in your PJs." He and Annie were obviously very different creatures. Even in the wake of his break-up, he'd refused to be beaten down, and though he could've been accused of partying to excess, he still thought it a better way to get over someone than wallowing as she continued to do.

"It's my first Christmas without Mum. I miss her like crazy, so excuse me if I don't want to celebrate by getting drunk with people I see way too much of already." Annie didn't appreciate having to justify her actions to David. She'd done enough of that over the years, but it was something a man like him would never understand or have to go through.

David Reece would never take orders from anyone. She knew how much it was killing him to be powerless now and couldn't imagine him ever being cowed by anything. On the flip side, she doubted he'd ever be able to empathise with her past. She'd spent so much of her time being torn between her mum and her boyfriend and constantly apologising for not giving either one her full attention that it was almost a relief to be on her own.

"You don't have to cut yourself off from the rest of the world. There's no harm in having one night out. You might surprise yourself and actually enjoy it."

"I just want to be left alone."

What if she and Kevin did fancy each other a bit? The flirting was fun, but asking him out or expecting him to make a move based on it was a step too far out of her comfort zone. She didn't know if she was ready to date anyone again, and if he turned her down or messed her around, she'd never want to repeat the experience.

"Do you think that's what your mum would want for you?" David's tone was much softer now, less confrontational as he tried to guilt-trip her into doing this. She knew why. Performing this good deed and playing matchmaker could be his chance to go wherever he was supposed to be. Surely that was what they both wanted, wasn't it?

She thought of her mum always apologising for holding Annie back when she should've been out having fun, or blaming herself for her daughter's boyfriend when he cheated on her — none of which was her fault. If he hadn't wanted to be with her, all he had to do was say. He hadn't been adult enough to discuss any troubles in their relationship. If her mother had seen Annie's state the previous night, she'd have beaten herself up over it instead of giving her the 'pull yourself together' talk David was attempting.

"No, it's not." She couldn't do anything about the past, but she could take a stand and wrestle back control of her life. With that in mind, she dropped the stack of jigsaws she'd been sorting into numerical order and walked straight over to Kev's stand.

"Will you be going to the Christmas party this year? I think it's at The River Room." Her heart was pounding so hard with adrenaline that she'd just wanted to get the words out, but she sounded so abrupt, so brazen. It didn't sound like her at all.

Kev choked on the tea he was sipping. "I, er...sure. Are you going?"

Annie gave him a curt nod. "I am now. I'll see you there."

"Wait! Do you mean like on a date?" This was the last chance for her to back out and laugh off the suggestion that she'd just propositioned him in their place of work. The stunned look on David's face helped her keep her nerve. It wasn't often she was able to surprise people when they expected so little from her.

"If you like?" She tried to make out it was no big deal by hiding her shaking hands behind her back and hoping he couldn't see the sweat beginning to form on her top lip.

"Sure," he said with a grin, enabling her to breathe again. The world hadn't ended after all.

"Good." She simply turned and walked away, not daring to glance back and see his reaction. No doubt David, who was standing applauding her, would let her know.

There was a possibility she might barf once the belated nerves kicked in with a vengeance. She'd probably spend the rest of the night agonising over the consequences of what she'd done and what disasters she was leaving herself open to.

At least she'd made the move, taken a step forward. Now the rest was down to David and, of course, Kevin.

Chapter Seven

"I'm going to call in on Sam. He owns this place as well as the flat. Please don't make me look any more mental than he already thinks I am,"' Annie lectured him as they left her apartment and walked into Fletchers Café below.

"I can't make any promises on that score, but I swear not to interfere." He crossed his heart, though he couldn't bring himself to do the 'hope to die' thing with it. Neither of them needed to weird out the landlord and get her evicted, leaving them both wandering about with nowhere to go.

David had to admit that despite its less than salubrious surroundings, the café was a hidden gem. They bypassed the tables and chairs under the green-and-white striped awning outside to enter the bijou premises. He supposed it was cosier inside compared to sitting out in the December weather. Plus, the smell of fresh bread and coffee he imagined emanating from the kitchen had to be preferable to the inevitable diesel and cigarette smoke outside.

They'd made use of every available space in there. Along with the pretty French bistro-style tables and chairs, there was a breakfast bar at the window with a row of high-backed stools. The black wrought-iron furniture against the backdrop of white subway-style tiles on the back wall could've made for a stark interior, but was saved by the gorgeous crystal chandelier hanging from the ceiling, adding some glamour. The vintage French signs and framed Parisian scenes gave the place a splash of colour and an air of being somewhere more glamorous than a corner coffee shop. It was somewhere he wouldn't be embarrassed to be seen.

The festive garlands strung along the counter tops drew his eye to the goodies on display in the glass case. He just knew everything was made with a ton of butter, but all those delicious iced swirls and chocolate-laden breakfast munchies he'd kill to taste were off limits, just like everything else he'd taken for granted in normal life.

"Hey, Sam, just an orange juice, please."

David didn't have to check the menu to know she'd ordered the cheapest thing on it, likely to give her an excuse to come in.

"Morning, Annie. Do you want something to eat with that too?" The much-too-happy-for-this-time-of-the-morning guy behind the counter dazzled her with his dimpled smile.

"No thanks."

"I can't tempt you with anything at all? On the house." Handsome Sam was much more accommod-ating than he ought to be, and David was taking an irrational dislike to him, regardless that he'd obviously been good to Annie. *Better than her scummy employer who didn't check to see if his employees had enough to eat on the crappy wages he paid.*

"There's no need to do that. You'll go out of business if you keep feeding me for free."

"You know I make too much food anyway. Better than not having enough for the hungry hordes. Take a seat and I'll bring something over to you in a minute."

Without any further protest, Annie took the seat closest to the door, avoiding the mistletoe hanging from the ceiling.

"So, do you come here often?" David leaned across the table and waggled his eyebrows at her, not entirely in jest. Seeing her interact with Sam made him curious about the relationship the two had. For all the illusion of leading a lonely life, there were clearly several men who took a keen interest in her, even if she was oblivious to the fact.

"I try to call in at least a couple of times a week to see him. His wife died two years ago, before he opened this place. I know what how it feels to lose someone close, and I like to check in and make sure he's doing okay." Annie scraped her nail along a scratch on the table, avoiding his eyes, and David sensed this regular interaction was important to her. A little company went a long way to making a person feel part of life again after a devastating event. He'd found that out for himself.

"Here you go. That should set you up for the day." Sam slid into the seat beside David without invitation and loaded the table with a croissant, a pat of butter, a tiny pot of homemade jam and some chocolate spread.

"All calorie-free, I assume?" She didn't wait for an answer before cutting the croissant open and slathering it in the stuff. David loved that she didn't spend her time seriously worrying about that kind of thing. There were much more important issues to lose sleep over than having an extra pound or two on the hips compared to the next woman, and he'd found it boring listening to those neuroses from past partners. They might've looked good on the outside, but they clearly hadn't been happy in their own skin. That level of insecurity wasn't attractive. It was part of the reason David didn't stick around for meaningful relationships. He wanted to get laid, not become a therapist for those with major daddy issues.

Annie took a bite of the flaky pastry, crumbs falling everywhere as the melting chocolate spread oozed out and trickled down her chin. Sam reached out at the same time as David to dab at the chocolate but only one of them was of any use to her.

"There was a woman in here asking after you yesterday," he said, sucking the chocolate from his thumb, a gesture which neither of them appeared to baulk at but that opened David's eyes to the easiness of their relationship.

"Really?" Annie swiped a napkin from the table to wipe away any further remnants of her breakfast from her chin.

"Yeah. Not one of my regulars. She isn't one of the mums from the school run, and I didn't recognise her as one of the office workers from around the corner who are in here every day without fail."

"Did she say what she wanted?"

David detected the note of panic in her voice, as though anyone looking for her could only mean trouble.

"She said she knew you from back in high school and had seen you about. I think she just wanted a catch up, since she's thinking of moving to the area."

"Did she give you her name?"

Sam blushed. "Sorry... I didn't get around to asking."

"Well, what did she look like?" The irritation was beginning to sound in Annie's voice now and David didn't blame her, if there was someone hanging around asking questions about her.

"Pretty, petite and...lovely." Sam smiled that boyish smile again, so utterly devoid of guile that David almost fell for him himself. He couldn't understand why he and Annie hadn't got together when they seemed so right for each other — so alike and with a lot in common.

"Ooh, he likes this mystery woman, whoever she is." It didn't take a genius to work it out, and perhaps a part of him said it to get a rise out of Annie, but if anything, she looked pleased.

"She clearly made an impression on you," she teased, increasing the red tinge to Sam's cheeks.

"I admit that we talked for a long time over coffee. She told me about her daughter and I explained about my, er...circumstances. I'm meeting her tonight to show her around town."

"I'm so happy for you, Sam." Annie reached out and gave his hand a squeeze, making David yearn for even that simple contact.

"You two really are just friends, huh? I'm just checking in case Sam's about to break your heart and I'm the one left picking up the pieces." David scanned her face for any signs of jealousy, finding only a look of annoyance flashed in his direction.

"I'm only showing her the sights, such as they are. It's not some mad, passionate love affair, Annie." With more customers filing into the café, Sam rose to his feet and began clearing the table.

"Yet. I'm just glad you've met someone again."

"Me too. I'll make sure to get her name this time, in case you do know her. She has the most amazing bright red hair and piercing blue eyes." Sam floated off then to serve his customers, leaving Annie and David staring at each other, their mouths wide open.

"Flame," they said simultaneously.

"Surely it couldn't be. Why would she be slumming it around here?" As much as David didn't want it to be true anymore than Annie did, he knew something about her that virtually no one else did.

"She has a daughter. She told me. It's possible she followed us here from the hospital." For what reason, he couldn't be entirely sure, other than a sudden interest in Annie, which wasn't good news for either of them.

"I can't see she's honestly willing to move here, so it must be me she's snooping about, but why follow her fake fiancé's hospital visitor?"

"Perhaps she thinks you're some kind of threat, about to expose her lies over our non-existent engagement."

"Great. All we need is someone stalking us. The next thing you know, she'll be having me sectioned for talking to myself."

"We're just going to have to be more careful from now on and keep pumping your friendly landlord for information, just as she is doing." He had a feeling poor Sam wasn't going to get the happy-ever-after Annie wanted for him, but hopefully he would keep Flame out of their hair long enough to deal with their own crisis. Whatever her motive, they couldn't afford to let her interference derail whatever journey they were supposed to go on to end this whole ordeal.

* * * *

"Don't you have anything else to wear?" David cast a critical eye over Annie's multi-functional uniform, which was serving as her hospital visiting outfit again.

"Nothing I'm willing to be seen in publicly. If I'd known I was going to be hob-nobbing with the rich and famous, I'd have had some sequins sewn onto my onesie. I don't see the point in splashing money out on clothes I can't afford and won't wear again. It's more important that I can pay the bills and eat once in a wonder." She certainly wouldn't have frittered her hard-earned cash on expensive nights out or drinking down at the pub, even if she'd had someone to go with.

"You're going to have to invest in something for the Christmas party if you want to wow Kevin. I think he's seen you in that outfit once too often for you to get away with it."

"Har de har." He'd be laughing on the other side of his face once they walked into that hospital room.

Annie knew very well she was going to have to break out the credit card for something to wear, though it still wouldn't be the kind of haute couture David was used to.

"I'm not saying you don't look good. Clearly Kevin thinks so too, but it wouldn't hurt to put a little effort in. You know, a trip to the hairdresser, some new lingerie..."

"All right, I get the message. Although I can guarantee no one will see what underwear I've got on." Asking someone out was a far cry from having sex with them, and she wasn't the sort to put out on a first date.

"Except me." He reminded her that any illusion of privacy had vanished the second he'd appeared in her flat.

"Then I'll be sure to don my biggest granny pants and greyest bra."

"Can't wait." He scrunched up his nose in disgust at the image and she considered the matter closed, along with any thoughts of her in racy lingerie. He'd seen quite enough of her already, and it wasn't very comforting to have him insisting she needed assistance to snag her man.

"You're one to talk about my wardrobe. It's a bit disconcerting to see you in a dinner suit every time I turn around, as if you're here to take my order or about to launch into some Frank Sinatra number." The last time she'd had men around her in suits had been at her mother's funeral, so he projected a kind of doom and gloom without even opening his mouth.

"You prefer the hospital gown with the slit at the back? Perv." He was grinning as they exited the lift, but beneath the joking, she was certain he felt just as exposed and vulnerable as she did right now.

He was lying in that bed like a museum exhibit, people coming and going and talking over him as though he didn't exist. All the while he *was* there, listening and hurting and unable to do a damn thing about it. Her plans for the night weren't going to improve his sense of helplessness either.

"Maybe I should get one myself for the party. Now that really would get Kev's attention."

"Honestly, for the amount I'm probably paying to be here, you'd think they'd provide something with more class. Is it asking too much to have a breathable fabric?" He tilted his nose up in the air and Annie had to stifle a giggle as a nurse passed them in the corridor.

"Ssh-h. You'll get me in trouble. We don't want the staff getting suspicious that I'm not a grieving relative after all."

"What are we doing back here anyway? There doesn't seem any point, and *he* gives me the heebie-jeebies." It wasn't good that he taken to referring to himself in the third person, the detachment almost becoming acceptable to him now. That could make it more difficult for him to be reconciled in body and spirit, although that wasn't the main reason she'd brought him back.

"You made me confront my fears and tick one thing off the list. Now it's your turn." She opened the door to find his parents and a young girl sitting around the bedside. Only one of the visitors came as a surprise to her.

"Hey, Annie. Thanks for texting us back." Nicholas Reece got up and shook her hand, and Annie could feel David's eyes burning into the back of her head.

"Traitor," he spat at her.

She'd known he wouldn't appreciate the ambush, but that meant they were even. Both had been put into awkward situations that they weren't allowed or able to simply walk away from. It was his turn to do something brave and out of his comfort zone. In this case, she was going to force him into a room to hear his parents out.

"Any change?" Annie was compelled to ask, regardless that she knew nothing had changed since their last visit, apart from him becoming her dating guru. Not only had she phoned this morning to check, but she had the non-living proof standing right next to her.

David's mother shook her head and proceeded to plump up the pillows under his. "I keep hoping he'll open his eyes and that seeing us here will be enough for him to get back on his feet. I don't care if he screams and shouts or throws us out, as long as he wakes up."

She was very convincing as a concerned parent. They both were. That was the reason she'd agreed to come back again tonight when they'd texted her. She wanted to get to know them and give David a chance to see what was going on with them there. Even if it didn't make a difference, at least she could say she'd tried.

"He'll wake up. He has to." The little girl, who Annie imagined to be about ten or eleven, stepped out from the corner to comfort Melanie. She was still dressed in her navy school uniform, her dark hair braided and hanging over one shoulder. It was heart-breaking to see her obvious distress.

Annie looked to David for an explanation, but he remained unmoved by the scene before him. He hadn't mentioned a sister, and she assumed this wasn't a long-lost daughter he'd misplaced. In the end, she introduced herself to satisfy her curiosity.

"I'm sorry. I don't think we've met. I'm Annie, a friend of David's."

The child moved behind Melanie, spooked by being addressed directly, and let the older woman intervene on her behalf.

"This is Emma, our daughter."

Annie slowly turned her head towards David, unable to believe he'd concealed this piece of information from her. "David has a sister?"

"He didn't tell you about me?" Emma's face fell, and Annie began to side more and more with this side of the Reece family before she found out what had caused the rift between them. It was one thing for him to be pissed at his parents, but it was cold to have abandoned a little sister who was an innocent bystander to whatever had happened.

"David's a very private person. He hasn't told me anything of his family circumstances."

Annie hoped that was enough to prevent the young girl from taking the slight personally. He'd been equally dismissive of the whole family. However, a heads-up about a sensitive kid sister would've been appreciated. "I'm sure David didn't intentionally neglect to mention a sister."

Nicholas laid his hands on Emma's shoulders. "Emma was born after David left home. No matter how many times we tried, he refused to give us a second chance to be better parents to him."

Annie thought they were all being perfectly affectionate with each other. It wasn't that she didn't believe David's stance that his parents had done a terrible job raising him, but people could change. They must have been very young when they'd had David. Not that that was an excuse for any ill treatment towards him, but it might explain it. Perhaps their presence here was proof that they were desperate to grab hold of an olive branch...if only for Emma's sake.

It was clear that she was fond of her big brother by the way she was straightening his bed covers and brushing his hair off his face. It was difficult to figure out why he would hold a grudge against her too.

"Do you see much of your...David?"

"Not really." That bombshell didn't put her off as she tucked a tiny teddy bear into bed beside the patient, and Annie's heart broke for the child who only wanted him to return some sort of affection and treat her as family.

"You've got to understand, Annie. They were so useless at being parents that I'm sure there was a strong case for child neglect. They were never at home. I had to feed myself most nights while they went out partying, and I was a lot younger than Emma. Fair play to them if they're off the booze and 'parents of the year' candidates now, but they did nothing for me." The more David talked about his upbringing, the more his voice began to shake from decade's worth of pent-up rage, something Annie knew had to come to a head before he could fully deal with it.

"I don't blame David for cutting us out of his life. We weren't the best parents."

"Understatement of the century, Dad." David was right up in his face, though Nicholas couldn't see him.

"We were young and stupid and too immature to deal with the responsibility of a child. If we could go back and do it all over again, we would, wouldn't we, Mel?"

Annie guessed having Emma had been a way of filling a void when David had moved out. A kid sister in the equation gave her some leverage to work on a reconciliation. Even if he couldn't find a way to forgive his parents, there was a little girl here who needed him.

"When David left home at such a young age, it was a wake-up call for us. We've been honest with Emma about why he doesn't visit and the sort of parents we were to him. Believe me, we would never have had Emma if we were still the same people. I wish David could understand that. I don't blame him for hating us, but I guess he's done very well for himself, despite our failing him." Melanie was very much the proud mum as she continued to list all his achievements, and it was obvious that they'd kept track of their son, regardless of the breakdown in their relationship. They hadn't lost hope of getting their family back together, even if he considered them out of his life for good.

"He did give me my own phone and he calls me every week to see how I'm doing at school."

David threw his hands up as Emma let out another one of his secrets. "It's not her fault she's caught in the middle. I want to make sure she has someone looking out for her, because I sure as hell didn't."

"He won't talk to us, but he's been very good to Emma, never misses her birthday. She idolises him, even keeps his photo by her bed." If David really was the perfect big brother being portrayed by Melanie, Annie was crushing on him a little herself. She wouldn't mind a hunky older man regularly checking on her welfare and sending her presents. They clearly had a strong bond, despite David denying it. Why else would he refuse to meet up with a child he'd accepted as family? Unless he was afraid that by letting her further into his life he'd have to confront the issues he had with his parents, and he'd been clinging on to that anger for so long that perhaps he didn't want to let go of it.

"I hope he wakes up soon."

"I'm sure he will, sweetheart." Now that David had seen for himself how much Emma thought of him and how much he meant to her, he couldn't refuse her. Annie would make sure of it. Contact might only be the matter of a weekly phone call, but to this little girl, it was a symbol of her big brother's love.

It would be harder to walk away and deny that connection now, as it would also be for Annie. These were the first people she'd seen outside working hours for weeks, even if it was at the side of a hospital bed.

"Is that Flame person around? They gave me David's personal possessions, including his house keys. I wasn't sure if she should have them." Melanie dangled the keys from her finger as if she were afraid to touch them. It was surprising when David had pegged her as some sort of gold-digger, who, if it were true, would surely have been rifling through his possessions already?

"No!" David was so emphatic that he forgot himself and tried to grab the keys out of her hand.

"I don't think that's such a good idea. They aren't as close as she's making out." Annie played Devil's advocate, safe in the knowledge that Flame wasn't about to storm in and claim ownership, because she was out with Sam. Although, it wouldn't surprise her if she cancelled because a better offer came up. From everything Annie had heard, it wouldn't be beyond her to do a photo shoot draped over the wreckage of the crash in her underwear to capitalise on her fifteen minutes of fame.

"Oh, good. I didn't really take to her when we saw her last night. She didn't have time to talk to us about what happened. She's too full of herself, if you ask me. David needs someone supportive in his life. I know he doesn't make it easy for people to get close to him, but we all need someone, don't we? I'm glad he has you,

Annie. I'll let you keep these safe, and if there's anything we can do, let us know." His mother handed over the keys to David's kingdom, but Annie felt more of a fraud than Flame accepting them.

David didn't know her any better than Nicholas and Melanie. She might appear supportive by being here, but it was only because she had her own interests at heart too. All of this was to get David out of her life, not make space for him and his ever-growing family in it.

* * * *

David was more than a teensy bit pissed off at Annie as they drove to his house. She knew he had no choice but to follow wherever she went, whoever she met, and she'd used it against him.

"You're going to have to talk to me sooner or later or you'll stay in limbo forever." She kept her eyes on the road and saved him from seeing the smug look on her face when he admitted she was right. Nothing would be solved by his sulky silence, but it was maddening that she was the only person he could talk to, when she was the one who'd put him in this mood.

"You ambushed me," he eventually accused once his blood had settled back down to a simmer in his veins.

"Okay. I knew you wouldn't be happy to see them again, but we did agree to tackle all aspects of those lists, no matter how uncomfortable."

"You didn't have to be so underhanded about it," he huffed, arms folded and feeling defensive, due to how much of his personal information had been revealed tonight without his permission. He hated this powerlessness, being at someone else's mercy, when it made him so vulnerable.

He'd been so used to making decisions on his own, fending for himself, that it was hard to get to grips with his current status, beholden to Annie. The only option he had was to accept her help. To trust her, no matter how difficult the journey was proving to be for him on a personal level.

"Emma seems very fond of you." Apparently deciding they'd endured enough silence, Annie brought up the subject he'd been avoiding since leaving home. His family was out of bounds, but now that she'd enabled them to cross into his world unchallenged, he had no choice but to face those things that caused him so much pain.

"I don't know why."

"You're her big brother. I know you don't want contact with your parents, but it's a good thing you're doing for her, simply by being there." He could hear the surprise and admiration, but he didn't believe he deserved it when he'd abandoned Emma in that toxic environment with his parents.

"Having someone checking on their welfare is the least a child should expect in life."

Annie let out an exasperated sigh. "Could you just take a compliment? Or admit you like the child? Would it really kill you?"

No, but it would confirm an emotional attachment he wasn't ready to deal with yet.

"She seems like a good kid—smart, and not one of these brats today who think they should have everything handed to them on a plate. It sounds as though she's appreciative of everything you do for her."

"I know. She tells me every time we speak on the phone." That did make him smile. Emma wasn't like everyone else who took him for granted. He was simply her big brother.

"Maybe next time you could actually speak to her in person." Annie's hint that she intended to prolong this contact with his family didn't sit well with him. Things were fine the way they were — apart from the obvious complication of him and his split personality.

"What else are you expecting from me, Annie? Let's make one thing clear. A heartfelt reconciliation with my parents isn't going to happen. Even if I said I forgave them in the hope that we'd complete this *mission*, I wouldn't mean it. I certainly wouldn't be gaining anything from it. They can't change the past and I don't particularly want them to be part of my future. I'm simply lumbered with them at present because of your interference. Once Emma is old enough to leave home, I won't have anything more to do with them."

"If you could stop thinking only about yourself, you'd see that child is crying out for you to love her. You're keeping her at arm's length, and she hasn't done anything to deserve that kind of rejection. Think about taking her out for a milkshake once in a while or going to watch her in a school play. Some acknowledgement that she's family would mean the world to her."

It was a shock having someone talk to him in such a fashion, holding a mirror up so he could see his faults. There weren't a lot of people willing to be so blunt with him and literally putting themselves in the firing line. Annie didn't care who he was or what he represented, only about what was right and wrong. Sometimes it took brutal honesty to keep him grounded and remind him that not everything was about maintaining that safety net around himself.

"I'll add being a better big brother to my to-do list, although I don't see that there's much I *can* do about it now." At this rate, he was going to have to write a book on things he needed to work on for whenever he did make it back into his own body. There were some business decisions he needed to take another look at, as well as aspects of his personal life.

This had been a real wake-up call to the way he'd been living, oblivious to those struggling around him who could be helped with his intervention.

He just hoped he got that second chance to start his life over and make a better job of it next time around.

Chapter Eight

Once David began talking again, appearing to have forgiven her for forcing him to see his family, Annie was able to relax again. The only thing worse than having a spirit haunting her every move was one in a huff, refusing to speak to her.

The exercise at the hospital had proved more fruitful than she'd expected, hopefully bringing him and his sister closer in the process. Now they were on the way to David's house — at his instruction, not solely so she could have a nosy around.

"I want to make sure no one's been here helping themselves to my stuff."

"You really are paranoid about people stealing from you."

"Is it any wonder?"

"I guess not. Perhaps I'm better off not having anything of value. I don't have to stress about being ripped off."

"I think you're safe, unless there are any guinea pig rustlers waiting for their chance to pounce."

"George Bailey would fight them off, don't you worry. He's got a black belt in gnawing and a high-pitched squeak that could make your ears bleed." Driving along, teasing each other, it was easy to forget they were anything other than a normal couple.

Until his imposing mansion came into view and highlighted the vast difference between their lifestyles, other than the different planes they were currently inhabiting. The building looked out of place in this strip of countryside, which should have been the setting for some grand manor house in the style of a mock castle, complete with ancient battlements and a matching title.

Instead, David's house was all glass and angles, lit from the inside out and made for showing off. A beacon for potential burglars, scavenging estranged family and girlfriends, it suited him perfectly. It reflected the superficial, shallow man she thought she knew. However, she was beginning to realise there was more to David. His whole arrogant persona was shielding that young boy who was so desperate for his parents' love.

If Annie had the chance to lie around in the luxury of this place night after night, the responsibility of its upkeep and protecting the contents would negate any positives. She'd worry herself sick that something would happen. There was something to be said for a dingy flat that most people didn't know existed. No one, except transient spirits, bothered her.

"I hope you've got a half-decent security system." There was no way of telling how long the house was going to lie empty, and it was no secret to the world that the owner wasn't at home. She didn't want sole responsibility of protecting the contents, when life was stressful enough right now.

"The second you set foot on the property, your mugshot will be uploaded to every police station in the country." It was difficult to tell if he were joking or not. He could have told her he had a trapdoor that would drop her into crocodile-infested waters if she was too slow typing in the security code, and she would've been inclined to believe him. He had enough money to make that happen.

"Seriously, won't my presence arouse suspicion around here? I don't want anyone calling the police on me. How on earth would I explain being here when I'm nothing to you? You weren't even aware I was one of your employees, for goodness' sake. I don't think anyone's going to believe we're besties." His parents had swallowed that lie because they didn't know any better. They hadn't been part of his life for a very long time. However, those who knew him might ask questions about who she was, why she was here and other things she couldn't answer truthfully without having alarm bells ringing.

"We won't stay long. I just want to check that there's nothing missing. Don't worry. I'll give you the security codes."

Annie was certain he'd change them as soon as he was able, but it was a miracle he trusted them to her at all. Although there were so many that she would never remember them anyway. Once she bypassed the main gate, complete with security cameras, there was another set of gates farther up, closer to the house. Then there was the alarm code for the dream-house itself. David's secure hold on his privacy felt like something out of an Indiana Jones movie. As she hurried across the entrance hall—which was bigger than her entire flat—she was afraid to look behind her in case there was a giant stone ball rolling her way.

"You might want to think about your electric bill and switch a few things off." Every light in the house was blazing away. The cliché chandelier lighting the path across the marble hall alone must have been diverting supplies which could have lit up half of London. It would be nice not to have to worry about mundane things such as bills or a budget, but it was a waste when there was no one here but her.

"That'll be Mrs. Davies, the housekeeper. She likes to put the lights on for me coming home after work because she thinks it makes the place cosier." He cringed at the idea, one Annie knew was wasted on him. David wasn't the sentimental type to appreciate the gesture, but she would like to meet this Mrs. Davies, who seemed to have a soft spot for him. Maybe Annie could talk her into dropping by her flat for five minutes every night to make her place more inviting to come home to after work too.

"Surely she knows you're in the hospital?" Apart from the obvious absence, his accident and subsequent coma had been all over the news.

He cleared his throat, and it was difficult to tell if it was through embarrassment or a sign of real emotion. "I would say so. This is likely her way of keeping hope alive that I'll be home soon. She'll have the hospital on speed dial, checking up on me."

The merest upturn of his lips suggested an affection there that he'd deny if pushed on it. It was becoming clear to Annie how far out of his comfort zone he was about being reliant on her when he was reluctant to show an emotional connection to anyone.

"I'm glad you have someone looking out for you."

"What's that supposed to mean? I'm not some sort of sad case living out here on my own, away from civilisation. I have plenty of people around me." His sudden defensiveness said otherwise. If it wasn't for Sam and his food parcels arriving frequently at her door, he could have been describing her circumstances too.

"I wasn't implying anything other than my jealousy that you have someone to do things like that for you. I wonder if I can train George Bailey to put the kettle on for me?" She employed a little humour to diffuse any potential animosity, but there was some truth in what she was saying.

Since her mother had died, she'd had no one to ask how she was or to talk with about soap characters on TV as though they were real people. A simple thing such as having someone leave a light on was a reminder that a person wasn't alone in the world and why she came home to a darkened flat every night. If anything happened to her, she doubted anyone would notice, never mind hold some sort of light vigil for her.

"I'd kill for a drink of anything right now. This is so weird." David glanced longingly at the crystal decanters on display atop one of the many cabinets lining the lounge walls. She wouldn't hold out much hope he'd have some of the fruit-based alco-pops she favoured anywhere in the house if she decided she wanted to take the edge off.

The large reception room she'd wandered into was dominated by a Christmas tree — a white Christmas tree with matching lights and baubles. Coupled with the fluffy arctic carpet and white leather couch, Annie was in danger of going snow blind.

"Wow. You should warn a girl, or at least provide sunglasses before she comes in here."

"Sorry. Mrs. Davies' insistence — the tree, at least. The rest was chosen by an interior designer."

"It figures. There isn't anything here that feels very…you." In fact, there was nothing to indicate who lived here. At the very least she'd expect to see paperwork strewn around, or some evidence that a businessman was in residence there. There weren't any knick-knacks, paintings on the wall or even photos to suggest anyone lived here permanently — although there was an empty rectangular space above the fireplace, which indicated something had hung there once upon a time.

"Wedding photo." He followed her line of sight. "It, er…met with an accident once I discovered she'd cheated on me."

"Ugh. What is it with people who can't keep it in their pants? Was it a one-time thing? Sorry if that's too personal. You don't have to answer. It's just that I've spent the last year trying to figure out why assholes get into relationships if they have no intention of being monogamous." She wouldn't say it to his face, but she would've bet money on David being the one to cheat on a spouse. Unless it was the betrayal that had morphed him into the self-centred prima-donna she'd first come across. Cheating exes had a way of changing a person for the worst. In her case, she'd become more cynical and retreated further into her own world, away from anyone who could get close enough to hurt her again.

David's sad smile was one she'd seen in the mirror many times herself when she'd tried to convince herself that Jim's abuse of her trust was for the best in the long run.

"That's the million-dollar question, isn't it? Literally, in my case. Fool that I am, I was blindly in love with Linda. The same couldn't be said for her—at least, not with me. She was seeing someone else the whole time we were married. I hear they've got a nice set-up now, financed by the settlement she received from the divorce."

"That's crazy...and horrible. Jim was a cheating scumbag, but at least all he stole from me was my time, my heart and my trust. Quite a lot, in the scheme of things, but I don't think he set out to do it. According to him, he turned to other women for attention he wasn't getting from me." She didn't know how someone would ever recover if their relationship had been a lie from the start. By drinking too much, partying too hard and not committing to anything other than their own happiness, she supposed. She was beginning to understand the man behind the social pages and playboy reputation, and was thankful she was getting to know the real David Reece.

"That doesn't make it all right. You were looking after your mother. He should've understood that. It's just selfish to blame it on you."

"I did tell him that, and followed it up with a swift kick in the nuts that he won't forget in a hurry." She wasn't prone to violence and she wasn't proud of her actions, but it had been her first reaction to Jim's attempt to apportion fault with her. He'd called her a crazy bitch and staggered away clutching his bruised balls—never to be seen again, thankfully.

"Good. Remind me never to cross you unless I want to start a new career as a soprano. Unfortunately, I didn't get any form of revenge — only a house clearance." He spun around gesturing to the empty shelves, which had surely housed priceless antiques if his ex had seen fit to take them with her.

No one would ever dream of coveting her collection of Beanie Babies and seaside souvenirs taking up space in her apartment. In saying that, when Jim had gone, it had felt as though she'd been robbed of everything with any importance in her life. Looking back, it was possible she'd mixed up the grief over her mother with the break-up and afforded it more significance than it deserved.

"Linda took everything here of worth, along with the villa in France. I was too heart-sick to even contest her demands."

"That sucks. I'm sorry." It was comforting for Annie to have some of her mother's possessions around her, but that initial wrench — out of the home they'd shared, away from everything she'd ever known — had taken an emotional adjustment. Her mother hadn't chosen to leave, but it had broken her heart all the same. Couple that loss with a betrayal and it made that time even harder to move past, so she was able to sympathise with David to some extent.

"I wasn't feeling very Christmassy. I'm not in the mood to celebrate much these days, so I let them work away with the decorations in here. What's your excuse?"

"Do I need one?" Even without the spectre of an ex-wife haunting festivities, David didn't strike her as the type to be bothered with the season outside of increased profit margins at his stores. If he could forego the pretence of enjoying the holiday, she didn't see why she should be denied the same privilege.

"No offence, but I think your place could do with some festive cheer too. If I'm going to be stuck there for the holidays, I wouldn't mind having something else to look at other than your rodent friend."

Which part of that is supposed to be inoffensive?

"George Bailey is a guinea pig, a dearly loved pet, not a household pest. That's your department." She was a bit put out that he saw fit to slag off her house, when it was his home too for the length of this supernatural bonding.

David held his hands up in mock surrender. "I apologise for any slur against George Bailey's character. I will endeavour to get to know him better."

He was taking the piss now and making her angrier by the second.

"If my apartment is so offensive to your senses, perhaps I should move in here until things between us are resolved." Given the tight rein he kept on his private life, she doubted he'd see the funny side of her moving in and having access to all areas of it.

Despite her increasing annoyance at David, she tentatively lowered herself onto the pristine sofa and immediately worried she'd sullied it in some way simply by touching it.

"That's not a bad idea. You'd have everything you need, and you have my blessing to bring George Bailey with you."

Gah. He was being unreasonably reasonable. She'd be terrified to breathe on anything in here, never mind treat the place as a second home. It was fine for him—this show house was familiar to him—but she wouldn't be comfortable knowing she was intruding, with the rightful owner looking over her shoulder.

"It might look a bit suspect if I rock up here with all my belongings. It's not as though I can prove to anyone you've given your permission." She was awkward enough during hospital visiting. If she was expected to answer the door to anyone, it would be obvious she was out of place here.

"It's your choice. I just want you to know it's an option for you." The way he was looking at her, his head tilted to one side as though pitying her, made her think this mightn't be a one-time offer. Her personal circumstances might have shamed him into offering to take her in as the poor orphan she was. Whilst she appreciated his generosity, and as terrible as her pad was in comparison to this, it was hers, and she wasn't in a hurry to lose her freedom again. It was taxing enough having him around all the time and being constantly forced to interact with someone other than her pet at home.

"I'll keep it in mind," she said diplomatically, not wishing to sound ungrateful or completely rule out the idea when her personal circumstances were so precarious. She was a survivor, after all, and, unlike David, not too proud to ask for help if it came to it. Her problem was not having friends or family around her to rely on in the first place.

That seemed sufficient to ease his conscience and he carried on with his inspection of the ground floor, directing her to go wherever he needed her.

"I want a quick look upstairs, too, to make sure nothing's been disturbed there either."

Annie complied, led the way up the vast floating staircase and proceeded to open the doors to the many bedrooms along the corridor. "All present and correct?"

"As far as I can tell. My room's the one at the end of the hall."

She took that as an invitation, but it still felt intrusive, intimate even, venturing into his bedroom.

If this was a film set, it would've made the perfect backdrop for an illicit love affair. It made her think of those eighties dramas where powerful businesswomen took their young lovers to bed, still wearing full makeup, matching diamond earrings and necklaces and not much else. It was a room furnished and decorated to impress, to seduce. In contrast, her bedroom was somewhere to weep and wallow alone.

David's bed was impressive on its own, at least twice the size of hers, making it a dominant feature of the room. Confronted by it, it was impossible not to let her mind wander to thoughts of him lying there. The plump pillows and the luxurious grey silk bed linen were so inviting that she'd have thrown herself onto the mattress if he hadn't been watching. She was exhausted, and the high thread-count sheets she was sure he had on the bed too guaranteed a good night's sleep.

She opened the closet doors to reveal rows of tailored shirts and suits. The drawers were filled with perfectly folded and co-ordinated underwear and socks. It was a bit pernickety. He must have been having palpitations over her haphazard attitude to clothes storage. Well, he would if he were physically able to do it.

"I don't think anyone's been rifling through your drawers except me," she said with a grin, having only ventured into that particularly personal space because he wanted to see if his favourite watch remained tucked away at the back.

"In which case, we can go back to your place if that's what you want?"

She nodded. Although it had satisfied her curiosity about David's setup, the visit made her more self-conscious about the accommodation she was offering as a poor replacement.

Perhaps she could run the Hoover around the next day and not let the dirty dishes stack up until there were none left in the cupboards before she washed them. There were some advantages to living alone, which had soon turned into bad habits when there was no expectation of company to witness her slovenly worst.

"I do have an early start in the morning." Unless someone decided to call in sick at the last minute, she was on a half-day tomorrow. It meant she wasn't entitled to any breaks, but getting to leave early was as good as a holiday. She didn't have any Christmas shopping to do, so she could sleep all afternoon if she chose. At least she'd get a break from David then too.

"There are some leftover Christmas decorations in one of the spare rooms if you want to take some back with you."

"That's very kind of you, but I have some of my own tucked away, vintage ones passed on by my mum. I simply haven't had the motivation to put them up this year." To her horror, tears were burning the back of her eyes again. She'd got so used to crying when the loss of her mum made itself known, unseen from the world outside her apartment, that it wasn't easy to switch off the overwhelming emotion she'd been drowning in for over a year.

It was more disturbing dealing with a visibly distressed Annie than the usual spiky version — not least because David couldn't do anything to comfort her. He knew that lost feeling, being separated from everything he'd ever known, to be plunged into an unknown future. It was his good fortune fate had pushed him into Annie's arms and provided him with some company.

He wanted to hug her, squeeze her tight enough to smoosh all the broken parts inside her back together again. She'd done so much for him, and the most he'd managed to do in return was to set her up for a date.

Financially, he had the means, the contacts and the desire to help her out of the rut she was in—just not at the present time. Now that he was getting to know Annie better, he could see she needed more than a cash injection. Money wasn't going to solve all her problems when she'd been hurting so much. That brusque exterior was protecting a soft, vulnerable side of her that really deserved compassion. She needed someone to remind her who she was before life had worn her down.

"I can't help with the decorating, but I can supervise if you promise to make an effort—if only to honour your mother. I can tell how much she meant to you, but please don't put your own life on hold. I know it mightn't seem like it now, but you didn't die with her. You have your whole life ahead of you. Please don't waste it." That one small measure of empathy for her loss and concern for her well-being triggered the tears to fall in earnest, her shoulders heaving as her sobs filled the room.

David couldn't bear to see her in such pain and moved towards her. He tried to brush away her tears, but of course, they remained untouched. Nevertheless,

Annie closed her eyes as if he had and the sound of her heartbreak began to subside.

"I wish I could hold you," he whispered in her ear.

"So do I." She opened her eyes to look at him, their bodies so close that he should've been able to smell her perfume, feel her breath on his face, and there'd never been a greater reminder he was nothing more than a projection of his true form. He'd never wanted to kiss a woman more in his life, if only to remind them both that they were more than the lost souls they'd become and find some comfort in one another.

The shrill ring of the doorbell interrupted their moment and jolted them back into the present. Unfortunately for David, it hadn't jolted him back into his body, but he was beginning to think that was never going to happen anyway. "Who the hell is that?"

"Who else knows your gate codes?" Annie took a step back to reclaim her personal space and swiped the tears away with the back of her hand. The shutters were back in place again, covering up her moment of weakness.

"No one except Mrs. Davies — and she has a key." It had taken years to build that trust between them and he knew she wouldn't ever betray it by handing over his security details to someone else, not even if he was at death's door.

There was a prolonged ring as someone leaned heavily on the bell.

"Whoever it is clearly knows there's someone in here. I'll have to go down."

There was a thumping on the door. "I know you're in there. The hospital told me they'd passed David's house keys on with his other personal effects."

"Flame. Un-fucking-believable." Not content with having her face splashed over the newspapers, she was apparently trying to make a claim on his property too. He was sympathetic to the situation the woman was in with regards to her daughter, but that didn't mean he was going to hand over his house to them. This time around, he intended to fight for what was his, including his life.

"How did she get this far?" Annie was whispering, obviously afraid this psycho ex—he was dumping her as soon as he was able—could hear her. If all the lights hadn't been on or her car visible in the driveway, David imagined they could've got away with pretending no one was home.

"I have no idea. I've never given her the codes, although it's not impossible she's seen me keying them in. I'm going to have to increase security when I get the chance, and that'll start with getting you to change the codes before we leave tonight." Annie was the one person he knew wouldn't screw him over, when she'd had plenty of opportunity to do so already.

"Maybe you should stop bringing random women home with you if you don't want them turning up uninvited," she tossed back as she went downstairs to open the door.

David could have sworn he detected a teensy bit of jealousy mixed in with her judgement. He hadn't brought that many women home with him, but the idea that Annie was piqued amused him more than it irritated him. Perhaps she liked him more than he'd ever have guessed by the way she spoke to him.

"Whatever you do, don't let her over the doorstep or you'll never get rid of her." Flame had a habit of forgetting her personal effects, until she seemed to be moving in with him piece by piece. He could practically have built a clone of her from the false eyelashes, nails, boobs and hair pieces she'd left behind. Eventually, he'd bundled up the clothes and toiletries she'd left behind and driven them to her house to put a stop to any such notion of them living together.

Without him in residence, he dreaded to think what she was capable of doing next.

"How am I supposed to do that?" Annie was no pushover, but Flame was a force of nature who almost always got what she wanted, taking it by whatever means necessary.

"Put the security chain on and keep your weight behind the door in case she tries to push her way in."

"Your girlfriend sounds delightful," Annie grumbled as she tried to slide the catch on without making a sound. She took a deep breath and eased the door open. Immediately, the chain rattled as Flame tried to barge in and a gold stiletto wedged itself into the small opening.

"Who are you?" she demanded, regardless that she was the trespasser on the property.

"I, er…"

"Tell her you're the housekeeper."

Annie frowned at him, clearly not flattered by the comparison to his elderly employee.

"They've never met." A matter which confirmed he should never have been with Flame in the first place, when he was embarrassed to introduce her to the motherly figure in his life. She most definitely would not have approved, always telling him to find himself a nice girl who thought about him as much as herself. If she knew everything Annie had done for him these past few days, she'd have been picking out the wedding china by now. She was exactly the no-nonsense kind of woman Mrs. Davies would've approved of to help him heal after the last disaster.

"I'm Mr. Reece's employee. Who are you and what do you want?" The authority with which Annie answered was impressive, yet it still wasn't enough to put off their visitor.

"You're the housekeeper?"

He couldn't see Flame from his position behind the door, but he could hear the disdain in her voice and imagine the judgemental assessment she was giving Annie with her cold shark-eyes.

"Yes. Now what do you want?" Annie bristled and stood taller instead of shrinking under her scrutiny, sticking two fingers up at a woman who couldn't hope to hold a candle to the sort of person she was.

If David had ended up at her apartment after the accident, she'd have sold the story and tried to twist this situation to suit her at every turn. Annie had thought only of what he needed, including that set-up with his parents. He owed her big time.

"I'm Flame, David's fiancée. I'm staying here until he's well enough to come home. I want to make the place look pretty for him." She turned on the charm now that she realised she'd met her match, using that babyish voice that always made his skin crawl. He was questioning his sanity in ever getting involved with her. Clearly, his hormones had overridden all common sense when they'd hooked up. Although he hadn't seen it at the time, he'd been vulnerable and hurting, in need of an ego boost, and Flame had provided it.

"Mr. Reece doesn't have a fiancée. I'd be the first to know if he ever entertained the idea of marrying again. I also happen to know he didn't give you any of the security codes, and I guarantee you're the last person he'd want to see when he gets home. Now, totter back to your car and get out of here before I call the police." The full blast of Annie's ire staggered Flame back out onto the porch, and she slammed the door in her face.

He could hear Flame's enraged mutterings as she walked off, followed by the over-revving of her car engine before she tore away down the drive. Annie leaned her forehead against the back of the door, breathing heavily, as though the confrontation had sapped all of her energy.

"Please don't ask me to ever do that again. I've done more lying over these past couple of days on your behalf than I have in my entire life. I don't think my conscience will allow me to keep on in this vein."

"That. Was. Awesome." Despite her obvious discomfort, he faced Annie with a reverent sense of pride in standing up to Flame. She continually surprised him when she seemed to fly below the radar in her everyday life, but she was able to step up so magnificently when he asked.

It made him believe there was so much untapped potential within her that really should benefit more than just him. Annie could really break out of this safe cocoon she'd created around herself and onto greater things. If only there was someone to support her and whom she trusted enough to let them. No matter why he was here with her, he knew it was going to be his job to at least try to break down those barriers she'd built up.

Chapter Nine

Watching the clock tick down was like waiting for the school bell to ring on the last day of term. Every second was interminable agony, holding out for that much-anticipated freedom, even though Annie was merely swapping the confines of work for the four walls of her flat.

As soon as the hands hit their target, she was off. She slung her bag and coat over her shoulder without so much as a glance back. As soon as she stepped outside, she was swept up in the tidal wave of tourists and shoppers flooding the busy street.

"Where do you think you're going?" That ever-present devil on her shoulder piped up to remind her that he was there. She was still coming to terms with everything he'd said and made her do the previous day and would've preferred a time out from him for a while.

It wasn't like her to get so emotional in front of anyone. Then again, she hadn't expected David to be so lovely to her, so understanding. When he'd come to her, she'd almost felt his arms around her. He'd done such a good job of comforting her.

They'd connected on a level that had taken them both by surprise, and she'd seen a depth to David that he worked hard to suppress.

They'd seemed to recognise something in each other in that moment — a loneliness, a meeting of souls, which made her wish they were on the same plane — whichever one it took for them to be together properly. He was the first person she'd truly opened up to since her mother's passing, and whilst cathartic, it also marked a change in her relationship with him. Somehow, he'd changed from being an unbearable irritant to becoming the most important person in her life. The only person in her life, really, and that wasn't a good portent when he was halfway to heaven — or hell.

"Er, home to put my feet up." She was on autopilot now, her legs carrying her on that familiar route to the nearest tube station because she had no life in between the two destinations. Work and home — they were all she had to fill her days, only now with added commentary.

"I don't think so. How many days until the big date?"

It took Annie a moment to figure out what he was referring to. She fell out of step and went against the current of bodies around her to seek solace in a nearby doorway.

"You mean the Christmas party?" She stood facing the window display of an exclusive boutique showcasing the latest winter party fashion, all silver glitter and snow-white fur. It reminded her of David's lounge, and she wondered if there were any leftover remnants of his carpeting that she could borrow to fashion an outfit she could actually afford.

"Yes, I mean the Christmas party — unless you have another social engagement planned that you haven't told me about?" He was trying to be funny, but her lack of social life was too tragic to find any humour in the comment.

"Two days." She'd wiped out the pittance in her bank account to pay for the overpriced meal, which would be prepared and microwaved for the masses in the belief they'd be too inebriated to notice. Annie hoped something positive would come of this investment, something other than a hangover and cringeworthy exploits she'd regret when she sobered up.

"We need to get a move on. That doesn't leave a lot of time for me to work my magic." David waved his hands in front of her face like some second-rate magician at a holiday park.

"Why don't I like the sound of this?" She hated change, and whatever he had up his sleeve definitely meant nudging her out into a world she wasn't sure she was ready to face again. To be fair, she knew she'd done the same thing to him, insisting he spend some time with his family, so she couldn't very well back out of whatever he had planned.

"Because you're a control freak and you're going to have to trust me on this?" The dimple in his cheek deepened as his smile grew wider, and she knew he had her pegged. Up until last night, he would've been the last person she'd trust with her personal life.

"What do I have to do?" she sighed, resigned to spending her time off doing something else she didn't want to do. She may as well have stayed at work.

"We're going clothes shopping!" He stood waiting for an enthusiastic response she wasn't feeling.

"Ugh." What else did he expect? She was obviously not one of his clothes-horse girlfriends. She had a shape, a curvy figure that she couldn't simply drape a flimsy piece of fabric over and think it was going to look good. It took hard work and many, many changes of outfit to find anything she was remotely comfortable wearing—although she supposed comfort was never going to be a factor in this outing.

"Any other woman would be only too glad to have an excuse to splurge." He seemed genuinely puzzled by her reluctance, giving some insight into the women he was used to—confident, beautiful women, comfortable in their own skin, who wouldn't be the slightest bit guilty about throwing money away on frivolous purchases.

"Any other woman could probably afford to splurge. I'm not sure I have money to cover my bills this month." She lowered her voice, so ashamed of her financial status that she didn't want to share it with passers-by. It was humiliating enough admitting it to a multi-millionaire.

David's shoulders dropped, and she could see he was taking a lot of the blame on board for her circumstances. He was her employer, but it was also the system at fault, making it legal, if not moral, to exploit workers and giving them barely sufficient wages to keep them off the streets. If it weren't for Sam's generosity, she might even have been forced to join one of those food banks to keep her cupboards stocked with basic supplies in between paydays.

"You could put it on a credit card, and I'll reimburse you when I can." It was sweet of him to offer to treat her, but there was more than her pride preventing her from accepting.

"The credit card is for emergencies only, and no harm to you, David, but we don't know if you will ever be able to pay it back." It was a stark reminder that this might not have the happy ending they wanted. At the end of the day, she had to be sensible. There was every chance she'd be left footing a bill she couldn't pay, all so she could look good for one night of the year. She still had to think of how she was going to support herself after David had gone. The one thing they had in common was that the future looked bleak for both of them.

Deep down, she knew he was trying to do something nice for her, even if it was only hypothetically speaking. "We could do with the budget version of your *Pretty Woman* fantasy. There are a few cool charity shops we could try. Sometimes they have some lovely vintage dresses at bargain prices."

She used to enjoy those trips out with her mum when she'd been mobile, poking around and hoping to find a few treasures in other people's cast-offs. They'd picked up a few nice items along the way and it meant she'd been able to indulge her book habit at a fraction of the cost. She wasn't too proud to take advantage of a bargain or two.

"Second-hand clothes?" The concept was clearly alien to him as he displayed his blatant snobbery with a scowl. No doubt he'd see it as another form of her peasant practices, scavenging through someone else's trash. Annie didn't see it like that when shopping at one of those stores saved her money and at the same time also contributed funds to the named charity running it.

"Well, if you're happy to shop there…"

"I am."

"Then think of me as your invisible Richard Gere." He gave a mock bow, and though he might not be seen as her personal shopper, she was sure he'd make his opinion heard.

* * * *

Annie was assaulted by a blast of not overly pleasant odours as she opened the door to the charity shop. It smelled fusty, like that time she'd taken a caravan holiday with her mum and the smell of the mould inside had permeated everything, including their clothes. As their neighbours had lent them the use of their static caravan in Camber Sands, they couldn't complain. Instead, Annie had spent that first day scrubbing everything and leaving all the doors and windows open for some fresh air. After that, they'd had a great time and forgotten all about that bad first impression. It had simply taken a little effort to reap the potential rewards.

Something clearly needed a good airing out in here. The sickly-sweet perfume wafting from the lady manning the shop counter wasn't helping. It merely amplified the need for some open windows.

Annie walked over to the clothes hanging closest to the door.

"Step away from the old women's slacks." David's voice was an alarm ringing in her ears as she gravitated towards the rail of black trousers.

"All right, Gok Wan... When I want your opinion, I'll ask for it." Annie was getting too used to chatting to him and it was easy to forget herself. Thankfully, the shop assistant was engaged in conversation with a white-haired pensioner on the other side of the counter, who was regaling her with tales of mutual acquaintances to hold her interest.

Her matching lavender cardi and camisole, teamed with fine gold chains, didn't look as though she did her own shopping on the premises. "Did you hear Tommy's in hospital again? Agnes hasn't wasted any time. I saw her heading out the other night. Mutton dressed as lamb, if you ask me."

Annie filtered out the rest of the character assassination of poor Agnes and prayed the gossip session would drown out the arguments she knew she was going to have with David.

"Even Julia Roberts needed some help with her wardrobe. Although I could see you in a pair of thigh-high boots..."

"I'd be less self-conscious wearing trousers, thank you very much." She reached for a pair of non-descript, boot-cut, black leg-coverers, but David stepped between her and the rail.

"That's because they render you invisible, and that's not the look we're going for here." He dazzled her with that full-beam charm of his that made her heart flip. It was a different sensation to that flirty excitement she experienced when talking to Kev, reaching deeper inside to leave a longer-lasting impression.

She put it down to the fact that she saw him twenty-four-seven. He was working his way under her skin, but she was sure it was nothing she couldn't be cured of with a David-ectomy, when he finally went back where he belonged.

"I'm not really your leopard print or sequins kind of girl. I prefer something in a wallflower pattern. There isn't much call for dressing up alone in the flat. To be honest, I don't know where to start." Anything other than her uniform or comfy casual was going to be weird enough for her without purposely drawing attention to herself.

"It's Christmas and you'll want to impress Kev. We need something to make him notice you. Won't you at least try a dress? Pretty please?" He fluttered his long, dark eyelashes and turned her insides to putty. It was hard to ignore someone that pretty making eyes at her.

"Fine." She flounced over to the rail with all shapes and sizes of frocks to choose from, to flick through the clothes. The click of the plastic hangers as they slid rhythmically along the metal rail detailed her instant damning judgement. *Too long, too short, too gaudy, just too much...*

"What about this one?" She picked out a pretty floral swing-dress, very fifties in design and something she could wear again should she dare to venture out of the flat in the future.

"You're not going to a tea-dance." David was aghast at her choice and she knew he would've snatched it out of her hands and tossed it over his shoulder if he could have.

"I want something that makes me feel pretty, not something I'm going to be tugging at and adjusting all night, worried I'm showing too much cleavage or leg."

"Spoilsport."

They moved farther back into the recesses of the store, careful to stand far away from the gentleman staring at the shelves of dusty DVDs and muttering to himself. It crossed Annie's mind that he might have had his own invisible friend criticising his personal choices too and wondered which of them would make a purchase first.

The search began again, and she did her best to stay away from the romantic florals that offended David so much. As she inspected the new row of possibilities, her gaze lingered on a plain, khaki-coloured shirt-dress.

"Very Sunday-school picnic," David snorted before he was asked for his opinion.

This was going to be a very long afternoon when their tastes were so far apart.

"What do you suggest then?"

"Keep going and I'll tell you when I spot something that doesn't remind me of an outfit my nan used to wear."

"Your nan must've been one hell of a stylish lady," she snarked back and worked her way around the shop, bypassing what she deemed perfectly acceptable outfits.

"Stop." Eventually he called a halt to the garments she was swiping, and Annie was as horrified at his choice as he had been at hers.

Red. Lacy. Clingy. Everything she avoided.

"It's not exactly subtle."

"It's hot and we men are visual creatures. We don't do subtle."

It really wasn't her. There was no escaping anyone's attention in that get-up. "I don't know, David. Doesn't it scream 'desperate'?"

"No, it says, 'I'm sexy and I know it. Now you know it too.'" The flirty wink he gave her, along with the unintentional compliment, made her want to try it on for him and draw more of his personal interest.

She took a deep breath and selected the vampy outfit to take to the changing room. There was no way she was buying it if it showed off all the wrong lumps and bumps she might've gained from her chocolate binges.

They'd eventually discovered, through trial and error, that she could be awarded some privacy if any doors or barriers were left ajar. As long as there was some open connection, she was saved from having David up close and personal in confined spaces. It was only when that barrier was closed that he snapped back to her side as though on elastic.

She was able to strip, leaving a small chink through the door, safe in the knowledge that David wouldn't appear to cast a critical over her practical, but uninspiring, underwear. Although, she doubted she'd end up in a position where Kev would see it either. She had no intention of getting hot and heavy with a man, only for David to appear at the end of the bed giving them marks out of ten on their performance. Besides, liking Kev wasn't enough for her to jump into bed with him.

It would take a long time for her to build a level of trust where she was comfortable enough to get intimate with someone again. She was only going along with this because David thought it was what she needed, and she couldn't argue when she'd forced him into an uncomfortable situation with his parents.

Annie considered that he might have a point about investing in some new underwear, when seeing herself in the mirror proved more depressing than she'd imagined. Her once-white cotton bra was comfortable, but it didn't do anything to boost her assets and wouldn't get anyone hot under their boxers.

She wanted to feel good, pretty and confident from the inside out. Her pride was at stake too, when David had only seen her at her worst so far. For once, she wanted him to look at her as a woman instead of the pitiful creature she'd become lately.

It took some wriggling and adjusting body parts to get the dress on, but the transformation was shocking, even to her. The fabric clung to all the right places, showing off her figure at its best. She'd simply have to work up enough courage to share it with the world, starting with David.

Once she shut the door to the cubicle tight, he was there with her in a heartbeat.

"Hubba, hubba!" His caveman response turned her skin the same hue as the dress.

"Is it too much? Not enough?" Doubt crept back in as his eyes swept over her again and again, assessing her with an expert eye. She was tempted to open the door and send him packing. There was no way she could ever hope to measure up to the supermodels he was used to on his arm.

"You're perfect." That gravelly response in the tight space sucked the air from her lungs until she thought she might pass out.

She did a double check for signs he was taking the piss, but instead he was nodding his appreciation. "Far from it, but if you think Kev would like it, I suppose I should splash out."

That amber fire she'd sworn she'd seen flash in his eyes dimmed as he stepped back. "What's not to like? You're hot."

This time the compliment sounded a bit flat, and though Annie had a wobble in confidence, she'd seen that flicker of admiration. She was buying this dress.

* * * *

"You know, I'm beginning to regret suggesting this whole *Pretty Woman* makeover. Who would ever have imagined that I wouldn't enjoy lingerie shopping? I should be in my element here, with all the eye-candy stock and a fashion parade of women in barely there undergarments, but I feel like a pervert when they don't know I'm here." He was doing his best not to look, but it was particularly uncomfortable because it was Annie he was accompanying.

There were certain urges he was developing towards her — ones he couldn't possibly act on and which he was sure wouldn't be appreciated in her quarter, even if he could. Annie was stunning, and not simply because he'd talked her into dressing up as every horny teenage boy's fantasy.

The dress highlighted all her attributes, but his fondness for her had increased because of her obliviousness to her own charms. He was so used to dealing with people full of their own self-importance that it was refreshing to be in her company, albeit on a more permanent basis. If he'd been tied to, say, Flame, for this length of time, he would've been exhausted by her constant need for attention. Annie was the opposite, almost shrinking into the background any time the focus was on her. That dress would certainly test the self-confidence he was hoping to inspire in her when it would make her centre stage in any room.

She was a mass of contradictions, both frustrating and intriguing to him. There were signs that even if they hadn't been pushed to search for a better type of life for her—and him—that it was something she wanted for herself. It was clear she was unhappy, not only in her work but also where she was living and generally fed-up with the life she had. Yet she'd been so hurt in the past that she was obviously afraid to go out and find something different. These spiky defences she'd put up to protect herself and keep predators from her door were also preventing her from moving on to something better.

This spiritual intervention had left her no choice but to let him into her life, where he'd witnessed her underlying vulnerability. Behind that bolshie façade, she was fragile, requiring nurturing he hoped this Kevin was capable of giving her.

"Well?" Annie stood before him now in nothing but scraps of black material purporting to be underwear. He'd created a monster, one who was a million miles away from the shapeless blob he'd first met in the dark. With his gaze trained on her enhanced cleavage, he was inclined to zip her back into that onesie until he could think straight again.

"Yep. I think we're good." It was impossible in this cubicle to look anywhere but at the soft swell of her breasts rising from their lacy support, reminding him exactly what she looked like beneath.

Despite his *condition*, David was sure his temperature—along with other parts of him—were rising at the sight. The quicker she let him out of here, the better.

Annie turned around, hands on her hips, to study herself in the mirror, leaving him with the perfect view of her sweet backside and long legs.

"I don't know... Maybe I should go all out for the red cliché? You know, matching red lace bra and panties, and maybe some stockings too?"

This was so unfair. He'd had the tables well and truly turned on him, when the whole point of this exercise was to make her more attractive to Kev, not him. It crossed his mind that perhaps that was what this little display was about, showing him she didn't need any help in that department. After all, she'd gone from screaming and shouting at him every time he popped up unexpectedly to parading in front of him with barely a stitch on. He swore she smirked when she caught him ogling her in the mirror.

"I think this is perfectly adequate." He kept his tone measured, trying not give away how uncomfortable he was, but not being able to either act on this growing attraction or walk away from it.

"If you're sure..." She unhooked her bra and David was forced to turn away before he combusted altogether.

"I am," he growled. What he would give for a moment to touch her, feel her soft skin beneath his fingertips or kiss her with the fervour she apparently evoked in him—the sort of passion that was steadily rising the longer he spent in her company. At least her confidence appeared to be on the up, even if it had come at the expense of his resolve.

Chapter Ten

"Retail therapy was exactly what I needed." Annie had driven to the hospital with her purchases packed into the boot and a triumphant grin on her face. Her self-esteem had risen a few points, and it wasn't only due to the small fortune she'd spent on herself. It was also because of the effect the exercise had had on David.

"Hmm-m, I'm not sure I can say the same," he muttered.

"Yes, I did think you looked a little uncomfortable back there." It had taken every ounce of her courage to strip down to her smalls, but it had tested her theory sufficiently to prove her right. He'd been flustered for the first time since coming to terms with his mortality, more so than when they'd inadvertently showered together.

"Rummaging through dead people's clothes does tend to have that effect on me."

David wasn't fooling her. It wasn't merely the fact that he'd lowered himself to set foot in a charity shop that had unnerved him. She'd seen the flare of lust in his eyes and stoked the fire, eager to revel in its warmth. It had been an age since she'd felt wanted, sexy, and it was intoxicating. She wanted more and was reluctant to believe David's sudden interest was merely because she was the only woman who knew he still existed on this plane.

The one way to validate these new powers would be at the work Christmas dinner, watching to see if they had the same effect on Kev. Yet, David's reaction was the one she cared about most. It gave some credence to her growing feelings, which seemed to be progressing from irritation and pity towards something more dangerous to the man currently in her life.

As they trekked along the now-familiar hospital corridors, the staff nodding at her in recognition as they passed by, David continued to make his displeasure known. "I don't think there can be anything more depressing than visiting your own half-dead body night after night."

"It should be life-affirming for you. This is proof you're still hanging in there, and there's a good chance of you pulling through." She was hoping another trip to his alter ego's bedside would also remind her what a bad idea it would be to become attached to him in any shape or form. It had taken her so long to recover from her last losses that it would be foolhardy to set her cap on someone hovering between life and death.

There was a high probability he'd leave her, even if he did survive his injuries, when he came from a completely different world, moved in classier circles and was only with her because the powers-that-be willed it.

Once that tie was severed, he was bound to go back to that life where half-naked women were plentiful and of a much higher grade than the one he was lumbered with now.

"Or I'm watching myself gradually fading away..." Hands in his pockets and shoulders slumped, the dejected David was a world away from her earlier personal shopper. That version had been so buoyed by the possibilities for her future that guilt tapped on Annie's shoulder because she couldn't do the same for him.

Later at home, she could mock up a few hairstyles for herself on the laptop and get his opinion on a new look. He seemed to get a kick out of creating his own Frankenstein's monster, and she'd much rather see that spark of energy back in him than his resignation to a pessimistic non-future.

"Do you want me to give you a haircut and a shave?" It was clear he was a man who took care of his appearance, and though it had only been a few days, the man in the bed was looking unkempt. The staff would be doing their utmost for him, but David could direct her to achieve the look he wanted.

"I'd prefer a wax." His impish face lit up again with a mischievous grin which suited him better than a scowl.

It took her a moment to register which direction his wayward thoughts had travelled, and when hers caught up, she blushed, questioning if his personal grooming really extended south of his beard.

"TMI, David." She kept on walking, giving no indication that she was contemplating taking a peek under his hospital gown to satisfy her curiosity and call his bluff at the same time. He took pride in his appearance, but she believed he was secure enough in his masculinity that he didn't need to go bare down there to give the illusion of making something bigger than it already was. That was the only reason for man-scaping, wasn't it? It didn't make a difference to her where a man had hair on his body, except for the back and shoulder areas. The gorilla look did ick her out a bit.

Wait…was *she* supposed to wax down there? It was so long since she'd dated that she was out of the loop on these things. David would know. Then again, she didn't fancy having him sit in on a bikini wax with her. It was intrusive simply having him in the room when she was shaving her legs.

"What? Surely you're not a prude, Miss Marlowe?" He was getting too much of a buzz out of teasing her, but it was a small price to pay to distract him from his own mortality.

"Not at all, as I believed I showed you today how much of a non-prude I am. I simply don't see the point in grooming your nether regions when there's no one to see you, bar the nurses. In case you've forgotten, you're in no fit state to do anything, even if they were impressed by your baby-smooth groin."

His belly laugh succeeded in ending the deeply disturbing conversation as they reached his room. There was plenty of time for him to be despondent when they were on the other side of the door, but at least she'd put a smile back on his face where it belonged—albeit that she'd prompted several images in her head which could never be erased.

"This Christmas party can't come soon enough so you can pull the toy rep, get your leg over, and the earth will move for all of us." When he was winding Annie up, David didn't have to think about what was waiting for him in that room. He was more alive in the moments out here, trading innuendo with her, than those monitors attached to his body would suggest.

She made him laugh, she frustrated him and, most recently, she'd made him horny.

"You're assuming a lot. We don't know that anything's going to change, even if Kev is interested in me. I'm not pinning all my hopes on a second-hand dress being a miracle worker, and neither should you."

"Trust me... We'll make sure Kev will be knocked off his feet. Men are fickle creatures. The sexier you look, the harder we'll fall. The hair and makeup aren't going to be easy on a budget. I know the amount of money my ex used to spend on a haircut alone. Don't get me wrong... You're pretty, in a homely sort of way."

"Gee, thanks. You make me sound like a comfortable sofa."

"It wasn't intended as an insult. I mean, I've seen what we're working with and I have absolutely no complaints. I'm simply talking about adding a few embellishments to an already-great starting base." He backtracked on that misjudged comment when he saw her fold her arms in preparation for another verbal battle.

"You know we're not allowed to talk about the shower incident, but I get the gist."

"Perhaps you could volunteer as a model for trainee stylists to practice on, or go to one of those cosmetic counters for a free make-up demonstration."

"Yeah, and afterwards I could send them here, because the Rip Van Winkle look really isn't doing anything for you at all."

"Touché. Okay, I'll stop now."

"Good idea."

He had scant time to mope about Annie's critique of his bedbound appearance, his attention diverted to the other visitor as they entered the room.

"Emma? What are you doing here?" Annie echoed the thoughts in his head.

"I wanted to spend more time with David." She was leaning over the bed, still dressed in her school uniform, with a book lying open on her lap. It was apparent she'd been reading to him and the scene immediately choked David up. He didn't even remember having his parents do that for him when he'd been little.

He was overwhelmed by his rush of emotions for her, proving there was a deeper connection between them than he'd ever acknowledged. Her distress made it clear she had formed an attachment, despite his best attempts to prevent it. If their roles had been reversed and if by some tragic accident Emma had ended up in this hospital bed, he knew he'd never leave her side. She was the only family who'd ever showed him real love and she deserved the same in return. It wasn't fair to make her suffer simply because he was afraid of letting anyone close again.

"I came straight from school. I didn't want him to be here alone and I've heard it helps to read to people in comas. Do you think he can hear me—or that he knows I'm here?"

Emma's bottom lip wobbled as she spoke, and David wanted to hug her and tell her everything would be all right. He couldn't be sure anyone in her life was capable of doing that for her and vowed then and there to be that emotional support for her, if and when he could.

"I know for a fact he can." Thankfully, Annie was clearly as touched by her presence as he was and put an arm around her shoulders to give her a squeeze. In that moment, he would have done anything to trade places with Annie and be the one to comfort his sister. She threw him a knowing glance and he had to concede that she was right. Emma was a sweetheart and he was the one missing out.

"I know. I know. She's my little sister and I'd do better to remember that in future." He mentally rapped himself on the knuckles for all the times he'd brushed her off, thinking she'd forget about him if he kept his distance. Seeing her here and the emotions it had brought to the fore were an indication of what a futile exercise that had been.

"I brought him a present too." Emma lifted her school bag from the floor and pulled something from it.

David couldn't quite see what she had in her hands until she hung it on the end of his bed.

"My sewing isn't the best, but I thought he should have one. It's not very Christmassy in here, is it?" Emma directed her gaze around the room, and he had to concede she was right. No attempt had been made by anyone to acknowledge the time of year and try to jolly it up in here…until now.

Okay, this body separation thing must've been playing havoc with his hormones too, because he was on the verge of tears seeing the crudely made red-and-white felt stocking hanging on the corner of his hospital bed with his name spelled out in gold glitter—a gift made purely out of love.

"That's so sweet." He wasn't sure if Annie was talking to him or Emma with her hand on her heart, obviously as touched by the thoughtfulness as he was.

"I can't remember the last time I had a stocking hanging up for Father Christmas." At least, not a personalised, handmade one instead of a store-bought, mass-produced, monstrosity an interior designer had purchased for purely aesthetic reasons. It hadn't seemed important to David until now.

"I've got one for you too." Emma delved back into her bag and produced its twin with a sparkly pink 'Annie' embellishment.

"For me?" Annie looked genuinely astonished that someone would've considered getting her a gift, and it was a revelation to see that not everyone expected an unending conveyor belt of gifts.

She clutched the large sock to her chest as though she'd been given a diamond bracelet.

These two were seriously the most adorable pair he'd ever seen, giving him a lesson in humility he knew he'd never forget. Annie was so happy with so little and Emma so loving to someone she barely knew. David was beginning to realise the important things in life. None of this was about money. It was about being around people who cared. The irony in this being he hadn't realised he had such people in his life until it was almost over.

"All right, it's only a Christmas decoration. There's no need to get overly sentimental about it," David snapped. He didn't want Annie getting carried away and getting too personally invested with his estranged family for them to detach themselves again when the time came. He was giving himself the same pep talk about the surprisingly thoughtful gesture.

Annie gave him a hard look from across the room as she tucked her gift tenderly into her bag.

"Thank you, Emma, for going to so much trouble. It was very thoughtful." She reiterated the last word, likely for David's benefit, but he'd already digested the motives behind Emma's visit and been suitably chastened by it.

"I love Christmas. Mum and Dad always make it special for me and I wanted to do the same for David…and you. What do you do on Christmas Day? I can't wait until I have my own place, then I can go mad with the decorations." Whilst she was talking, she placed a little tree, complete with fake snow, tinsel and tiny baubles, at his bedside as unobtrusively as though she'd turned on a lamp.

His stomach flip-flopped at the clear difference in upbringing she'd had compared to his. "I'm glad they've stepped up to provide a safe environment for Emma, even though I'm a little jealous they weren't capable of doing the same for me. They treated me as more of an inconvenience. My 'take it or leave it' approach to the festive season is based purely on my experiences growing up. The Christmas joy of presents, dinner and spending family time together playing board games was never guaranteed for me."

Sometimes, if he were lucky, he'd get one of those things, but not all simultaneously. Celebrations — or lack of — were dependent on his parents' moods and alcohol intake. Therefore, any so-called good times were tainted with his anxiety that they'd come to an abrupt halt at any given moment.

If his parents had changed—and he hoped for Emma's sake they had—it didn't alter anything for him. Over-compensating for their past mistakes wouldn't erase how they'd treated their firstborn. Annie might hold out hope a reconciliation was the key to this mystery, but that seemed too much of a stretch for him. No matter what they did now, or who they purported to be, he couldn't forgive them—and he certainly couldn't love them. There could be a chance of cultivating a relationship with Emma, but he couldn't have any more toxic people in his life.

With Emma and Annie's influence, he was learning that the dead wood in his life extended to so-called friends and acquaintances who, as far as he was aware, hadn't bothered to check in on him since the accident. He'd be setting those people adrift at the first opportunity and pulling those who had his genuine interests at heart closer—that was, if Annie still wanted him hanging around on a less-permanent basis.

"Do your parents know you're here, Emma?" It didn't go unnoticed that Annie deflected any talk of Christmas. He'd seen her fidgeting when Emma mentioned the holidays. It was understandable that she wasn't feeling the love for this time of the year, given her circumstances, but he was going to insist on putting some sparkle back in her life. With any luck, she'd rediscover her inner Christmas elf and get carried away with the tinsel again with some prompting. There was no reason they should both play the Grinch role.

The broken eye contact and head hung in shame were a dead giveaway. "No. I told them I had hockey practice after school."

"It's getting late and it's dark outside. I think you should let them know where you are." Annie was very good at being the responsible adult, and that most likely came from years of looking after her mother. He'd been benefitting from her grounded, no-nonsense approach too and it struck him what a good mother she'd make. Hopefully, with the confidence boost they were working on, she'd get herself back out there where a family of her own might be a possibility.

Once upon a time he'd had that dream himself, wanting to provide all the things he'd missed out on to a child of his own, but his ex had put that notion out of his head. He wasn't sure he'd trust another woman to the point he'd want to be tied to her for the duration of a child's life.

Besides, his behaviour over these last months had proved he wasn't sufficiently mature to handle that level of responsibility. His love of partying would be curtailed by a young family, but he was beginning to enjoy time spent with loved ones more than getting drunk with people he hardly knew.

If he was lucky, someday he'd have a partner at home who'd make him forego that hedonistic lifestyle to settle down, content with his lot and no longer seeking an escape from his loneliness.

"I guess…" Alarm bells rang for David when Emma didn't sound as though she wanted to go home.

"Ask her why she didn't tell them she was coming here? I want to make sure there's nothing untoward stopping her from going back. It wouldn't have been the first time I'd delayed going home at her age, anticipating another night of drunken arguments, or worse, an empty house."

"Is everything all right at home, Emma? I'm a bit curious as to why you'd come all this way without telling anyone?" Annie tackled the subject on his behalf and he waited with some trepidation about the circumstances which had brought his sister here.

"They didn't think David would want us coming here all the time and said we should just call the hospital from now on to check on his progress. I know they don't get on, but it doesn't seem right to leave my brother lying here alone. *I* haven't done anything." To David's horror, he saw tears welling in Emma's eyes, and as Annie moved to hug her, they splashed down onto her shoulder.

"Of course you haven't, and I'm sure your brother's glad to have you in his corner. Hopefully when he wakes up, they can make peace again, and in the meantime, don't be afraid to visit. If David has a problem with it, he can take it up with me."

There wouldn't be any need to incur Annie's wrath, because she was right, as usual. Poor Emma had been collateral damage in the continuing war with his parents. The adult way to deal with them would've been to have a proper conversation about his childhood and lay out for them the impact their actions had had on him, even if they'd had to have some sort of mediator or family counselling for Emma's sake. If they couldn't accept responsibility and express remorse, he'd have been within his rights to cut them out of his life. That didn't have to extend to Emma, who'd come to his aid of her own free will.

He had to stop his selfish, immature behaviour, since it had been made clear to him the serious consequences it had for others around him. Perhaps he'd been living out that childhood he'd never had, but it was time to grow up. There was nothing sadder than an ageing playboy who thought he was God's gift, when in reality he was a self-absorbed asshole with a fat wallet.

Ouch. This near-death caper was akin to looking into one of those funfair mirrors showing him an unattractive version of himself he didn't appreciate. Unfortunately, he was beginning to realise that the ugly David Reece was real, and if he didn't change his ways, he wouldn't even have a sister to weep by his bedside.

"Why don't I give you a lift home to make sure you get back safely? It'll give me a chance to have a word with your parents too." It was the sensible thing for Annie to do, but David knew her offer would have repercussions for him.

As Emma sniffed her agreement and gave her sleeping brother a kiss on the cheek, he knew he'd have to swallow his pride and go along with Annie's decision. Like it or not, he was going home to spend another evening in the company of his parents. The last time he'd set foot in that house, he'd sworn he'd never see them again as long as he lived. His one consolation was that he'd remained true to his word.

"Annie...I wanted your advice on something. It's just that I can't talk about it with Mum and Dad, and David can't help me until he wakes up. It might be too late by then." Emma hesitated in leaving the room and Annie wondered if this was the real reason she'd turned up here tonight. There was clearly something on her mind that she was struggling to deal with on her own.

"Sure. What can I do to help?" Annie perched on the end of David's bed and pulled the chair over for Emma to sit down again.

"I told you there was something going on." He came to stand over his little sister, the protective big brother Emma needed him to be. It was a shame she had no idea he was right by her side where she wanted him.

"Ssh!" Annie temporarily forgot herself and spoke directly to him, only to have both Reece family members look at her with wounded expressions.

"I'm only trying to look out for her," David huffed.

"Sorry, not you, honey." It had obviously taken a lot for Emma to ask for help from someone she hardly knew, and Annie didn't want her to think it had been a mistake.

"It's my stomach." She rubbed her belly and forced a laugh. "I've hardly eaten today and it's rumbling so loud I can barely hear myself think. Now, what was it you wanted to talk about?"

Emma settled back into the chair, mollified with the half-baked explanation of Annie's sudden outburst. "W-ell, there's this dance at school…"

Annie leaned forward in her chair, keen to find out where this was going, because it certainly wasn't what David had been anticipating. "For Christmas?"

"Yes. It's non-uniform, but I don't know what to wear. There's a boy I like…Jamie. He's going to be there." She ducked her head, but Annie had already seen the tell-tale blush of young love.

"And you want to impress him?" She had a flashback to her own school disco when she'd been desperate to get the attention of a certain Mark Hepthwaite in her class. He'd been so cool with his short, spiky blond hair and cheeky personality that all the girls had fancied him. Her mother had taken in one of her old dresses for her to wear and Annie had loved the glittery blue sheath. Unfortunately, Mark hadn't been as impressed by her efforts and he'd gone off hand in hand with Michelle Gardener, who'd worn crop-top and camouflage trousers. *There is no accounting for taste.*

Even though Mark had lost most of his lovely blond hair since then and she'd seen him collecting trolleys at the local supermarket, it still hurt. That disco had been the most important event in her young life at that time. She almost envied Emma her simple childhood social drama compared to the more complicated matters she faced these days.

Emma gave a shy nod.

"No. No, no, no, no, no!" David bent down to shout in his sister's face. "You're too young for boys. Tell her, Annie."

She didn't even attempt to hide her glee at the situation, both for Emma's first crush and David's about-turn on the entire 'impressing boys' situation. Clearly, he cared more about his sister's virtue than hers.

"Why don't you ask your mum to take you shopping? I'm sure she'd love the chance to pamper you, and she's much more glamorous than me." She had no intention of taking David's advice on this subject. He knew absolutely nothing about being a young girl and even less about subtlety, if his fashion tips to her were anything to go by. Melanie Reece would fulfil the role of personal stylist much better than she ever could, plus she had the means to do it. Annie doubted her thrifty habits and favourite charity shops would impress a young girl attempting to wow her first crush.

Emma zipped and unzipped her pink backpack until the rasping noise became unbearable and Annie reached out to gently still her fidgeting hands.

"Mum's great, but she, uh…she's old."

Annie stifled a smile, which was more than David managed as he laughed openly at the slight against his mother.

"What about going with a friend then? Surely there are others in your class who'll be looking for a party dress." She caught herself before she parroted her own mum by calling it a frock. Then she would only have had herself to blame if she was tagged with the same *old* label as everyone else over twenty-five.

"Mum wouldn't let me go shopping without an adult. I thought maybe... You're kinda cool..."

"Kinda cool?" As someone who'd never been part of the *in* crowd, she'd take it.

"Why are we still talking about this? She's a child." Big bro threw up his hands and walked away muttering in his best dramatic performance. If he ever did get back to normalcy, he might find it difficult to keep his opinions to himself when he'd become accustomed to ranting away without consequence. Mainly because she ignored him when there were other people in the room.

"Yeah. You're pretty and my brother likes you, so you're cool." It was all so simple to the ten-year-old, but she was under the misapprehension that Annie's relationship with David was of a voluntary nature.

Annie cocked an eyebrow at David for confirmation that there was a grain of truth in his little sister's observations.

He stopped flapping around like a headless chicken to acknowledge the reference. "All right. I suppose you are growing on me. That makes you cool by association."

While Emma was distracted by a text message pinging on her phone, Annie stuck her tongue out at the now-grinning spectre in the corner.

"That's Mum. She wants to know when I'm coming home for tea."

That was further confirmation that this was an unauthorised visit and Annie was going to have to be the one to smooth the way home for her. First of all, she needed to know what else Emma was expecting from her.

"Don't worry. I can give you a lift. Tell her you're on your way."

"So, you'll come shopping with me for a new dress?"

Annie didn't know how she'd ended up so involved with this family in the space of just a few days, but so far, she hadn't been able to say no to any of them. Emma was no exception.

"If your mum agrees to it, I don't see why not."

"Absolutely no way. She's not allowed to date until she's at least thirty." David continued to rant and rave as Annie led Emma out of the room towards the lift, but she paid him no more attention than usual. He was going to find out the hard way that impressing boys wasn't the be-all and end-all of a girl's life, and hopefully they could pass on some of that self-confidence he projected so easily to his sister. He did have enough of it to spare.

Chapter Eleven

"Why don't you go and check with your parents if it's okay for me to come in? I'll get your school bag out of the boot." It would give Annie a chance to placate David about coming back here with Emma. He appeared to be sulking in the back of the car, since he'd stopped calling her a bad influence on his kid sister a while ago. This wasn't going to help get him back on her side any time soon either.

She understood his reservations about being there and his reluctance about spending time with them. They'd hurt him, neglected him and now here they were in the running for parents of the year. It was a bitter pill to swallow — not unlike having her long-term boyfriend cheat on her, then get engaged to his bit on the side. The difference being that this was his family, and she knew better than most how it felt to lose them forever. He could give them, and himself, a second chance, and perhaps in doing so restore the natural order of this world they'd lost themselves in.

Emma skipped off up the path, much happier than she'd been at the hospital when they'd first found her.

"She's a great girl," Annie said into the rear-view mirror. David's face was turned towards the window, staring at the lights on in the house.

"I didn't say she wasn't. It's not her I have the problem with," he sighed, sounding more sad than angry about the circumstances.

Annie took that as a positive sign, when he usually couldn't talk about them without a following volley of expletives.

"Has it changed much?" The large house set back from the road looked more like a castle, with its pillars and turrets all made from grey stone. It should've been intimidating, but the orange glow from inside was welcoming in the winter darkness.

"Not really. It's still the stuff of nightmares." Sometimes it was hard to tell when he was being sarcastic, but given the tales he'd told her about growing up here compared to this picture-perfect scene before them, she didn't think he was exaggerating too much. Despite trying to give the impression he didn't care, Annie had seen and heard enough to the contrary.

She'd got to know him well enough over these past few days to understand that beneath that tough — sometimes arrogant — exterior, he was protecting a big heart, one that had taken a few blows over the years and made him naturally cautious of letting anyone near it again, much like her own.

"Are you ready to go in?" she asked him in the mirror.

"Do I have a choice?" They both knew he didn't, once she went inside, but his smile said he wasn't as bothered as much as either of them would've imagined.

"Come in. We're so glad to see you again." Melanie met Annie at the door with a welcoming hug and ushered her inside. Despite its size, she was struck at once by the cosy atmosphere in the home, the heat from the open fire in the living room already flushing her cheeks. It was a pleasant sensation after walking in from the crisp, cold atmosphere outside.

"Oh, it's lovely in here." As she stepped inside, it was like walking into Santa's grotto, with fairy lights and tinsel twinkling as far as the eye could see. The smoky aroma coming from the open fire and the pine scent of the Christmas tree, combined with the delicious smells emanating from the kitchen, served to make it even more appealing.

Nicholas was sitting in an armchair by the fireplace, slippers on and newspaper in his lap. With a real Christmas tree and pile of presents underneath, the scene could've come straight from a Christmas card — one she didn't think had been faked for her visit, nor one David had likely witnessed here before either.

A glance at his stony face confirmed it, and she was overcome with an urge to cuddle him. To have been denied this in his own childhood and walk into his old house to find a display which would enchant any child had to be a kick in the teeth.

"We like to go all out for Christmas now." Melanie sidled up to Annie, presumably so Emma, who was regaling her dad with tales of her day at school, couldn't hear. She wasn't to know her son could. "You know, we missed out on doing this with David. Our own fault. We were too self-absorbed to be good parents to him. It was only when he'd gone that we realised what we'd lost, what we'd driven him to. Emma filled part of that void, but I wish we had our son back too." Her voice cracked, and Annie was compelled to put an arm around her to comfort her as she'd done with Emma.

She dared to look at David again, waiting for his reaction and the inevitable snort of derision. Instead she watched him rake his hands over his scalp and refuse to meet her eye. If he was beginning to believe his parents regretted their actions of the past and wanted to make amends, it was definitely progress. Annie was afraid to hope the thaw was finally beginning to happen, in case she jinxed it.

"It's not too late." She gave Melanie a squeeze, believing every word of repentance and regret. That wasn't to undermine the impact their previous behaviour had had on David, but his parents were owning their mistakes. Not everyone had that level of self-awareness or the ability to change, and it was lonely without family. David didn't seem to have too many people around him who genuinely cared, and his parents seemed as though they would gladly fill that gap, if he would only let them.

"What if he doesn't make it?" Melanie's voice was nothing more than a frightened whisper. "I just want to talk to him, hold him again."

"I'm here, Mum." David's outburst made Annie jump. She'd been convinced he'd maintain his sulky silence until she left the house and certainly hadn't expected him to get emotional. Yet here he was, finally reaching out to his mother, for her comfort and probably his own.

It was breaking her heart to watch them, helpless to enable a physical reunion between them, and that made her miss her own parents more than ever. If it were possible for people to exist on a different plane, she wondered if they were equally as frustrated as David that they couldn't communicate with her. She'd never believed in the afterlife until she'd been stuck living with a man no one else could see. This whole thing was messing with her head, to think they could be shadowing her the way David was, unseen by the person who needed to see them most. Her only consolation was that he hadn't seen any other ghostly bodies hanging around whatever plane he was currently inhabiting.

"You know, we...I found Emma at the hospital tonight?"

Melanie nodded, since Annie had insisted the child explain her whereabouts before she turned up at their house uninvited.

"She told us you were afraid of visiting in case David heard and got upset about it." For now, she left out the part about the school disco and the cute boy dilemma she'd found herself involved in. It wouldn't be fair to overwhelm them with more worry if they reacted the way David had. That was a matter that could be discussed later, calmly and without making such a huge deal about a wardrobe choice. Although, not knowing this family, she couldn't tell how Melanie would respond to Emma asking her for help instead of her mother.

"He's made it clear over the years he doesn't want us anywhere near him. I think he's going to have enough to deal with when he comes around and I don't want to make things worse. It would be a shock if he woke up and found us standing around his bed, and we're the last people he'd want to be there." She was toying with the string of pearls around her neck, clearly anxious at the possibility of straining their relationship any further.

"Trust me. When David wakes up, he's going to want you at his side." This time David met her eye and nodded his agreement. It wasn't as though she'd expect some tearful reunion the second he was able to speak to his parents, but she did think he was open to a discussion, at least, which was more than he'd granted them since leaving home.

"I wouldn't want to put that Flame person's nose out of joint."

"Somehow, I don't think you'll have to worry about seeing her around, unless it's for another photo op. Please, feel free to visit David as and when you please. He needs people around who genuinely care for him. If anyone has a problem with that, including David, send them to me. I'll soon sort them out." She made Melanie and her son both smile at her semi-serious threat, but they needed someone to bang their heads together, something she intended to do as soon as it was physically possible.

"Bless you."

"I'm starving. When's dinner ready?" Emma interrupted their heart-to-heart to address the immediate problem of her empty stomach, reminding Annie that she hadn't eaten anything for a while either.

"Goodness, I'd forgotten all about it. It's in the oven, hopefully not burnt to a crisp. Set the table for me, sweetheart, and you're staying too, Annie, yes?" The invitation came out of the blue and it would be churlish to say no when they were getting on so well. Her empty stomach certainly agreed.

"That would be lovely. Thank you." It might make David a tad uncomfortable to hang around here longer than anticipated, but a home-cooked meal in company was too tempting an offer to turn down. Goodness knew when she'd get another chance to be part of a family dinner.

* * * *

"Good grief. She cooks now? Wonders will never cease." David could imagine the taste and smell accompanying the sight of the roast chicken with all the trimmings served up to the table. It was these simple pleasures he was missing the most, along with things such as having that much-needed conversation with his parents.

He was slumped now in the doorway, with his new friend the green-eyed monster sitting cross-legged beside him, listening to Annie ingratiate herself into his family. It had taken him to see this scene for himself, to hear his mum get emotional about him, to really believe they'd changed. If he'd made some concessions towards them before now, he could have been part of this. Perhaps if he'd stopped being too proud to accept an apology, he might not have hooked up with someone like Flame or even had that crash. Instead, he could've been here, helping himself to a home-cooked meal, laughing and chatting with his family and settled down with someone like Annie.

Still, this epiphany on the meaning of his life and choosing a better path hadn't changed anything. He hadn't suddenly awakened from his coma or materialised as his parents' surprise Christmas present. There were unresolved issues as to what had brought about this change or why they'd neglected him so badly in the first place.

"What are you doing for Christmas this year, Annie? Do you spend it with family?" It was a perfectly ordinary question for his dad to ask, a normal assumption for people—other than him—to spend the holidays with company. However, between mouthfuls of mashed potato, Annie shifted uncomfortably in her chair.

"It'll be a quiet one for me at home. My parents have both passed." She helped herself to the jug of water in the middle of the table.

"Surely you have friends to spend it with?" His mum seemed horrified at the notion and he wondered how she'd feel if she knew that was how he'd planned to spend the holidays too.

Annie shook her head. "It's fine. I only have the one day off work anyway, and I intend to make the most of it, lying around watching TV and catching up on some sleep."

"You're working Christmas Eve *and* Boxing Day? That's terrible. What sort of work are you in?"

Now it was David's turn to be embarrassed. Those two days were the busiest in the business. The twenty-fourth of December was when people were buying their last-minute presents and the day after Christmas was when their sale began, plus they were inundated with kids spending their Christmas money. Although personally, he'd never have expected an employee to work both days. He'd have hoped management would've had a much fairer system of designating those days between staff members.

"I work in retail, so we never really stop."

He mouthed his thanks to her for saving his blushes and not mentioning he was her sadistic employer, forcing her to slave away over the festive period.

"Can Annie come here on Christmas Eve? We can have hot chocolate in our PJs and watch Christmas films together." Emma was literally bouncing in her chair with excitement at the prospect.

It sounded as though this was an established Christmas Eve ritual, one which no longer included drinking themselves into oblivion and forgetting which day it was when they woke up—a family tradition which he had carried on, with no real reason to celebrate on his own.

It flagged up Emma's want of company too. He knew what it was to be the only child and want someone to share the excitement and anticipation of Christmas, regardless that the main event turned out to be something of an anti-climax. If things had been different, they could have had each other to make the day really special. He would've loved to spoil her with gifts and spend Christmas playing board games and eating too much with her. Perhaps he still could.

Annie choked on her glass of water at the invitation bestowed upon her, but David thought it would be nice for her to have the company and share the fun too. He knew how she spent her free time and was starting to think she needed some sort of intervention before she shut herself off completely from the rest of the world.

"Honestly, there's no need to pity me. Thanks, Emma, but that's family time." Annie tried to let her down gently, but it left his sister pouting and playing in her dinner rather than eating it.

"No, Emma's right. You must come and spend Christmas with us. You are family now." His dad asserted the plan by thumping the table with his fist, rattling the plates and cutlery and everything else that wasn't nailed down.

After seeing how fiercely Annie had defended her plans and protested against any insinuation that she should decorate for the season accordingly, David was surprised to hear her quiet, "Thank you. I'd like that very much."

This time apparently hadn't only affected him and his attitude towards the season. He was happy for her that someone had taken her in and made her part of their family, whether she agreed or not that she needed it.

"Hopefully, we'll have David here too," she added pointedly.

"I hope you're right," he sighed, confessing his change of heart for her ears only. The smile she was desperately trying to stop spreading across her face was in danger of making her look smug.

Then again, the matching one he was wearing might give away how much he was looking forward to spending that time with her too—in real life, without keeping his presence a secret and where he was hoping he and Annie would have a chance to be in each other's company properly.

"Wouldn't that be wonderful?"

"This near-death experience might prompt him to get in touch again. What do you think, Annie? You know him better than we do." His mother, then his father, jumped on board with the idea, though still sounding unsure he would be easily convinced.

Annie arched an eyebrow at him, waiting for his input.

"If, by some miracle we figure this thing out and I get my life back, I promise to come and spend Christmas here—on the condition that you do too." Suddenly the holidays no longer seemed something to dread, but something to give him a reason to live.

"I think you might just have a full house this Christmas." Annie was already starting to feel like part of the family, but it would be so much nicer to have David here properly, to get to know him without all their personal baggage getting in the way.

"Annie, would you like to come and see my room?" They'd barely finished eating before Emma got to her feet and beckoned for her to follow.

"I, er...I don't know." She looked to Melanie and Nicholas for an appropriate response to their daughter's request. It might come across as a bit weird for a grown woman they'd only known for a matter of days to be disappearing into their young daughter's bedroom.

"It's fine. She shows everyone her unicorn collection. She's very proud of it. David's to blame, of course. He gave her that first one. Do you remember, Nicholas?"

"Oh, yes. She toddled about everywhere with that thing. It was almost bigger than she was at the time. It's a bit worse for wear these days, but it still has pride of place on her bed. I only wish David could see it too."

"It wasn't anything special, just a stupid cuddly toy I got a discount on." He could deny it all he wanted, but David had obviously always had a soft spot where Emma was concerned. Understandably, he'd been guarded because of the history with the rest of the family, but now that they were making inroads towards restoring their relationship, it was important he saw for himself the impression he'd made on his little sister.

"Why don't I go up and take a picture to show David when he wakes up? Then he can see it for himself when he's well enough for visiting." That gave her a credible reason for being in Emma's bedroom without it seeming too weird for her to be hanging out with a pre-teen.

"That's so thoughtful of you, Annie. I'm sure he'd love it."

Annie didn't stick around to hear any more of Mrs Reece's effusive gratitude when she didn't deserve it. She hadn't managed to do anything of particular use to the family beyond lip service. The rest was going to be down to David.

Emma sprang up the steps ahead of her, leaving no time for her to marvel at the smooth mahogany banister under her fingers or the vast marble staircase she was sure was wider than her own living room. This was Cinderella territory, and though she wasn't wearing her glass slippers, she knew that by the stroke of midnight she'd be back in the dusty scullery where she belonged.

"Do you like it?"

It took a moment for Annie to home in on the source of the voice when Emma was obscured by the array of colourful unicorn bodies already in residence on her bed.

"It's very, ah...bright." The pink glittery walls were sparkling to the point of possible strobing, with the addition of fairy lights strung along the coving on the ceiling. She had her own silver Christmas tree perched on the corner of a desk littered with assorted unicorn trinkets and schoolbooks. It was the kind of room she would've loved as a child, but as an adult, it was beginning to give her a headache.

"Wow. Someone was allowed to run riot with the glitter glue." There was the slightest hint of jealousy in

David's reaction to the décor. Annie saw him out of the corner of her eye, wandering around the room, assessing every soft toy, family photograph and nod to a happy childhood. He paused at the doll's house, an exact replica of the Reece household, right down to the matching sparkle-fest in Emma's tiny bedroom clone. As relieved as she was sure he was that his sister was being taken care of, Annie knew there'd be a part of him who wished the same could've been done for his younger self too. Okay, so he wasn't the dollhouse type, but the little boy she imagined would have been grateful for any of the toys or gifts Emma had been bestowed by her parents. She wondered if his unhappy childhood had been part of the reason he'd gone into the toy business, bringing delight to children who were appreciated much more than he'd ever been.

Although she couldn't physically comfort him, she did walk over to where he stood for some reassurance that he had her support and understanding. The ornate white armoire bursting at the seams with triangles of pink and blue fabric caught in the doors was the rich cousin of the flat-pack, chipboard wardrobe barely hanging together in Annie's room.

"Emma, you've got more clothes here than the local branch of TK Maxx." It was doubtful any member of the family had ever set foot in a budget clothes store, and as Annie opened the doors to a world of quality kid couture, she wished she could fit into them herself.

"Mum says a girl can never have too many clothes." It was the first time a pouting Emma had shown any sign that her family's wealth may have had an adverse effect on her. Being spoilt might not have been something David had ever had to worry about, but they were obviously making up for lost time with their daughter. It could almost be as damaging as the neglect David had suffered if she became the sort of person who took everything for granted, not appreciating any of it.

"She should think about donating some of these to that charity shop we were in. It would be much better to raise funds for a good cause than have them gathering dust in there." David gave Annie hope he could be the one to rein in Emma's sense of entitlement and his parents' spending habits attempting to buy her affection. These new altruistic tendencies made him even more attractive, at the same time providing Annie with a sense of achievement at opening his mind to the idea of charity. Perhaps he was hinting she should do the same for his sister.

"You know, Emma, the world isn't all about how much stuff you have. I mean, your brother has all the money he could ever need, but that's not important now, is it?" She mouthed, 'No offence', to David, because she knew it wasn't a nice thing to hear after everything he'd worked so hard to achieve. He gave a shrug of indifference. After everything he'd experienced lately, he'd presumably worked that out for himself

"I guess not." Emma hugged her precious unicorn, whose horn wasn't as perky as it likely once had been and was more of a dirty grey colour than pristine white.

"I'm not here to lecture you, but some people aren't as lucky as you and your family. You don't have to buy new clothes all the time. You can wear the same things over and over again and the money you were going to spend could go to people who really need it. I'm sure you have plenty of stuff that doesn't fit you anymore either. I could take some things to a charity shop which could resell it and pass on the proceeds to a worthy cause."

"Is that what David does?" Emma jumped up off the bed and padded over to check out the contents of her wardrobe with Annie. It seemed as though emulating her big brother was the incentive needed to capture her interest.

"It's something he's looking into," she answered with a grin.

"I think you could give us all a few lessons in morality. Before you came along, I only ever thought of myself, Annie. I hope that's something that is beginning to change." David's kind words caused a lump in her throat that she might be making some small difference, in her own way. The Reece family could really boost the coffers in those shops, should they decide to donate some of their gorgeous clothes.

"It is," she answered him without hesitation. The selfish man who'd turned up and demanded her help had gradually turned into a considerate brother with a social conscience, and she was as proud of him as she was of herself for the transformation.

"It is what?" Like an inquisitive puppy, Emma cocked her head to one side and stared up at her.

"Whoops!"

Annie didn't need David to remind her she'd slipped up. She knew it the second she'd responded to him without that filter she'd been so careful to use around other people. "It is amazing how many lovely dresses you already have here. We might not need to go dress shopping after all."

She started chucking hanger after hanger onto the bed for them to have a good look at what was already available in 'the Emma Reece collection'.

"I think he's already seen me in most of these at the church youth club we go to on Friday nights. I want him to see me in something new...something special."

Annie pushed aside the colourful pile of tulle and velvet to make a space to sit on the bed and patted the spot beside her for Emma. "Listen... I'm way older than you and I've crushed on more than a few boys in my time. I want to share a few things I've learned along the way."

"Okay." Her eager pupil assumed the position at her right hand, waiting for her words of wisdom.

"Emma really needs to get some friends her own age." David looked as though he'd rather be anywhere than in his sister's bedroom listening to her talking about boys. Annie wouldn't put it past him to clamp his hands over his ears to block out the conversation altogether.

Although she agreed with him, this time Annie didn't say it aloud.

"Being with someone can be fun and exciting, but life's not all about making a boy like you. If they don't want you for who you are, they're really not worth your time. It's more important that you're comfortable with yourself."

Emma sat with her head bowed, contemplating what Annie was telling her. She had no idea if this was too heavy for a child her age, when she had no experience in dealing with this sort of thing. It should be her mother's job to talk her through the pitfalls of growing up into a young woman. Then again, she might be more qualified for this consultation when she was the one living alone in a one-bedroom flat.

"Do you have a boyfriend, Annie?"

There was the million-dollar question. She didn't, but she'd like to have one. Just not at any price.

"I don't. I used to, but he turned out to be a not very nice person. I'm better off on my own."

"Are you happy, Annie? Are you comfortable with who you are?" They were questions she'd expected to get from Emma but hearing them come from David threw her. He knew her circumstances. She couldn't bluff him, and neither could she lie to herself.

She gave a quick shake of her head, enough to dislodge a couple of unexpected tears that she quickly wiped away.

"I just want to look nice," was his sister's muted response.

"And that's fine, but do it for you, not anybody else. Okay?"

"Okay."

"Now, let's have a look at everything we've got and see if we can't cobble together something you like." It was clear as Annie sifted through the pile that there were some dresses blatantly too small for the girl. Yet it would be a shame to let all this good-quality fabric go to waste.

"This one used to be my favourite, but I guess it might fit someone else now." Emma stroked the lilac dress with the full organza skirt, embroidered with delicate pale blue flowers and rose petals.

"It's beautiful."

"I used to dress up in it and pretend to be a princess."

"If I could squeeze into it, I would too." The detail was exquisite, although it did look a little young for her now.

The wannabe-princess reluctantly sorted the dress into the pile for donation but kept stealing wistful glances back at it until Annie could stand it no more.

"You know, we could take some of the flowers off this and sew them onto...this one." She grabbed a plain pink shift dress that was more Emma's size.

"You can do that?"

"Sure. It's been a while, but I have a sewing machine at home I can use." It wouldn't take much to add some embellishments and she was willing to put the time into it if it meant making Emma happy. If she'd had anything halfway decent in her own wardrobe, she'd have done the same for her big night out and saved the expense there too.

"Annie, you're amazing. Thank you."

She found herself sprawled on the bed on top of the dresses as Emma launched a hug attack.

"How very *Pretty-In-Pink* of you," David mocked from above. "Let's hope you can create something more aesthetically pleasing than that monstrosity Molly Ringwald mutilated those two vintage dresses for. Andrew McCarthy couldn't have been that bothered by what his peers thought to be seen anywhere near her in that outfit."

Annie didn't know what she was more surprised by — the fact that he was a fan of eighties John Hughes' movies, or that she'd entangled herself further in the lives of the Reece family.

* * * *

"Hi, Sam. How did your date go?" He was locking up the café when they returned home, and Annie couldn't resist asking. She figured she had the right when Flame had been snooping around after her first.

"Good. Good." He turned his face away to pull down the steel shutters, but not before she'd seen the rise of colour in his cheeks under the glare of the streetlights.

"Did you get her name this time?"

"Beverley," he supplied as he knelt down to secure the lock.

"Yep. That's her. Beverley Smith." It was David who confirmed the secret identity of Sam's new love interest.

"Really? She doesn't look like a Beverley." The name didn't sound nearly as glamorous as the woman who'd graced countless magazine covers and red-carpet events.

Sam snapped around. "Why? Do you know her after all?"

"No, I, er...it was just that the way you described her, I expected her to be called something more...exotic."

"Hmm-m. When I mentioned your name, she seemed surprised too. She thought your surname was Davies."

"She must have me mixed up with someone else. Hopefully my doppelganger is some swanky, rich lady living the high life out there." She didn't like lying to Sam, but it would be impossible to explain what was happening without sounding crazy. Besides, this was the first time he'd shown any interest in a woman in the whole time she'd known him, and Annie didn't want to be the one to break his heart.

"It's early days, but I really like her, Annie." His lopsided smile was endearing, but it also spoke of his vulnerability. If he was willing to open himself up to this woman so readily after all this time mourning his wife, it was a sign he was in deep. She could only hope Beverley — and Flame — had good intentions towards him, that this wasn't some sort of ploy to find out what was happening between her and David.

"I'm so pleased for you, Sam. Just be careful, okay? I wouldn't want you to get hurt."

"Thanks, Annie, but I have a real good feeling about this."

What else could she do but smile and wish him well?

She waved after his car until the headlights disappeared into blackness.

"Does he really have no idea who Flame is? Has he been living under a rock these past couple of years?" David apparently wasn't as enamoured with Sam's guileless charm, doubting his motives as well as Flame's for the budding romance.

"Sam puts his heart and soul into the business. He works day and night, so he doesn't pay much attention to the whole celebrity nonsense. I don't even know if he owns a TV." It wouldn't be the first time she'd made a reference to pop culture that had gone completely over his head. Sometimes she wished she was more like him, uncaring about the lives of the rich and famous and concentrating on getting her own on track.

"I just find it hard to swallow that he wouldn't recognise her. You don't think they're cooking something up between them?"

"I don't know what Flame's playing at, but I do know Sam is a genuine guy. Besides, what juicy story do you think they're going to get out of joining forces to snoop on me? All they're going to find is a crazy woman talking to herself, spending money on outfits she can't afford."

"All for a good cause," he reminded her.

"I have to admit that I am starting to get into the Christmas mood." Annie opened the door to the flat in a better frame of mind tonight, after David's family had shared a little of their festivities with her.

That unexpected house call had done wonders for her, and it certainly seemed to have paid dividends for him too. Now she had the prospect of sharing Christmas Day with someone other than her pet guinea pig, she was looking forward to the time off, especially when David was planning on being there too.

"You might want to tell that to your flat," David grumbled in response as they set foot into the darkness. It was depressing coming home to this after the warmth of the Reeces' sparkling wonderland.

"I know that can't have been easy for you back there, but I think it could be good for both of us to spend Christmas with your parents if we can." She went around switching on all the lights in an attempt to make her sparse flat more visitor-friendly.

"I'm not promising anything," he warned, "but I'm willing to hear them out and spend some time with Emma."

He'd clearly given it a lot of thought, and Annie was over the moon, not least because she was fast becoming fond of the entire family. She gave a little squeal, itching to throw her arms around him for a tight hug. Even if reconciling him with his family didn't turn out to be his *mission*, she believed it would make him happier in himself. He needed people around him, a sense of family and security — all of those things money hadn't been able to buy him.

"That's all anyone's asking of you, and you're proving your maturity in agreeing to it. I know they hurt you, badly, but I truly believe they regret it. It's not too late to salvage a relationship with them. For some of us, that's not an option." The sadness crept into her voice as it did every time she was reminded of what she'd lost.

It struck her in that moment that she no longer included her ex in that category. He didn't feature in her thoughts much at all anymore. He was a lost cause and a waste of her time and energy, whereas David was very much a work in progress and someone worth fighting for.

He made some sort of unintelligible noise without actually agreeing with her. "Well, we can sit here being miserable, or we can try and inject some life into this place, no pun intended. Are we going to decorate or not?" he asked.

"You mean am I going to decorate? You won't be able to do anything other than supervise. Remember?" The idea was more appealing to her now that she'd been inspired by the Reece family and the nostalgia she was feeling for her parents. She was eager to explore the boxes of decorations she'd inherited and recreate the spirit of past Christmases with David.

"I'm good at that." David winked and took up his spot on the sofa.

It didn't take too long for her to get organised, since everything had been packed away so lovingly the previous year. The hardest bit had been assembling the six-foot artificial tree single-handedly, which hadn't seemed so cumbersome when helping her mum set it up in the corner of their living room in previous years. Now, trying to balance one layer of branches on top of another and trying not to decapitate her angel on the ceiling was proving tricky.

David's sole input had been shouting, "Left a bit. Right a bit. There's a big gap in the middle."

He'd been in serious danger of having a miniature resin reindeer lobbed at his head.

"I bet you could tell the story behind each and every one of these." He came over to inspect the assortment of oddities she'd hung on the branches, along with the many strands of tinsel and fairy lights.

"Yup. We bought new ones every year and some of these were handed down through the family. I think these go right back to the thirties." She pointed to a fragile lantern painted with a fireside scene reminiscent of the one they'd witnessed in his parents' living room.

Instead of the usual sadness that accompanied thoughts of Christmases gone by, it gave Annie a warm glow inside to remember the happier times they'd had playing out this scene together, probably because the Reeces had let her enjoy some of their family time with them tonight and reminded her that not all memories had to be sad ones.

"We bought this one when Dad died." She traced her fingers over the red robin embossed on a white porcelain heart. Her father had been a keen nature lover, and something about robins had always made her think of him. When she saw them about, she imagined it was a sign he was there with her. Fanciful, maybe, but it gave her comfort to think he hadn't disappeared from her life altogether.

She hadn't had such notions after her mother's death. The stress of her illness and caring for her had knocked that pie-in-the-sky thinking out of her. It had quickly become clear when she lost her mum that she was well and truly on her own. That had been when she'd bought George Bailey to provide some companionship.

David had helped draw her back to the outside world, forcing her to deal with his issues on his behalf. It had opened doors for her with his family and given her the confidence to think about life past her grief. For that, she'd be forever grateful.

"I would've been one of those street urchins with their faces pressed up against your window, wishing he could be part of that happy family." It was unusual for David to come across as emotional and vulnerable, and it had more impact than the anger Annie had come to associate with his childhood.

That image of him as a lost boy wanting to be loved caused such an ache in her soul that it physically hurt. It was obvious that all the peacocking he did as an adult was him trying to prove he didn't need anyone to be happy, when all along he'd been crying out for the affection she'd taken for granted from her parents.

"Now it's the other way around," she joked, but her eyes had already sprung a leak.

"You're very much part of my life, Annie." He held her gaze, his brown eyes not mocking her for once, but willing her to believe his sincerity.

He reached his hand up as though to touch her face and she held her breath waiting for that contact. It was only when his hand fell away again that she remembered his touch remained elusive to her.

She swallowed down her disappointment and the realisation of how much she'd wanted that moment of intimacy to happen.

"For now… I'm only part of your life because you don't have a choice." She handled a silver bauble a little too roughly and the worn thread she'd hung on the tree snapped, sending the fragile ornament hurtling towards the floor.

"That's not true and you know it," David snapped at the same time. His reflexes, though misplaced in this plane, were quicker than Annie's and he shot out a hand to catch the plummeting bauble.

She didn't know which one of them was more surprised when he caught it in the palm of his hand. Slack-jawed, he handed it over to her, their fingers brushing, bodies touching, for the first time. Electricity pinballed around her insides and he lit up at the physical contact too.

"Did you just—?"

"Uh-huh." A smile slid across his lips and he took a step closer to her as though he was about to take her in his arms. Yet she was denied another second of his touch upon her as the ornament dropped into her hand unaided.

"How...? Why?"

"I don't know." David tried again and again to replicate his actions, frustration and concentration furrowed on his brow as he attempted to retrieve the ornament from her grasp. The slightest brush of skin against skin had suddenly become the most significant event in both their lives.

Eventually, as had happened that first night when he'd attempted to leave her flat, he had to admit defeat. "Fuck!"

"There must've been a reason it happened. You reached out without thinking... You were pissed off at me. If that's a requirement, I'm sure we'll manage to do it again."

"It has to be a good sign, right?" His eyes were shining bright with hope — and with ample reason. This was the first time there'd been any indication he might be able to get back into his own body.

"Of course." She tried to match his enthusiasm, but with this new development came a sense of dread winding up from her gut to choke any excitement.

The sooner he returned to his body, the sooner he'd leave her, and she'd got used to having him around. If she were honest, she didn't want to share him with anyone else just yet. Once he'd found his way back to his life, she'd lose the one she'd just discovered.

Although she hadn't said it back to him, he was a huge part of her world and she didn't want to go back to living in one without him in it.

Chapter Twelve

"Tonight's the night." The Christmas party hadn't come a moment too soon for David. Standing by that tree the previous night, he'd wanted to reach out and touch Annie, hold her, kiss her.

Perhaps it had been a blessing that his wish had come true a fraction of a second later, when it was safer and less likely to complicate matters. If this was a step back into reality for him, there was no point in starting something he couldn't finish with her. He'd only hurt her and ruin the connection they'd fostered since the accident. She'd be better off with Kev, who was safe, reliable and alive.

He hadn't been able to move so much as a feather since that last amazing achievement. Goodness knew he'd tried, but he didn't know how he'd caught that bauble or touched Annie in the first place. The shock that had reverberated through his body at feeling her warmth for the first time had been immense and had convinced him it was the moment they'd been waiting for — that he'd come back to life solely so he could put his arms around her.

Apparently, that wasn't the true goal after all, as once again, he'd embraced only air and was left impotent when it came to being of any use to Annie. In hindsight, this likely wasn't about his happiness, when he'd spent years indulging himself, but Annie's. That would explain his brief venture back to solid form. It had enabled him to save one of her precious ornaments and make her truly happy in that split second. She was what he had to focus on. All this time, she'd been working to reunite him with his family, when she was the one with a crappy job, crappy flat and was as miserable as he'd been when he'd first left home.

"I wish I had a bit more time to get ready. Everyone else will have been off having their hair done and getting spray tans." Annie was flapping around her bedroom and David could hear the opening and closing of drawers behind him. He'd sworn not to peek as she changed out of her work clothes into the outfit they'd chosen for Kev's seduction.

This developing relationship with Kev was what needed his attention, and he'd have to set aside any petty jealousy. This was his one chance to do the right thing by her and achieve his personal goal at the same time. He was going to walk her through the perfect date credentials to enable her to blow Kevin's socks off, no matter if it killed him to see her walk away with another man at the end of all this.

"Sit down. Take a sip of the wine you poured and chill. You don't want to be too early. A late entrance will certainly get a man's attention. If there is one thing I've learned from past girlfriends, it's that they like to make an impression when entering a room. There's nothing Flame enjoys better than having people waiting around for her, then walking in as though she was doing them a favour by turning up at all."

He knew Annie had more regard for people's feelings than to treat them that way, but this was about transforming her into someone who turned heads. It was embarrassing to admit that he'd repeatedly fallen for those selfish, self-absorbed players with no consideration towards others' feelings — and more so to admit he'd eventually become one of them...until he'd met Annie.

She came around to his side of the bed, dressed only in a threadbare, faded pink towel, and sat down beside him with a sigh.

"This so isn't me." She eyed up the pile of new makeup, hair products and fake eyelashes and nails spread over the bed.

"I thought that was the point?"

As she looked at him, her skin pink from the hot shower, her hair damp around her shoulders, he honestly thought she'd never been more beautiful. David could only apologise for the shallow nature of his fellow men who hadn't been able to see it before now. This was simply to give her a profile boost. Once someone took the time to see beyond her outward appearance, they'd realise what an extraordinary woman she really was.

"Hmm-m. I hope it's worth the effort. I mean, are you sure I should wear these? I'm not the kind who'd let a man get far enough on a first date to see my underwear." She stretched the minute black thong between her fingers.

"It'll make you feel and act sexier." He thought of the accidental flashes he'd witnessed over the years that had caused him to follow women who favoured skimpy underwear like a hound dog.

"I'm not sure how sexy it'll be walking with a wedgie. I'd swap my granny pants for that any day. I'd rather be comfortable and not in danger of catching a chill in my nether regions or pulling my knickers out of my arse all night." She made him snicker as she pinged the thong at him. He'd never worn one himself, only appreciated them on an aesthetic level, and had never considered practicality or comfort levels. *Clearly only thinking of myself, as usual. Lesson learned.*

"You do whatever you want, but if things heat up between you and Kev—"

"I can guarantee he will not be getting into my pants tonight. As if I'm going to hook up with anyone when you're hanging around. Ew-w!" She lifted the glass of wine from her dresser and knocked it back, the thought obviously driving her to drink.

That clarification raised so many conflicting emotions inside David. Her disgust at the thought of him hit hard, but the pain lessened with the knowledge she wouldn't be sleeping with Kev tonight. If he could hook them up and get back to normal life, escaping that image of them rutting together, he'd be over the moon. He didn't want to imagine her with anyone, much less see it for himself. Yet that was the aim, wasn't it? For her to be happy, even if it meant changing her so Kev couldn't resist.

Why, then, was that shiny dream of leaving her flat smudged around the edges with sadness?

Annie's mobile phone rang, startling them both. He hadn't heard it ring the whole time he'd been here.

"That's probably him now, phoning to ask what you're wearing. Be honest with him. Although you might want to leave the bit out about the ancient towel ensemble you've got going on."

Annie scrabbled around in her bag, searching for the phone, giving him a glimpse of the smooth, soft skin of her inner thigh as she bent over the edge of the bed. Annie was right. It didn't take anything as cliché as skimpy lingerie to turn a man on. A discoloured, worn towel worked equally effectively. Although, since it had taken Kev a lifetime to make a move, it was best she did go all out tonight. He hoped the SOB deserved her, that this would be her happy-ever-after and that he didn't turn out to be another asshole who didn't treat her properly — or David would prefer to stay where he was.

That growing sense of loyalty to Annie extended so far that he was willing to sacrifice everything for her. *Wow*. He really had discovered what was important in life, and it wasn't flashy cars or wads of cash. In a way, this time with Annie had been his own moral makeover to ensure he got his priorities right in the future — the people he loved, and who loved him without condition.

"Hello?" Annie accepted the call, half-hoping it was Kev ringing to tell her he'd had a change of heart. She didn't recognise the number, but she'd welcome the chance not to have to go through with this charade. The fancy clothes, the makeup and the flaunting weren't her, but it was what David wanted to see and it was hard to say no when she wanted to please him.

They'd had a moment the previous night before he'd touched her, and she wanted him to look at her that way again, as though he were going to kiss her. If their time together was coming to an end, she wanted to make it hard for him to walk away from her in the real world, even if that meant transforming into the kind of woman he preferred to have on his arm.

She'd hardly given a second thought to Kev when her whole world now seemed to revolve around David, but if this date was the key to him staying alive, then she had to go through with it.

"Annie, I'm so sorry for phoning you. Mum and Dad said not to bother you because we don't know if it means anything or not and it wouldn't be fair to get your hopes up..."

"Emma, what is it? What's wrong?" The girl was rambling so fast it was difficult to make out the reason for the call.

"It's David. Oh my God. I can't believe it actually happened. What if this is it?"

Annie's heart was pounding in synch with the speed of Emma's voice.

"Calm down, take a breath then tell me what it is that's happened?" Only an emergency would have generated this frantic call, and now with mention of David, the crisis level was rising. Even he would be able to tell there was something wrong from her side of the conversation and he leaned in so he could hear too.

Although she was aware of his proximity, it was the simple human connection she was missing. She had to use her imagination to feel his hot breath on her skin and inhale the scent of the expensive, sexy aftershave she knew he'd be wearing, but her pulse fluttered all the same. The easiest thing, to put some distance between them and refocus her romantic inclinations towards the man she was actually going on a date with tonight, would be to put Emma on speakerphone, but she resisted. Instead, she and David sat side by side on her bed, waiting to hear the news together.

Emma inhaled and exhaled loudly. "Sorry. He opened his eyes last night. Only for a second, but the nurse swore she saw him do it. Maybe your wish is going to come true and he is going to be home for Christmas, Annie."

It was easy to understand why the Reeces were trying to play this down when the child was so carried away by this tiny development.

Annie instinctively knew this progress had happened at the same time he'd reached out and touched her the previous night.

"That...that's wonderful news. What do the doctors say?" They would have no idea what this signified, other than there could be a big change coming. Unfortunately, there was no way of telling what that would entail. If David returned to his body on a permanent basis, it would be a guessing game as to where he'd end up or what physical and mental damage he'd incurred during the crash.

"Well, they say it's encouraging, but that we shouldn't read too much into it." Emma's disappointment that they were trying to rain on her parade was evident and Annie didn't want to crush her even more.

"I'm sure it's a positive sign that he's on the road to recovery, but we've got to take one step at a time. It could be a long journey back for him." She was aware she was talking about David as though he weren't there, but neither of them knew what the future held for him. There was no point in giving anyone false hope.

"I knew you'd understand, Annie. You love him just as much as I do."

The words hit home for Annie. The pre-teen was clearly more aware of her feelings for David than she was, but she couldn't argue with the assessment. She'd fallen for this man who'd dropped so unexpectedly into her life, but she was afraid to admit it—to him or herself—when there was such a big question mark hanging over his future. If she gave in to those feelings, left her heart exposed and he didn't survive, she'd be devastated all over again.

David lowered his head, so she couldn't see how the nature of the conversation had affected him, then he tapped his watch to remind her of more pressing engagements than her developing attachment to a man in a coma.

"Let me know if you hear anything else, and you take care of yourself, Emma."

"Thanks for listening. I'm glad David and I both have you as a friend." She hung up, leaving Annie close to tears and more stunned by the revelation about herself than David's apparent progress at the hospital.

Whatever these feelings were, she knew she had a limited amount of time if she wanted to act on them. It wouldn't be long before she lost him to another Flame if she didn't make a move soon.

She gathered up the teeny-weeny lingerie and the contents of the department store make-up counter she'd been talked into purchasing. If she was going into battle, she was going in wearing her armour. One way or another, she was sure this night was going to change their lives forever. *No pressure.* It simply meant the first date she'd been on in over a year had to be a success. All she had to do was not be herself.

* * * *

"Are you sure this isn't overkill?" Annie checked herself out in the window of the hotel where Reece's Toys had hired a room for the party.

"Sexy as hell," David growled.

With her curves encased in siren red, her hair tumbling in loose waves around her face and her full lips painted to match her outfit, every man who walked past took a second look. If Kev didn't realise how lucky he was, then he wasn't worth the effort.

Annie tottered over to the elevator in her heels, and once the doors closed, resumed tugging at the hem of her dress, trying to pull it down farther.

"Stop fidgeting." It dawned on David as he watched her that she hadn't exaggerated how uncomfortable she would be dressing up. A huge part of being sexy came with confidence, and his feisty partner's insecurities meant she may as well have been wearing that God-awful onesie, not that it would have mattered to him what she was wearing. He'd seen her in various states of dress and undress, and she didn't need to do anything to impress him. He was already aware of how amazing she was, but apparently Kev was slow on the uptake and needed it spelled out to him.

"I can't help it. I feel so…exposed."

"Again, I think that's the point. We're trying to show Kev what's going on beneath that work uniform." David's stomach churned with disgust, even as he said it, when it sounded as if he was trying to pimp her out.

There was so much more to her than a great body, and he hated the thought that they had to create a brand-new cover for someone to take an interest and hopefully peek inside to find that out for themself.

The doors opened, and they were immediately hit by the noise and lights coming from the party already in full swing.

Annie took a deep breath before she entered the room, displaying the level of anxiety she was experiencing simply by being there. She was likely as uncomfortable as he had been returning to his childhood home, but they'd agreed to do whatever it took to restore natural order to his world, regardless that seeing the trembling hands clutching her bag made him want to spin her around and take her back home. They'd have a much better time curled up on her sofa watching those terrible soap operas of hers and taking the piss out of the plethora of murderers and kidnappings that happened on a weekly basis in such small towns.

She paused inside the room, presumably searching for a corner to hide in when all eyes were on her. He could sense her backing up, getting ready to bolt, when Kev lit upon her.

"You look great," he said, kissing her on the cheek.

He apparently hadn't gone to the same lengths to impress his date. The short-sleeved checked shirt, tucked half-in and half-out of his torn jeans and teamed with scuffed trainers, made him look scruffier than he did at work. It gave the appearance of having dropped in as an afterthought, not that he was meeting someone.

Way to woo a lady, Kev.

David had many failings, but he always made an effort on a date, and he was quickly turning against this fuckwit for not affording Annie proper respect.

"Thanks. I think I need a drink. I didn't realise there'd be so many people here."

"For the toy reps, the warehouse staff, as well as the retail sector of Reece's, this is the one time we can all get together. It's a shame Mr. Reece wouldn't put his hand in his pocket to give us a free bar, the tight git."

"Dick." David couldn't help himself, forgetting momentarily that Annie could hear him, even if her date couldn't. At least she didn't pick a side, refusing to acknowledge either insult.

"Where are we sitting?" The dance floor in the centre of the room was surrounded by long banquet tables for the sit-down meal, with rows of chatting employees already in attendance. The sheer number of party-goers and accompanying noise must've been overwhelming for Annie, who spent the majority of her time alone. David had only been out of the social loop for a few days and he was finding it difficult to acclimatise.

"Over there. Order me a drink too. I'm going for a slash." The smooth talker sounded like he'd had a few before she got here. That could explain why he hadn't taken any notice of Annie's obvious anxiety. David would never have left her on her own. He would've taken her hand and led her to her seat. In a more salubrious setting, he might have tipped a passing waiter to find them a quiet table in the corner. He was beginning to think it wasn't Annie who needed training on the art of dating etiquette.

All he could do in this instance was remind her that she wasn't completely alone, despite appearances to the contrary.

"There are two empty seats around that far table. I think that's where he was pointing, and the waitress is taking orders. It will save you having to fight your way through to the bar."

"Thanks," she whispered, and David yearned to put a steadying hand on her waist to guide her to safety and let her know he was truly there for her.

Annie weaved her way through the maze of tables and chairs and practically collapsed into the empty seat to escape the stares. Unfortunately, Kev had chosen to sit in predominantly male company, whose eyes lit up when they saw her join them. She nodded an acknowledgement before snagging a passing waitress to order a shot of Dutch courage.

Kev staggered back to the table as the same time as their drinks arrived and he helped himself to the pint from the tray, slopping some of the contents over Annie and the table.

"I wasn't sure what you were drinking."

"Anything at all, love."

David clenched his fists at this moron's behaviour, and he had no idea how Annie was managing not to pour that beer over his head. If he'd been a tenth as patronising or discourteous to her, she wouldn't have been long calling him out on it. Either she was so smitten by this guy that she thought this was cute, or she was so desperate to get with him that she was willing to overlook it.

If the price of his freedom was her tying herself to this arsehole, she was seriously overestimating his worth. Still, she hadn't given any suggestion that she was offended in any way, so he simply had to hang around and suck it up. The occupant beside her date vacated his seat for a smoke break, so at least David was saved from spending the rest of the night standing behind the couple, cringing at the interaction.

"Do you know everyone here, Annie?" Kev gestured around the table, pint still in hand, sloshing more beer and oblivious to Annie's attempts to blot the stains on her dress with a napkin. It pained David to see her attempting to rescue it when he'd been the one who'd talked her into buying the outfit she could ill-afford, all for this deadbeat to ruin it.

"No, sorry. I think everyone I know is at the table in the corner." Sure enough, David spotted the rest of the faces from the Covent Garden branch waving over at her, but Kev remained unmoved.

"These reprobates are the other reps." His companions jeered like a chorus of boozy public schoolboys, eyeing Annie up as though she was a prime cut of meat served to them on a plate. She smiled politely, but uneasily, at the middle-aged men across the table full of empty bottles and glasses. It was the sight of her nails digging into the palm of her hand that gave away her anxiety at the situation he'd found herself in.

Of course, it wouldn't have been the first time David had introduced a woman to a similar band of drinking buddies, but it was only from this point of view he could see how intimidating the scenario could be to the only woman present. Everything about it flashed danger signs, yet Kev appeared to care more about impressing them than Annie.

"Everyone, this is Annie." It was a half-arsed attempt at an introduction, as he didn't seem bothered about making her comfortable. The other reps held up their glasses to acknowledge her then resumed their bawdy conversation.

"Gagging for it, she was. I shagged her right there in the stockroom. Wham, bam, thank you, Pam." The red-faced, obese narrator prompted another round of raucous laughter, but David reckoned the only action he'd had seen lately was from his own *palm*. This lot weren't doing much for the reputation of the brotherhood.

Annie ignored the titillating anecdote and tried to engage Kev in conversation, ignoring the fact he was still looking past her at the rest of the group.

"So, uh, Kev, what are your plans for Christmas?"

"What? Oh, I don't know. I won't have the kids this year, so not much." He knocked back the rest of his pint and clicked his fingers at the waitress to order another.

Annie spluttered into her wine. "You have kids?"

"Yeah. The wife has custody because, you know, one of us has to work."

"You're married." It was a statement rather than a question as Annie attempted to process this new information.

"Not anymore. I'm young, free and single again. Isn't that right, guys?" He raised his glass and his voice to gain his peers' approval.

Annie's strained smile was getting tighter by the second. Surely she wasn't still planning on going ahead with this date? It was a shambles. Kev wasn't the knight in shining armour riding in to save her. From everything David had seen, the guy was an alcoholic, misogynistic prick she could do without. David despaired of the company she'd been dragged into tonight and it occurred to him that men over a certain age might be single for a very good reason. They were dicks most women had already grown tired of, and he included himself in that band of merry men who would undoubtedly go home alone and cry themselves into a drunken stupor at night.

The rest of the dinner didn't go much better than the pre-drinks, with Annie trying to make all the conversation and Kev showing no interest in her at all. He did more drinking than eating, whilst Annie didn't do much of either.

David hadn't interjected with his opinion of the man they'd pinned their hopes on for both of their happy-ever-afters. Not only was he shouldering most of the blame for pushing her towards him, but it remained Annie's decision what she wanted to do next.

When she excused herself to go to the bathroom, David was relieved to get away from the dick-measuring contest going on around the table too. Naturally, he would have won if they'd been competing in the literal sense. These bell-ends were so boastful that they had to be over-compensating for something. He followed her out and waited until they were alone in the hallway before he spoke.

"So, are we climbing out of the bathroom window?" She'd shown her face, had dinner, and unless she was dying to strut her stuff on the dance floor later, there was no reason for her to hang around. Since she didn't strike him as a disco diva with her aversion to the spotlight, he didn't think she'd be prolonging the date from hell. She certainly didn't owe Kev more than the company she'd already given him.

Annie blinked her spider-lashes at him. "Why would we?"

"I just thought... It's going well then?" He bit his tongue so hard that he almost severed it in two. Surely she wasn't falling for this display of macho bollocks when she didn't put up with it from him? She'd been able to see past his playboy façade and be honest about who he was, with her and himself. If it hadn't been for Annie, he'd still be angry with his parents and the rest of the world. She'd been as stubborn as he was, forcing him to really examine his life and see what it was he wanted, and that wasn't anything money could buy. It was hard then to watch her sell herself short and believe Kev was the fulfilment she needed in return.

"I'm doing everything you told me — hanging on his every word, laughing at his jokes and touching his knee to let him know I'm interested."

Ugh. This was his fault. He'd taken a funny, fiery, independent woman and turned her into a simpering fool, ripe for the picking for men like Kev…men like him, all because that kind of woman was less of a threat to him. They wouldn't hurt him because he'd never love someone so shallow again. Annie shouldn't have to pretend to be someone else for a man to fall for her when he knew he already had.

"You can't be that fucking desperate to get your leg over, Annie. The guy's an arse. He'd shag himself if he could and film it for his mates to wank over. You can do so much better than bloody Kev."

"Apparently not. Now, I need to pee. I suggest you stick your fingers in your ears and close your eyes." She flounced off, shoving the door to the ladies' loo so hard that anyone standing behind it would've been splatted against the wall.

David couldn't believe she was actually going to go through with this. He couldn't bear the thought of that prick with his hands all over her or being forced to watch him bang her up against a bus shelter somewhere. That seemed his most likely seduction technique, if he could get it up at all after the amount of alcohol he'd downed.

The most galling thing about all this was watching it unfold and being helpless to do anything about it. In normal circumstances, he wouldn't hesitate in calling

Kev out on his behaviour. As for Annie, if she couldn't see sense, it wouldn't be beyond him to throw her over his shoulder and cart her off to save her from herself.

Forced to stand and watch her apply another slathering of vixen lipstick and adjust her cleavage in the mirror, he was able to identify the simple reason behind his growing resentment of Kev. *Jealousy.*

Deep down, he wanted to be the one to wine and dine her and take her home at the end of the night and that's what was colouring his judgement of the evening. With that in mind, he kept further opinion to himself as they made their way back to the table. Annie was practically vibrating with rage after their exchange and she was entitled to do so. She was an adult, after all, and capable of making her own decisions—no matter how stupid.

It wasn't as if he would've taken anyone's advice on his past relationships, for those very reasons. The more someone told him what to do, the more he would've been inclined to do the opposite to prove a point.

"I hope you didn't miss me too much." On her return, she dropped a kiss on Kev's cheek, who took the opportunity to gawp down the front of her dress.

"Pig."

It was only when Annie frowned at him that David realised he'd said that out loud.

"I was just telling the guys here I'm the luckiest man in the room tonight." He swatted Annie's backside, and she didn't punch him or kick him in the balls as David would've expected her to.

There were a few titters over the beers across the table and he suspected the conversation about Annie hadn't been rated PG.

Kev's phone screen lit up with a text notification and he grabbed it before Annie could see it. Convinced it was a message from a wife or girlfriend, David peeked over his shoulder.

Lucky all right. You're on a promise there, mate.

Kev smirked over at his chubby friend, who gave him a salute.

Bile rose in David's throat at the way they were objectifying her, hating himself for doing the same in making her dress for their pleasure.

Not usually my type, but beggars can't be choosers. Good for a knee trembler after last orders.

Kev punched out a reply, but David couldn't bring himself to notify Annie and crush what was left of her confidence.

When she bent down to set her bag on the floor and Kev mimed shoving her head into his crotch, David did lose his shit. It was instinct which propelled his fist forward in an effort to save Annie's blushes. He wasn't expecting to connect with anything, much less Kevin's hand as he attempted to take an incriminating picture of her. In that split second, he was able to land a blow, sending the phone skittering across the floor.

"What the fuck?" Kev's thoughts echoed his own. He'd hit Kev, made contact and punched the phone right out of his hand.

"What's wrong?" Annie snapped her head up to see what was going on around her.

"My phone…"

"Holy shit!" David was still trying to come to terms with what he'd managed to do and what it could mean.

"What?" She was glaring first at Kev, then him, demanding answers.

Kev shook his head. "I thought something hit me there. Maybe I've had a bit too much if I've started imagining things."

"Or you've got the shakes," Fatty suggested helpfully.

Kev got up to retrieve his phone and Annie whispered to David, "What did you do?"

All he could do was shrug when he had absolutely no idea himself. Rage had overtaken thought as he'd lashed out, because they'd been disrespecting Annie so badly. He thought back to the last time he'd become solid matter for a brief period, when Annie had been dissing herself. She was the key, along with the strong emotions she evoked in him.

As Annie and Kev fussed over his phone, checking to see if the screen was smashed, David took the opportunity to test his theory. He tried to push an abandoned knife lying on the table with his fingertip. No joy. He thought of Kev having his hands all over Annie and the red mist began to descend. One more rage-fuelled push and the knife slid comfortably across the tablecloth. He could really do this!

If Annie wasn't going to listen to him and rate herself worth more than a handsy drunk, he was going to take matters into his own hands. Literally. He was going to have some fun and teach cocky Kev some manners along the way.

Chapter Thirteen

This was more painful than Annie could've imagined, and considering the anxiety dreams she'd had leading up to tonight, that was saying something. Okay, so she hadn't looked down to find herself standing starkers in the middle of the dance floor, but the way Kev and his lecherous mates had been staring at her, she may as well have been. She shuddered, her skin crawling at the idea of letting any of them anywhere near her. Kev included.

"Are you cold? Why don't you come over here and let me warm you up?" Her date slapped his thighs, but he was deluded if he thought she had intention of sitting on his lap. She wasn't going to lead him on any further when she'd known from the moment she'd walked in here the whole thing had been a mistake. There was nothing remotely attractive about him and she didn't know what the hell she'd been thinking agreeing to this. That was a lie. She'd gone ahead with this charade to keep David happy. Now that he'd decided he was the keeper of her virtue, she was calling his bluff.

How dare he accuse her of being desperate? She wasn't the one who hooked up with a different bed partner every day of the week. Until he'd come along, she'd been perfectly content to remain single. Skint and exhausted maybe, but her relationship status hadn't been the problem, not for a long time. It was in her nature to do exactly the opposite of what David wanted, when he'd been the one who'd insisted she tart herself up, then had a change of heart when it suited him. He'd tried to turn her into the kind of automaton he dated, without considering what kind of man Kev would turn out to be.

It was hard enough having David as her employer dictating her working conditions and finances, without having him wedged into her love life too. If Kev got out of order, she'd sort it out herself. She'd been taking care of things for a long time before David appeared on the scene.

For now, she'd let Kev continue to wind him up and help him learn how to treat a lady. So far neither of them was doing a stand-up job of it.

"I have a seat right here, thanks."

"Aww, come on. Don't you wanna give me a lap dance?" He thrust his crotch upwards and Annie realised he was getting dangerously close to that line. She chose to ignore the sexist comment, but it was David who reacted.

"That is fucking it!"

She could only watch in horror as he swiped Kev's bottle of beer on the table and knocked it onto his thrusting crotch.

"What the hell are you playing at?" she yelled at David before she could check herself.

Kev's head snapped up from investigating his wet crotch at the sharp tone of her voice.

"I didn't do anything." He traded the macho talk for whimpering like a little boy. It was easy to imagine he'd never grown up, when this mob had behaved worse than a group of adolescents.

"Not you," she barked, glaring at David, then cursed herself for slipping up again. To take the heat off her actions, she began trying to mop up the spilt beer.

"I don't care who you're talking to, just keep on doing what you're doing, baby." Kev leaned back in his chair, balancing it on its back legs with his hands behind his head and his eyes closed in mock ecstasy.

Annie tutted and dumped the sodden napkins in a pile on the table, no longer caring where the beer soaked in.

She turned around in time to see David kick the legs of the chair out from under him, sending Kev sprawling onto the floor.

"Pack it in!" she shouted at him.

"He deserves it, and if you weren't so blinded by the thought of hooking up with him, you'd be the one doing the arse-kicking. Ignore everything I told you about how to act on this date. All you should ever be is yourself, and if that's not good for the likes of this piece of shit, then he doesn't deserve you." It was an impassioned speech from David and she was touched that he thought so highly of her, even if it had taken tonight for him to realise it himself. He'd risked a lot to get his point across, but he was right. She'd let Kev get away with too much in her attempt to make David jealous. They'd all been acting like children tonight.

Kev lifted his head up from the floor. "Did you see that? Something kicked my chair. First my phone, then the beer... I think this place is haunted." He wasn't far off the mark, but there was no way Annie was going to give him credence after the way he'd treated her tonight. It was his turn to be humiliated.

Annie rested one stiletto on his chest and pushed him back down onto the floor. "Go home, Kevin. You're drunk."

She stalked away, back across the dance floor, with her head held higher than when she'd come in, and didn't even look to see how David had reacted to her move. The uproar of Kev's boozed-up cronies was interrupted by his yell of, "Crazy bitch!"

Annie stopped dead in her tracks, a statue in the midst of her bopping colleagues. Her usual reaction to anyone shouting at her would be to hang her head and scuttle out of view, but time with David had taught her to stop being a wallflower, a doormat or any other inanimate object not relevant to the world. He'd pushed her, driven her to be more, and she was no longer prepared to languish back in the shadows.

Calmly and deliberately, she pivoted back around and headed back towards Kev. He shut up when he saw her coming. David trotted behind her, clearly enjoying watching the monster he'd created come to life.

She wasn't afraid to square up to the man who'd thought he was good enough for her to date and poke him in the chest with one of her fake red talons.

"I must be a crazy bitch to have seen anything remotely attractive in a sexist waste of space like you." She grabbed a pint off one of his mates lounging beside him and poured it slowly over his head until his hair was plastered flat to his face. "Grow up."

For the first time in her life, she felt powerful as she left the party and the sea of shocked faces in her wake. She didn't even care that she'd have to face them all at work. At least half of them would be too drunk to remember, and she didn't speak to the rest much anyway.

"Wow. Remind me never to piss you off." David gave her a round of applause on her dramatic exit.

The truth was that she was more determined than ever to get a new job. Life was too short to drag herself to a place every day that made her hate her life. Her New Year's resolution was to find something better, even if she had to go to night classes and further her education to achieve it. After everything she'd done for David, she'd be expecting a glowing reference too.

"What? You mean like calling me desperate?" She wasn't about to let that one slide and banked a beer shampoo for him in the future too.

David grimaced. "You know I didn't mean it. I just couldn't believe you were falling for that guy's bullshit."

"I wasn't." She hadn't worn a coat tonight in case she spoiled the impact of her outfit, but despite the cold, she didn't regret the decision as they stepped outside. The cool air was refreshing after the exhilaration of her contretemps with Kev. As she breathed in a lungful of fresh air, it felt like the start of a new exciting Chapter of her life.

"I should've trusted you knew what you were doing. Sorry."

"I wouldn't even have let it get as far as it did, except you were pissing me off as much as Kev. I don't need any man telling me what to do or how to behave."

"Message understood." His knitted brow evened out as he smiled, sending Annie's pulse into another merry jig.

She wouldn't have been a bit interested in Kev, even if he'd been the perfect gentleman tonight, when she only had eyes for one man these days. Unfortunately, he was the one man she would never actually be able to get her hands on.

She set off home, keen to get back to normal and slip into something more comfortable than her scarlet woman outfit. There was no point following that path with David when, far from being the answer to their prayers, tonight had been a disaster for him too. With one exception.

"I liked your party tricks, by the way. When were you going to tell me you could do that?" It hurt that he hadn't shared that progress with her when they'd gone on this journey together and made her think he wasn't keen to keep that connection between them. One day she might wake up to find him gone, without giving her the chance to say goodbye, proving he didn't care for her as much as she did for him. If there was a solution to getting him back, she wanted to be there to help him find it—be part of the process so he'd never forget her. Maybe, just maybe, there could be a chance for them to get to know each other in the real world too.

"I didn't know I could. I swear I haven't done that since that night by the tree. I took myself by surprise."

If she took him at his word, then there must be a common thread linking the two incidents. "You decided you wanted to mess with Kev and it just happened?"

"Pretty much. That first time, when I wanted to slap the phone out of his hand, all I was thinking... Well, I wasn't really thinking. I just lashed out."

"You only become solid form when you want to hit something?" That stifled any thoughts of a romantic kind.

"That's how it worked tonight. I don't know how that translates into progress for my *condition*. Unless some major, life-changing event pisses me off so much I turn into The Hulk, I don't know how this information helps."

"We could get Flame to stop by your hospital bed and have you married off in some morbid wedding ceremony. That ought to get your blood pumping." She hadn't forgotten about his alleged girlfriend who might or might not have feelings for him, regardless of David's view of their relationship.

"Yeah. Why don't you drag my ex-wife along as bridesmaid to make doubly certain?" His droll response went some way to erasing any of her fears that he might have any residual feelings towards his past lovers.

"It could be arranged if you think it's worth trying?" Intense anger seemed an odd catalyst if they were being taught some cosmic life lesson. The opposite might've been more constructive in David's case, when it had taken this long for him to get over the negative feelings he harboured towards his parents. The same could have been said about her and her ex, who she barely gave a second thought to now that her life was so full of other people.

David paused to mull that over all too briefly. "Nah."

The two of them burst out laughing, tonight's faux pas seemingly forgiven and forgotten. It was only the odd stares from the smokers and brawlers outside nearby clubs that reminded her she was still the only one who could see and hear David, despite his new talents.

"We should try and stay away from the busy end of town. I don't want to draw any more attention tonight."

David had already risked a lot by doing what he had to preserve her dignity. It had been an unnecessary exercise when she had been capable of doing that herself, but now that red mist had dissipated, she could see that it had come from a good place — perhaps with the help of a certain green-eyed monster, and hadn't that been her plan all along? The ultimate game-changing make-over, the knockout dress and the racy lingerie had been for his benefit and no one else's.

She'd wanted David to see her in a different light than a go-between for him with this world he couldn't be a part of, but to what end? If he wanted to be anything other than her over-protective spirit bodyguard, they couldn't do anything about it anyway. All tonight had succeeded in doing was emptying her bank account and alienating her from more people.

"Are you sure this is a good idea?" Once David saw the route she intended to take home, he voiced his concerns.

"I come this way all the time." Okay, the alleyway was less like walking into a black hole during the daytime, but it was familiar to her. The high fences either side of the path provided shelter on blustery afternoons and the schoolkids she often passed deemed it safe enough to use.

"Not dressed like that, you don't."

He doesn't see the irony in his disapproval of my dress when he was the one who chose it.

"It's a shortcut and I'm cold and tired. Don't worry. There's usually no one around."

"Or any light, or traffic…"

Ignoring his protests, she set off down the alleyway, not caring about anything other than getting home as quickly as possible.

"I am regretting not bringing the car. If not for the couple of drinks I did have and the lack of available parking, I could have made a quicker getaway." She was contemplating taking her shoes off, but the fact she couldn't see what she was walking on put her off. The thought of God-knows-what squidging between her toes was too terrifying to risk. Once indoors, she could kick off the crippling heels and soak her feet in something much more pleasant.

"You could have got a taxi." He was still trying to tell her what to do, regardless that she'd got through the past twenty-odd years without his interference.

"I'm not made of money. Don't forget I'm already in debt from this little escapade."

He might have grown up in poverty, but he'd forgotten that everything he took for granted now remained out of her reach.

"The Tube then. I want you to be safe."

"I thought we'd already covered the 'I'm a big girl and I can look after myself' talk." She heard his sigh as he disappeared into the darkness, along with everything else down this back street.

Now that it had been pointed out to her, it seemed like the perfect hunting ground for would-be serial killers. The farther she walked, the more eerie the solitary sound of her heels on the pavement became. The hairs on the back of her neck pricked up when a second, then a third, set of footsteps joined hers.

"I don't like the look of this. There are two young guys behind taking a keen interest in you." David's warning made her heart race faster, because she knew he couldn't do anything if she was in trouble.

She reached a stretch of footpath which did have working streetlights. It opened up into a more exposed area, but there were no other signs of civilisation. The two men could've diverted down a number of other streets, but the footsteps followed her with a quickening pace. She didn't want to run and escalate any potential threat to her safety when it could all be in David's imagination. Annie didn't even look back, trying to give the impression that she was confident and in control, although she was trembling.

The wolf whistles summoned her attention, but she kept walking. "Hey, baby. Wanna come to a party?"

Annie didn't want to engage with them, although she knew ignoring them would piss them off more. She wasn't wrong.

"Bitch, we're talking to you."

Any second, things were going to turn nasty, and she had nowhere to run to for help.

"Quick, in here." As she rounded the corner, a hand grabbed hers and tugged her off the main path.

It was only when she was safely hidden in the shadow of a nearby doorway that she realised it was David who'd come to her rescue.

Before she could question what had happened, he put a finger to her lips to quieten her. She could actually feel the pressure of his touch upon her. They were nose to nose, pressed together in the cramped shop entrance, and for the first time, she could feel his breath on her skin. In that second, she and David were in their own little world and she barely registered the footsteps running by or the swearing before her pursuers gave up trying to find her.

They remained holed up together, staring at one another, long after the danger had passed.

"Is this real?" She reached tentatively out to stroke his face. He was warm beneath her fingertips, his jawline bristly with the scruff of his beard.

His touch was equally exploratory as he rested the palm of his hand against her cheek. "It feels real."

She closed her eyes, revelling in the comfort of truly having him here with her. The tears running down her face were happy ones.

"How? Why?" She was afraid to fully let herself believe this was happening, in case he was ripped away from her again. If they could uncover the reason he'd materialised now, perhaps she could find a way to make him stay for good.

"I only know I was experiencing the same emotions as before—angry at the thought that they wanted to harm you in some way and desperately wanting to protect you."

Despite claiming she didn't need him or anyone else in her life, she was overwhelmed with relief to finally have him there in person, not just in spirit.

"Whatever it is, please hold that thought until we get home." She wanted to talk, really talk about what this meant. There was no way to deny the strength of her feelings when this was the equivalent of winning the lottery for her. She needed to know if he thought of her in the same way or if she'd simply become a convenience to him.

The last thing she wanted was to wake up tomorrow and find he'd gone back to his old life, expecting her to return to hers. She couldn't cope with that level of loss again. If he was free to leave her now, it was important to find out if that was what he wanted.

"I've had enough of hiding in the shadows. Come on." He took her hand again and stepped out under the glare of the streetlights with her.

"I'm alive!" he bellowed, breaking through the still night to make Annie jump.

"Ssh! Someone might hear you." She thought primarily of the two lads who'd been following her, though she knew David would take them on if he had to. That was what had finally brought him to her, after all.

"I hope so," he said with a great big grin. Then he cupped her face in his hands and landed a smacker of a kiss on her lips, which definitely wasn't in her imagination when she felt it right down to her toes.

She practically floated home with David's arm around her, and the thought that their life together could truly be about to begin.

Chapter Fourteen

All David's senses were assaulted at once as he re-entered the real world again. He noticed the cold seeping into his body first, but he didn't care when it made him feel alive. The smells emanating from the fast food places on the way back to the flat made his stomach rumble and his mouth water, and he could almost taste those fried onions and greasy burgers.

Best of all was the warmth of Annie's body pressed against his, the scent of her delicate perfume and the wine he'd tasted on her lips. *Heaven.* He didn't know what had brought about this transformation or if it would last, but he wanted to make the most of it before everything was taken away from him again.

"So, now what?" Annie kicked off her shoes as soon as they walked into the flat, and David was overjoyed to find he could do the same. The jacket and tie followed.

"I can't tell you how good it is to do that. I'd kill for a shower too. It's the simple things you miss most when they're taken from you." He didn't care about the luxuries in his million-pound pad. He simply wanted to wash away the traces of his time spent in limbo.

"I'll put the water heater on for you. Do — Do you think this is permanent?"

David could hear the worry in her voice, her concern matching his own, but there was no sure way of knowing what was in store next.

"I don't know. Perhaps we should check in at the hospital and see what's happening there." If patient Reece had vanished from his sick bed, then surely that meant this ordeal was over and he was where he was supposed to be?

"I'll give them a ring in a minute. In the meantime, can I get you something to eat or drink?" Annie had launched into polite hostess mode after days of treating him as her unwanted house guest. It was funny, but he didn't want anything to change between them. For now, he was content to be right there until he figured out his next move.

"Food. Alcohol. Oh God, I feel as though I've been wandering the desert for a month. Can I go help myself while you phone the hospital?" Suddenly he wanted to taste everything and savour all the things he'd been denied.

"Sure. Unfortunately, my tastes aren't quite the same as yours. I don't have champagne or caviar, but I can offer beer and crisps." Annie was teasing him as she opened the cupboards for him to inspect, but he preferred that to the polite stranger routine.

"Anything. I'm ravenous." He stuck his head inside the fridge, searching for treats as though he'd been let loose in a sweet shop. "Go. Go." He waved her off so she wasn't around to witness his scavenging.

"Okay, Oliver Twist, help yourself." Annie went off laughing to make the phone call that could change their lives in an instant.

As David carried armfuls of food over to the kitchen worktop, it occurred to him that they were apart for the first time in days. He was tempted to run in and out of all the rooms, opening and closing all the doors simply because he could. On the other hand, there was nowhere else he wanted to be. He was in no rush to go back to his old life. Perhaps it was a sign he'd become institutionalised that he still didn't want to leave her side — or there could have been another reason.

His armful of spoils tumbled onto the counter as he became distracted by thoughts of Annie. He could put his behaviour tonight down to being protective, unwilling to see anyone treated the way Kev had treated her on their supposed date...except he knew he'd been driven primarily by jealousy. He should've been the one taking her out, when he knew and appreciated her better than anyone. Annie didn't have to pretend to be anyone else when he'd fallen for the person she was at heart. They'd had a moment in the shop doorway when he'd wanted to kiss her longer, but he'd known that the touch of her skin would only make him want more.

However, Annie wasn't the kind of woman he could bed and move on, even if she'd wanted that. They'd developed such a strong emotional bond that he didn't want to jeopardise it. That didn't make it any easier to forget the softness of her lips against his.

He popped the lid on a beer and chugged it down, the refreshing liquid a poor substitute for the last thing to cross his lips. Not even the cold cuts of meat or spicy potato crisps could satisfy the craving which had awakened inside him.

"Well, your alter ego is still in bed but showing signs of returning to the land of the living. I'm expecting another ear-blasting phone call from Emma any minute." Annie tossed the phone down beside the debris from his food binge, not appearing overjoyed by the development. He knew the implications as well as she did. There was a chance this could change in a second or he could disappear altogether from her life. Their unconventional time together was coming to an end.

"I'm making the most of whatever time I have left." He indicated the array of junk food and leftovers that he'd purloined in her absence.

"You're doing it wrong. How can you possibly enjoy that simply by gorging on it?" Annie tutted as she began tidying up the mess of crumbs and ripped packets he'd discarded all around the kitchen surfaces in his haste to satiate his appetite.

"Sorry." This had become his second home, and he'd forgotten his manners along with the life he'd left behind.

Annie bustled around behind him, retrieving a clean tea towel from the drawer. "I mean, you're just mixing everything together, not savouring every morsel."

She fashioned the tea towel into a bandana, totally confounding David.

"They say if you lose one of your senses, the others are heightened." She held up the triangular fabric for his attention.

"You want to blindfold me?"

"Uh-huh. Best way to do a taste test."

David had to fight to supress the stirring in his nether regions as his thoughts ventured in that direction.

"You know, if you're into the kinky stuff, you don't have to be coy about it." His voice was a tad more gravelly than he'd anticipated, but they were treading dangerous ground.

She tutted and advanced into his personal space with her makeshift blindfold. There was a second as she lifted it to cover his eyes when David thought how easy it would be to slip his arm around her waist and pull her to him for a proper kiss, but she hadn't given him any indication that she was up for that. Since she'd done so much for him, he didn't want to disrespect her the same way Kev-the-cock had.

"I need you to trust me. I'm not going to give you anything disgusting. We're simply heightening the sensation for you." She reached around to tie the towel around his head, enveloping him in her sweet scent and letting the soft waves of her hair brush against his cheek.

Yup! His sensations had definitely been heightened.

"Do whatever you want to me," he said, and thought he felt her shiver against him in response.

"Okay, an easy one to start with. Open up."

David did as he was told and parted his lips to accept her food offering. The spicy seasoning and crunch of the potato crisp was instantly recognisable and very tasty.

"Crisps."

"That was a baseline test to get our bearings. Drink?"

He nodded, and Annie put the bottle of beer to his mouth and tilted it for him to drink, cupping his chin so it didn't spill.

"Now, something trickier."

He waited, his mouth open and vulnerable as he put his trust in her not to leave him there in the dark as a prank. She traced something soft across his lips and when he bit down, juice exploded into his mouth.

"Orange," he said with confidence as he chewed the delicious tangy segment of fruit.

"Okay, next." This time she popped a small, cold chunk into his mouth. It was creamy, smoky and instantly recognisable.

"Cheese."

"Good. Now, just take a bite of this one. Don't be greedy." He crunched the cool, hard shell and the smooth, sweet confection was heaven on his tongue.

"Mmm-m, chocolate. How I've missed you." He heard Annie's giggle and hoped she was enjoying this as much as he was.

The contrast of sweet and sour on his tongue, combined with the sensual experience of having her feed him, was just what he needed to remind him he was alive.

"Drink?"

He waited for that fizz of beer on his taste buds. This time as he drank, some of the liquid spilled at the side of his mouth. He was about to swipe it away with the back of his hand when he felt Annie press closer to him and the tickle of her tongue on his skin as she lapped the beer from his lips.

His body went into overload, begging for more. Annie's hands were on his chest, and when she made no move to back away, he anchored his arms around her waist the way he'd been longing to do. He found her mouth in the dark, so hot and wanting against his. If this was limbo, he didn't ever want to leave.

His body was hard with need for her and as he sought her tongue with his, there was only one place he wanted to take her—the bedroom. This attraction, coupled with the emotional journey they'd been through, had reached a boiling point, but if they weren't careful, they'd get burned. It was one thing being cocooned together here away from the realities awaiting outside, but sooner or later he had to return to his own world.

He didn't want to hurt Annie by leading her on if they couldn't follow up on this time together. His life was crazy, and it didn't seem fair to drag her into it before he knew what was waiting for him.

With great reluctance, he pulled away and tore off the blindfold. "The water's bound to be hot enough for that shower now."

It didn't matter if it wasn't. A cold shower would do him just as much good. David didn't look back as he walked to the bathroom and closed the door behind him.

Annie must have misjudged the situation, and now she was humiliated about making advances towards David. The signs had been there—or so she'd thought. The flirting, the coy glances and lingering touches had apparently been exaggerated in her fevered imagination. Why else would he have bolted after she'd kissed him?

David Reece was not the shy, retiring type to be intimidated by a woman making the first move. From everything she'd heard, he wasn't the sort to turn down sex handed to him on a plate, and that was what she'd been offering.

She wasn't under any illusion they were going to have a happy ending but she did hope that letting that chemistry flare into life might have given him cause to think about her after he'd gone. What she'd been afraid of most was opening her heart to him, only to lose him the way she'd lost everyone else she'd ever loved — and that was exactly what had happened.

Far from prolonging contact between them, she'd sent him running. She had confused his remaining presence for want, rather than necessity, and embarrassed herself. If he didn't fancy her now, all dressed up and so obviously 'desperate' for a bunk-up, he never would.

The sound of the water running behind the firmly shut bathroom door was a reminder to her as she made her way to her bedroom that he was free to do as he wished. That didn't include her. It would come as no surprise if he decided to make a solo dash to the hospital now to see if he could resolve his situation without her. Although, he'd have to be careful not to let anyone see him in both incarnations at the same time.

Employing her contortionist skills rather than ask David for help and let him think she was trying to seduce him again, she undid the zip on her dress.

It represented a waste of time, money and energy and she knew that every time she saw it hanging in her closet she'd be reminded of the night's events. That dress was a tangible record of her triumph and heartbreak. Tomorrow she might see if she could return it and let some other poor woman think she'd found the answer to her prayers. She stroked the sultry fabric which had held so much promise when she'd bought it with David in mind.

"Sorry. I didn't think... Sorry." He burst into the bedroom, the ever-present tuxedo swapped for one of her worse-for-wear towels wrapped around his waist.

Her first instinct was to panic that she'd been caught standing here in her underwear and she looked for something to cover herself. Then she remembered he had no interest anyway and brazened it out.

"I couldn't wait to get out of that dress. It's not really me." Goosebumps pricked her skin, and it wasn't due to the cold. She was staring at his naked torso and the rivulets of water trickling over the smattering of dark chest hair, over the ripple of his abdominal muscles and down...

"No, it's not." The towel slipped farther on his hips as he moved towards her.

She swallowed the mixture of emotions surging up inside her like a tsunami, threatening to wipe out everything in their path. She hadn't been able to fool him any more than she could fool herself. He was gorgeous and would never be interested in her in *that* way. He'd only spent time with her because he'd been forced into it.

"I...I don't know what I was doing, thinking a dress and some makeup would magically turn me into someone Kev—or any other man—would find attractive." She hiccupped, the words and taint of rejection catching in her throat.

"That was my fault. I should never have suggested any of it." David reached out and brushed her hair off her shoulders. "Well, maybe apart from the lingerie."

He'd seen her in less than she was currently wearing, but the way he was looking at her made her feel exposed.

"Because you can't polish a you-know-what?" There was a metaphor about glitter and dog poo, but this wasn't the time to quote it verbatim.

"No, because you don't need any of it. You're perfect the way you are."

Annie swallowed down the sob threatening to erupt at the romance of the moment. She was wondering if this whole scene was in her head when a half-naked hunk was telling her he preferred her *au naturale*, especially when he'd seen her at her snot-covered, onesie-wearing worst.

"Do you really mean that?"

David smiled as he dipped his head and wound his hand into her hair. "Yes, I really mean that."

This time he took control of the kiss, a tender exploration of her mouth with his until she was sure she was the one made solely of air. When he let her go, she was in danger of floating away altogether. Her lips tingled with the memory of him there, so fresh, but so too was that earlier rejection.

"Why did you run out on me earlier?"

He sighed and sat down on the bed next to her, the mattress dipping with his weight and giving her some comfort by reminding her that he was really there.

"I want this. I want you. I do." He rested his head in his hands as though he were going through some sort of existential crisis. Maybe he was, slumming it with her instead of his usual calibre of female acquaintances. Stockholm Syndrome, that was probably what it was. He'd spent so long locked up under her control that he'd imagined he had feelings for her and was conflicted about acting on them.

"We don't know what's going to happen from one minute to the next. How do we know how much of this is real between us? What happens when I do return to my body? I don't want either of us to regret sleeping together. I'd rather wait until we know for sure it's what we want instead of rushing into things."

"You mean, like date and stuff?" It was absurd to be thinking of a first date when they were in her bedroom, practically naked and hungry for one another.

"Yeah. I mean…this is kinda new for me. I don't usually need, or want, the whole romance deal, but I figure we're due some quality time at our own pace."

"You want to woo me? You know that's not necessary?" She glanced down at her scant attire and actually made him blush.

"Yeah. I haven't felt about anyone like this in a long time and I don't want to ruin what we have by rushing things."

She was bowled over by his honesty in opening up about how he felt. Most of all, she wanted to be more than a convenient shag to him, even if her body was telling her something different. That didn't mean she wanted this to end.

"Can we at least cuddle? I want you to hold me as long as we're together."

"I'm not going anywhere," he promised, and lay with her atop the covers, the first time she'd shared her bed here with anyone.

They spooned together and the solid warmth of David's chest at her back made her feel safe. She was content, happy and the door to her heart was wide open.

That security David had provided with his honesty and sheer presence prompted her into saying those words she thought she'd never utter again.

She turned in his arms until they were but a breath away from each other. This was it. All or nothing.

"I love you."

He instantly tensed, and she worried shed blown it completely. Then he rubbed her nose with his in an Eskimo kiss. "I love you too, Annie Marlowe."

He kissed her on the lips and Annie thought she'd implode with pure joy. Eyes closed, lips parted, she gave herself completely over to fate.

The last thing she expected was for David to pull away again. With a frown wrinkling her brow and her body aching for his renewed touch, she opened her eyes to see what was wrong, only to find David's side of the bed empty. The bedroom door was still closed and all that remained of him was a dent in the pillow and a wet towel where he'd lain.

David was gone. The dream was over. The bubble had burst.

Chapter Fifteen

"David? David? Are you awake?"

That wasn't Annie's voice. David opened his eyes, but the glare of fluorescent lights almost blinded him. He tried to shield his eyes with his hand, but it was refusing to co-operate. Every time he attempted to lift his arm, it fell limply to his side again. Only a rasp came out when he opened his mouth to speak. *What the hell is going on?*

"You've been asleep for a long time. You'll feel a bit weak for a while." That unfamiliar female voice wasn't making any sense. He hadn't been asleep. Two seconds ago, he'd been in bed with Annie, confessing his love for her.

He tried again to say her name, find out what had happened to her now that he was alone in bed, but the croaky words weren't even recognisable to him.

"I'll go let the doctor know you're awake and get some ice chips to wet your mouth." The stranger in the room walked away from his bed, her rubber-soled shoes squeaking on the floor mapping her journey.

Squinting against the bright light, he struggled to recognise his surroundings. It was the annoying beeping sound coming from the machine next to the bed that finally helped the penny drop. He was in hospital, back in his own body. It was over.

He laid his head back down on the pillow and laughed, tears of relief streaming down his face that this nightmare had come to an end.

Annie. He had to get to Annie and let her know what had happened. It took some effort to swing his legs over to the edge of the bed, but the solid feeling of his feet hitting the cold tiled floor was wonderful — except, as he tried to move towards the door, his legs were trembling, and he was jerked back by the leads attaching him to the bank of monitors.

"What are you trying to do, Mr Reece? You must get back into bed." The door burst open and the nurse who'd been there when he'd woken up returned with a gaggle of medical staff.

They fussed around him, taking readings, poking and prodding him, like the medical miracle he would appear to them. *If only they knew the half of it.*

A benevolent bystander moistened his dry lips with a wet cotton bud and gave him some ice chips to suck on. It was strange having to adjust to simple tasks such as drinking and talking, when only minutes ago he'd been sharing an erotic feast with Annie.

"Phone," he managed to croak out to the attending staff, needing to convey the urgency to get word to her about where he was. Obviously, he wasn't going to be able to communicate with her effectively, which was weird in itself when they'd practically become one person these past few days, but once she was informed he was awake here, she'd understand what had happened.

He wanted her here with him when she'd become such a huge part of his life recently. Without her, he was lost, a vital part of him missing. It gave him some peace of mind to know she'd be here soon, but he wasn't happy about lying here, still unable to do anything of any meaning. Not only did he have to make reparations with his employees and family, but he and Annie needed some space to see what the future had in store for them as a couple.

He closed his eyes, exhaustion suddenly swamping his whole body as though he hadn't slept in months.

* * * *

His muddled dreams were full of thoughts of Annie, memories so vivid that he swore she was kissing him now, but her lips felt different, hard and coated in sticky gloss instead of soft and sweet.

"Annie," he groaned and deepened the kiss, but he couldn't shake the notion that something wasn't quite right.

With great effort and a promise the payoff would be worth it, he dragged himself back to consciousness.

"He's awake! David, I'm here!" Instead of being gently coaxed awake by the woman he loved, it was Flame whose face was inches away, screaming his name.

Before he'd had time to ask any questions, there was a series of flashing lights dazzling him and Flame grabbed his hand.

"Oh, darling, I'm so glad to have you back again." She sobbed and threw herself dramatically across his chest, setting off another series of flashes in his peripheral vision. He didn't have to see properly to understand this visit and declaration of relief was being witnessed by a battery of photographers. He wondered how she'd smuggled them in past the gatekeeper downstairs, but she must've had some inside help anyway to have got here, press-ready, so soon.

"Flame, I don't want paparazzi in here." His voice was still raspy, but he deemed it sufficient to get the message across. He didn't want her in here either, and he'd tell her that in private. At least he could communicate now, and he hoped it was enough to get Flame out of his life and call the woman he actually loved.

"The whole country has been praying for your recovery and we need to document it for them." She smiled for the cameras, all traces of tears gone in a second.

"Done. Now, can we talk? Alone." He gave the photographers a wave to illustrate the story they'd print, with or without his co-operation, to get rid of them.

"If it's about the wedding, I've got it all in hand. We can do it here with a special licence." The room lit up again like a nineties rave as David's nightmare refused to end.

"You're getting married?" Emma's face at the door, along with the those of his shocked parents, made him want to fall back into unconsciousness.

"No."

"He's still a bit confused, bless him. I don't think he's up for any more visitors." Flame cast a disapproving eye over his family, and David knew that if it hadn't been for the money or the name he'd made for himself, she wouldn't have looked twice at him either. Annie, on the other hand, had accepted him and his family without condition.

"In that case, I think your entourage should be on their way. David has family who wish to spend some time with him." It was his mum who attempted to put her in her place, which in her opinion wasn't by her son's bedside. He already knew from snippets of conversation she'd had with Annie that she wasn't a big Flame fan. Still, he knew her well enough to realise Flame wouldn't give up a photo op without a fight.

"I have every right to be here. I'm his fiancée." She stood up, hands on hips, trying to intimidate his mother with her six-foot-in-heels stature.

"I'm his mum and I'd prefer if you let him get some rest. We haven't seen you around here much before now, and if he's confused, I don't think this circus is going to help." She gestured to the cameras and strangers surrounding his bed.

"I'm his fiancée and I know what's best for him," Flame screeched and all but stamped her foot as this became a battle of wills he could do without.

"Mr. Reece, is it true you've been estranged from your son until now?"

"Do you think you'll be invited to the wedding?"

"I've heard you'd taken out a life insurance policy before the crash. Care to comment?"

The press did what they did best when they smelled a juicy story and inflamed the situation for a better headline. He was barely awake and here he was, back in the circus of celebrity — only now his family had been dragged into the craziness with him.

Annie would hate this level of attention and it was part of the celebrity package. He'd been selfish thinking they could be together simply because that was what he wanted. The implications of exposing her to this level of scrutiny finally hit home. It would destroy that self-confidence he'd been trying to build up in her, and for what? Realistically, how long could they last as a couple when they lived in such different worlds?

Emma ducked past the scrum and ran over to give him a bear hug, and in that moment all he wanted to do was keep the people he loved safe.

"Annie didn't tell me you were engaged."

"I didn't know." The woman herself appeared just as he'd done that first night at her home, unexpectedly, before he'd turned her world on its head. It wasn't fair to keep her spinning on that carousel forever.

He took a deep breath, believing deep down he was doing the right thing for her. Love had brought him back and he was sacrificing his heart so he could bring her more happiness in the long run.

"Who's Annie?"

Annie began to back out of the packed hospital room, but Melanie took her by the hand and pulled her centre stage.

"You must remember Annie? She's your best friend."

She didn't want to have her heart broken in front of an audience. If David didn't know who she was, that meant he wouldn't have any recollection of the time they'd spent together, the declarations they'd made to one another only hours ago. When he'd disappeared from her bed, she'd known exactly where to find him. She just hadn't imagined their blossoming relationship would've vanished along with him. All of it may as well have been in her head if he didn't remember any of it.

"Obviously, this woman is delusional or some sort of stalker. She told me she was his housekeeper, let herself into David's house." Flame looked satisfied with herself as she blew Annie's cover wide open.

"Right... You lot have got your story. Now bugger off before I call security." David's dad chivvied them out with a threat, mumbling about the place being a waste of money if they let anybody wander in off the street.

Annie was certain Flame had employed her wiles to get them in with her, but kept her mouth shut when she hadn't gained legitimate entry in the first place either.

"That includes you." Even Flame wasn't immune to Nicholas's ire.

"If she's staying, I'm staying," the redhead whined as Melanie and Emma wedged Annie between her and the bed.

"Annie's family."

Annie was chuffed they still saw her that way after Flame's outburst, but that was a fraudulent claim if David couldn't provide that precious link for her with the trio.

"So. Am. I." Flame was about to blow a gasket, by the sound of it, and wielded her huge diamond ring in their faces. There she was, flaunting that fiancée label again, and David was yet to correct her. From the minute they'd met, he'd insisted to Annie that their romance was fake. Even if he didn't recall those days together, working towards their goal of his recovery, surely he would've remembered *not* having a fiancée?

It was all too much for Annie, who wanted to grieve for the man she'd loved, not end up in the middle of his engagement to someone he'd told her he didn't care for.

"David, do you really not remember me?" She edged up to the bed. It was odd seeing him in his hospital gown, vulnerable and pale, when she'd been used to cocky tuxedo-man.

He glanced at her then shook his head. "Excuse me, everyone, but I'm really tired now."

He turned away as another nurse came in to shoo them all out of the room.

"Don't worry. They've said it could be a while before he comes around. I'm sure he'll remember you in time." It was Nicholas who tried to console her, but there were no words that could ever mend her broken heart.

As she said her goodbyes to the Reece family in the carpark, she knew it would be for the last time. When she'd looked David in the eye, she could see the shame blazing bright before he'd turned away from her. Then there was the clue that all was not what it seemed when he didn't kick off at seeing his parents in the room. He'd remembered how contrite they'd been about his upbringing, and that was why he'd accepted their presence so easily.

He remembered it all and had decided to take the easy way out rather than admit his mistake in leading her on. David Reece would never choose her over the gorgeous Flame, and she was a fool to have ever thought otherwise.

They'd had their fun and now it was time to go back to their own lives. David had made it very clear that his no longer included her. The main problem for Annie now was that everything she had left, including her job and her flat, would be forever associated with another man who'd voluntarily abandoned her. Far from having her happy-ever-after, this little interlude into the paranormal unknown had left her more miserable than before. Two words summed up her feelings about love now. *Bah, humbug.*

* * * *

"Flame, I'd like you to stay." David reached for her as the others trooped back out of his room. He wanted to rip out the wires keeping him tied to the bed as callously as he'd ripped out Annie's heart so he could run after her, but he didn't. That brutal dismissal of her and everything they'd experienced together — everything they'd felt for one another — had been for the best, though it didn't seem like it now.

He'd seen that same soul-crushing pain in her eyes that he felt in his chest at losing her. It was a clean break this way, letting her get back to normal instead of forcing her to live in his crazy world. That didn't make it easy, watching her walk away dejected as Flame gloated over her perceived victory.

"Why is that frumpy nobody trying to force her way in here anyway?"

"I have no idea." The lie caught in his throat. Annie was everything to him, but he'd have to learn to live without her. There was no way back now, even if he thought they stood a chance of making it. By lying, he'd done the one thing that guaranteed Annie would never take him back.

"We should talk about the wedding. I'm so glad I got to meet your family, and is that your little sister? She'll be adorable as a bridesmaid." Those cold blue eyes lit up with pound signs and David could only imagine what glossy magazine deal she'd been working on behind the scenes. He could've gone along with the whole thing, perhaps even as far as a marriage of convenience to boost their careers. After all, he'd been through one sham of a marriage already. It was his guilty conscience preventing him from stringing Flame along anymore.

He hadn't been fair to her regarding his true feelings either. "We both know there's not going to be a wedding. I never proposed, and we didn't get engaged. If we're being totally honest with each other, I think we've come to the end of the road as a couple." It was on the tip of his tongue to say they'd only been together for appearances' sake, but he didn't wish to humiliate her. He saved that for the woman he loved, to make sure he'd completely burned that bridge.

"B-but I've told the papers now." She appeared genuinely upset by his revelation when she must've known deep down that he was never going to go along with this charade. He knew he'd made the right decision if she was this deluded about the nature of their relationship, but he didn't need a scene. If he decided to tear into her over her lies and actions, she was going to cause more drama. It would also make him a hypocrite, considering what he'd just done to poor Annie.

"A near-death experience has given me a new perspective on life. I don't want to continue living a lie. Look… We don't have to do anything now. When the fuss dies down, we can quietly announce that we've split, or if you prefer, you can tell the press you dumped me." It didn't matter to him how he was portrayed. Flame could do her worst. He deserved it and he didn't care if it put the rest of the female population off him, because he'd never risk what was left of his heart with anyone who wasn't Annie.

Flame pulled up a chair and sat down. "Is it because of Little Miss Fake Housekeeper?"

Okay, he hadn't been as subtle about the situation as he'd hoped, but decided to neither confirm nor deny her suspicions. It wasn't going to change things for either of them.

"We've both got as much mileage as we can from this thing and I'd rather we part as friends than wait until we hate the sight of each other. We can do this on our, or your, terms." Actually, it would distance him even further from Annie if she believed he and Flame were a real couple after all. That level of betrayal would prevent him from reaching out to Annie when he realised what he was giving up, because she would never trust him again.

"Can I keep the ring on?" Flame admired the glint of the diamond dwarfing her slender finger.

"Sure." Whatever kept her happy, and she hadn't had access to his bank account, so he hadn't paid for it.

"Look, David. I'll be honest with you. I need this to happen to make sure I can provide Selena with a proper home." She finally dropped the act for the first moment of honesty they'd probably shared since getting together.

"Flame, be realistic. It's one thing posing for photographs together, but I'm not going to marry you just for the sake of cashing in. I know you're doing this with the best of intentions for your daughter, but I don't want to be a part of it anymore. I've had enough of pretending to be someone I'm not." His priorities had changed, and he had a lot of worthwhile, genuine relationships to work on. Unfortunately, that couldn't include the one with Annie.

"Then we're on the same page. I-I've met someone." She played with the ring around her finger, slipping it on and off, likely trying to decide if she wanted to give up this bling lifestyle after all.

"Oh?" He knew it was Sam, but he couldn't tell her that — or even confide in her that he knew the feeling was mutual. If she was willing to walk away from Flame's world, she was obviously as smitten as Annie's landlord.

"He's just an ordinary, working guy, not interested in any of this reality TV nonsense. I could really see us together, you know?" She was wearing that same dreamy smile he'd seen on Sam, and David envied her conviction to make it happen.

"He knows all about what you do? As Flame?"

She grimaced. "No. That's the sticking point. I don't think he'd want to be part of that and I'm not really sure how I'd explain it. As far as he's concerned, I'm just Beverley, a single mum with a penchant for his chocolate eclairs."

"Wouldn't it be better to start off being honest with him?" He had to wonder if it would've made any difference between him and Annie if she'd been upfront with him and told her she was one of his employees. Probably not. That chemistry had been there even though neither of them had wanted it.

"I don't want him to think badly of me. It would be a complete fresh start. He knows about Selena and he's looking forward to meeting her. One last magazine deal would simply give me something to put by, so we're on an even keel. He runs his own business and I don't have anything to offer."

"Stop putting yourself down. You're a great girl and I think some time away from the spotlight will remind you of who you are and what's important." It had worked for him.

"Thanks. I just wish I'd met him earlier."

"Out of curiosity, how did you two meet?"

"It's silly, really. I saw that alleged housekeeper of yours that first night at the hospital and followed her home. Sam runs the café below the flat and we got talking. It wasn't long before I forgot why I was there. It was nice to meet someone who didn't want anything from me."

"I hear that."

"You and Annie, you're together then?"

"No. We could've had something, but I don't think it's a good idea."

"That's a shame. That first night, I was worried you and her might have had something going on and all the lies to the press would catch up with me. Sorry about that, by the way. I'm not as cold-hearted as that makes me sound, but I was desperate. Your recovery was never in doubt, as far as I was concerned. I know what a stubborn asshole you can be." She reached out and give his hand a squeeze.

Not for the first time, David wished it was Annie's touch he could feel now that he'd come back from the almost-dead.

"It's okay. We've all done things we're not proud of."

"Yeah. Pretending to have amnesia was harsh, David." Her lips pursed into that thin line of disapproval.

He hadn't fooled anyone with that act, least of all Annie.

"You should think about settling down too, with someone normal like her. It'll stop your ego getting out of control."

"Too late on both counts," he said, his eyes closing as fatigue set in for real.

"In that case, can we go ahead with an engagement party before we call the whole thing off? That should be enough to secure us a double spread in the glossies." She pouted, and he was too tired to argue any more. Flame could have her party, Annie would hate him more and eventually they'd all move on without him.

He knew now what had brought him back from the ether, and it was to make the people he'd wronged ultimately happy again. Although, it could take Annie some time to see that. Unfortunately, the price of his freedom had cost him his heart.

"The party of the year," he agreed, though he'd rather spend the rest of the year crying in bed, eating gallons of ice cream and mourning the love of his life. When David Reece went down in flames, he did it in style.

* * * *

"How can you not remember Annie? She's amazing, and, like...your best friend." Emma remained undeterred in her quest to make him remember her new bestie. She was helping him pack his few belongings to go home. He'd had a talk with his family in private to resolve past issues. With a lot of apologies, hugs and tears, they'd all agreed to move on and leave the past behind.

"I think she exaggerated. Apparently, she's one of my employees. I don't even remember meeting her."

The lies fell too easily from his lips, but he knew each one cast a black stain on his conscience. He lifted the bag containing what was left of his tuxedo and vowed to bin the thing as soon as possible. Thankfully, his parents had brought him a change of clothes when they'd come to pick him up. Flame was off party-arranging somewhere and that suited him fine.

"Are you sure you don't want to come and stay with us for a while until you're feeling better?" His mum was making the effort to reclaim that parenting role, but it would take some getting used to.

"I'm fine, Mum. I just want to get back to normal." He'd accepted the offer of a lift home at least, a compromise that said he was willing to let them play some small part in his life.

"That's so weird. Annie seemed to know a lot about you, but she didn't strike me as some sort of obsessed stalker." Emma wasn't willing to let Annie slip out of her life as David had done. Her question was becoming a constant reminder of his betrayal and loss but also forcing him to prolong the lie.

"Obviously, she's read something into a brief meeting that wasn't there." He shrugged but couldn't shift the weight of guilt from his shoulders.

Annie hadn't come back or been in contact with anyone since that night. She'd taken the hint that he didn't wish to pursue the relationship. He hoped she'd get over it quickly. It was the same wish he had concerning Emma and her Miss Marple act.

"Lovely girl, Annie. Such a shame," his mum chipped in. They'd all been smitten with her. Even his father kept asking after her, and he got the impression that they'd practically adopted her too.

"Okay, I'm ready to hit the road when you are." Not only was he keen to get back to the peace and quiet of his own home, but also to escape all this Annie-appreciation. He didn't need anyone to tell him how amazing she was when he'd seen her funny, kind and compassionate nature for himself. Without waiting for a further post-mortem on the relationship he'd killed stone dead, he picked up his bag and moved towards the door.

"Darling, I'm so glad I caught you."

David was prevented from escaping by the arrival of his fake fiancée-to-be, who greeted him with double 'mwah, mwah' kisses on the cheeks.

"We're actually just on our way home."

Flame ignored his blatant attempt to leave and pushed past, forcing him to do an about turn.

"Royal Court have had a last-minute cancellation for Christmas Eve. I need to get back to them ASAP to secure the booking for their Secret Garden room. So, what do you think?" She was bouncing up and down, high with excitement and in danger of breaking her neck in those killer heels she was wearing, but David had no clue what she was rambling on about.

"Have I missed something? Why would I want to book anything in the Royal Court?" It was the kind of pretentious, over-priced venue Z-list celebs frequented in the hope the paps outside would catch them wearing next to nothing—definitely not the kind of establishment he was keen to visit any time soon. He'd quite enjoyed his time away from the limelight—apart from the whole half-ghost, half-man ordeal—and wasn't in a rush to launch back into that lifestyle.

"Our engagement party, silly." Flame hit him on the arm, hard enough for him to know she was serious.

"Oh yeah. Isn't that a bit soon?" He'd agreed to the idea to keep her happy, but deep down he'd been praying she'd lose interest before they actually made it that far. *Wishful thinking.* Christmas Eve was only a couple of days away.

"You promised." Her eyes glinted with something dangerous, threatening consequences if he went back on his word. David had had enough of putting that look of disappointment on faces recently.

He kissed her on the cheek. "I did. Go ahead and book it." *What's one more night of hell?*

"You can't have a party on Christmas Eve. We've asked Annie to stay over with us." It was Emma who threw a spanner in the works with yet another reminder of the woman he was leaving behind. He knew how much it would mean to Annie to spend Christmas with everyone and how much it would hurt to have it taken away. Then again, with everything that had happened and was still to come, it would've been awkward for her to be at his parents' house for the holidays. This could make a convenient out for her too.

"I'm sorry, Em." David vowed to make it up to them all as soon as he'd fulfilled his obligation to Flame first. He was giving her Christmas Eve, but he'd go all out to make Christmas Day special for his family. There was one person he could never make amends with, because making her hate him was the only way he could get her out of his life for good.

"Don't worry, son. We'll be there." David's dad was every bit as intimidating as Flame without having to insinuate anything other than his sincerity about being part of his life again.

It was his mum who tried to reason with Emma. "It would be a bit awkward to have Annie staying now, love. I'm sure she'll understand."

Unfortunately, it was going to take longer for his little sister to come to terms with the new arrangement. She flounced out of the door, showing the first signs of that teenage temper. The look of disgust she shot David on the way out suggested the shine had worn off her big brother's halo as far as she was concerned.

He didn't blame her for thinking badly of him when he was so disappointed in himself.

Chapter Sixteen

"Talk about over the top. It looks as though Tinkerbell and Mrs Claus have been decorating whilst drunk on eggnog." There were fairy lights and fake snow glittering on every available surface in the Royal Court. David thought back to Annie's jest about his living room, suggesting he should've been providing sunglasses on the door to prevent snow blindness.

"Isn't it magical?" Flame spun around in the centre of the room, dressed to fit the theme—whatever that was—in a white, lacy catsuit. He'd drawn the line at her suggestion of him wearing a white tux a la John Travolta and donned something a little more understated from his existing wardrobe. It was strange having to put on a suit again, but since coming back to the land of the living, he'd given more consideration to his spending habits, with this party being the exception.

After seeing the conditions his employees had to endure, he felt guilty about frittering away huge amounts of money on frivolous purchases and was putting some new guidelines in place to increase wages. That was one reason he wasn't overjoyed about this whole debacle, the purpose of which was entirely for Flame to show off.

He no longer felt the need to gloat over material possessions, having realised there was much more to life. Once their engagement was over and he was free to sever ties, he wanted to channel the kind of cash wasted on this vulgar display towards something more meaningful, such as funding scholarships for under-privileged kids, giving someone else the chance to improve their lot in life. His priorities had changed because of his experience, and he no longer thought solely about himself—a transformation Annie had played a huge part in.

It was impossible not to think about her, how she was doing and what life lesson she was supposed to have taken from their time together. *Don't trust another man, regardless of what he says? Guinea pigs make better life companions than a man who swears he loves you then denies all knowledge of you?* No matter what spin he tried to put on his actions, he knew she'd ended up with the shitty end of the deal.

It brought him scant consolation that she'd quit her job too. When he'd given in and made some discreet enquiries, he'd discovered she'd handed in her notice at the store the day after the incident at the hospital. He tried to convince himself that she'd move on to better things, but he worried that her resignation was a knee-jerk reaction to what he'd done. She was already struggling financially, and he'd hate to think he'd been the cause of more hardship for her.

"Hello? Could you at least pretend you're enjoying this?" Flame folded her arms, her face thunderous as she glared at him.

"Sorry, what?" He waved at a passing champagne-carrying waiter, because he was going to need something to get him through this night.

"It's our engagement party. Bloody well engage!" She locked those blue laser beams on to him and David was sure she'd vaporise him on the spot if she could. He wished he'd never agreed to this charade, because now she could dictate to him as she pleased.

As the doors opened and the chosen ones were granted admittance to the select gathering, which included a multitude of Z-list celebrities he'd never heard of and only a handful of people he actually knew, including his family. He was glad to see some normal, familiar faces among the surgically enhanced, Instagram-ready strangers parading past.

"Are we under-dressed or over-dressed? It's kind of hard to tell." His mother surveyed the room and tugged at her silk blouse, clearly self-conscious around the clotheshorses and their almost-there fashions worn for maximum press exposure.

"You're perfect, as always." David kissed her cheek and led his family away from the champagne-guzzling set to somewhere they'd be more comfortable.

"She can't stay. She's underage." Flame blocked their path to the corner booth David was guiding them towards and gestured dismissively at Emma. He recognised the dress she was wearing. It was a mash-up of the two outfits Annie had taken to create a bespoke piece for a little girl with a crush. He didn't reference it, knowing that despite what he'd done to her, she'd kept her promise to his little sister.

"She's family, and if anyone has a problem with her being here, they can see me." Emma wasn't going to cause any more trouble than the reprobates they'd already let in.

"Keep her out of the way," Flame demanded before swanning off back to the other guests.

"Ignore her, Em. You're the most important person here, as far as I'm concerned." Not a liability who should be locked away out of sight, according to Flame.

His parents wandered off towards the buffet, but Emma stayed with David, clearly needing to get something off her chest as she fidgeted beside him.

"Are you really going to marry her?" Confusion was written all over her face as to why he'd want to spend his life with someone who treated her fiancé's family with such contempt.

The whole purpose of this trial was to protect the ones he loved, so he could start over with no more pretence, and he couldn't bring himself to lie to her face.

"Flame's not so bad when you get to know her." Despite her blunt manner and flamboyant lifestyle, David knew she was as insecure as the next person. If he'd turned up at her house instead of Annie's on the night of the crash, perhaps he would've taken the time to look beyond her outward appearance and forge a better bond with her, not Annie. It was possible, but he doubted it, when she didn't have the same compassion and kindness that had challenged him to become a better person along the way.

Fate had paired him with Annie for a reason, and she'd brought love and understanding into his life, even if they hadn't been able to continue this journey together. For a short time at least, he'd known what it was to love and be loved unconditionally—an experience that could never be rivalled, even if he spent the rest of his life trying to replicate it. It was that time with Annie that had taught him the importance of having love and support in his life—something he could find with, and provide for, his family. It was a pity he'd thrown away the chance to do the same for Annie.

He had so much more in common with her than the person he'd tried to be all these years to fit in with those he believed epitomised success, like Flame.

"I already know Annie. *She's* nice," Emma huffed, and David couldn't argue with her logic.

"This isn't Annie's world. She wouldn't be comfortable here." He took in the ostentatious surroundings and thought of how much she'd hated leaving her flat to visit the private hospital. Flame was in her element playing hostess, showing off her diamonds, being the centre of attention as everyone congratulated her as though this was a solo venture—which, of course, it wasn't.

"It's not our world and we're not comfortable, but we're here for you. Annie would be too if you let her. Flame's only here for herself."

David thought back to that first night in the hospital, when Annie had done battle with the receptionist and overcome her fears to help him. Flame hadn't even been in the hospital room, too busy securing her front-page coverage to be concerned with his injuries. Annie had also reconciled him with his family, with no hidden agenda or pay-off for herself. She'd given him everything he'd asked of her and more. To anyone who might've witnessed the proceedings, it could appear that he'd spurned Annie's selflessness and chosen Flame over her.

He couldn't defend his decisions without explaining everything that had happened, and the chances anyone would understand were nil. Only Annie knew, but she would've struggled to understand his motives too. She'd have been the first to tell him she could make decisions for herself.

"Flame is very...popular." He struggled to find a positive and didn't succeed in convincing Emma that he was madly in love with his fiancée, as she raised an eyebrow in disbelief.

"Why do you want all of this anyway? We'd have had a nicer night at home playing board games and drinking hot chocolate."

A tempting scenario he couldn't envisage Flame wanting to take part in.

"When did you get so wise, Em?" He ruffled the top of his little sister's head.

"Around the same time you got so stupid," she mumbled with a grin.

He counted himself lucky for getting a second chance to know her too, when she would always keep him grounded. *Come to think of it, it's no wonder she gets on so well with Annie.*

At that moment, another familiar face walked into the room, and he knew the game was up.

"Excuse me. I have guests to go attend to." David tried to intercept Flame's suitor before he could approach her but he didn't make it in time.

"Sam? What on earth are you doing here?" Flame's face went as red as her hair as her secret life gradually unravelled.

"I know I didn't get an invite, but I thought I should come and see this for myself. You didn't think to let me know you were engaged to another man?" The agony was written all over the man's face as he took in the scene, a world away from the one he and Annie inhabited, highlighted by the stained shirt and slightly wrinkled trousers he was wearing, having obviously come straight from work.

Champagne fountains and winged-angel sculptures carved in ice were a stark contrast to the wares in the high street café David had been frequenting in their neighbourhood recently.

He scanned the room full of reality stars, wannabes and their entourages, including several camera crews following the events of these so-called personalities. He thought of the unending self-promotion and attention-seeking behaviour that kept them relevant, and it no longer held appeal to him either.

"It's not what you think, Sam. We'll talk later." Flame tried to usher him away from the partygoers, who, if Annie was to be believed, Sam wouldn't recognise as being famous anyway.

"You lied to me, Beverley — or should I start calling you *Flame*?"

"You know, then?" Her perfect posture sagged at the revelation and David could swear part of that was sheer relief that the secret was out.

"A friend thought someone should tell me I was being taken for a fool."

"No guesses as to who that was." Flame glanced at David, as though this was somehow his or Annie's fault.

"To be fair, Flame, the whole point was to have this splashed all over the papers. What did you expect?" It was impossible to be sympathetic when they'd concocted this whole charade between them, without considering the implications it would have on those around them, something he'd sworn not to do again.

"You're the fiancé, I take it?" Sam looked him up and down, the same way Annie had that first night they'd met and written him off as a lost cause.

"Mate, we're not together. This is what they call scripted reality. We never had any intention of getting married. I know it's mad, but this is what passes as a career these days. Anyway, I think it's safe to say we're both retiring as of tonight." He slapped Sam on the back, showing him there were no hard feelings, on his part at least.

"Definitely. Sam, I'm so sorry. David only agreed to go along with this because I knew we'd get a magazine deal. The money for the photographs alone will set Selena and me set up in a house of our own. That's all I ever wanted out of this. I never expected to meet someone I genuinely cared about." Flame was holding on to his arm as though it were a lifeline, obviously afraid to let go of him in case he left her floundering in this sea of so-called celebrity.

"You're really willing to give up all this?" It was clear Sam was beginning to weaken when he stopped struggling against her touch.

"Yes. I never wanted this life, but I would like to start one with you."

"I don't know, Bev. This is a lot to take on."

"Don't let something good slip out of your life. Trust me. You'll regret it." David was having something of an awakening of his own.

With his parents, Emma and Annie, he could've had something real—a support system that wasn't based on how many likes he got on a video of him falling out of a club with a woman on each arm. He could be himself now, and though he might seem boring compared to playboy David, he was no longer angry at the world. There was no need to act out the way he had, now that he'd found peace.

At least, he had until he'd been ripped out of Annie's bed. In that second, lying with her and confessing his love, he'd never been so content. There was no place, no person, no feeling, which could compare. *So why the hell am I wasting precious time here?*

"Good luck, guys."

"Where are you going?" Flame shouted across the room as he ran off to find Emma again.

"Home," he shouted back, sure Flame would style this out in her inimitable way. He no longer cared now that he'd fulfilled his obligation.

"Where are Mum and Dad?"

"They're over at the buffet. What's going on?"

"I'm taking control of my life again. Tell them to take you home and I'll see you there later." He ran off towards the exit, dodging dancers and waiters lest they slow him down.

Out of the corner of his eye, he saw Sam and Flame slip out of the side door after him. Apparently, he wasn't the only one who'd woken up to everything life had to offer and wanted to grab it with both hands.

He could only pray it hadn't come too late for him.

* * * *

"You're a selfish knobhead, Clarence, taking what you wanted and buggering off, leaving poor George to fend for himself." Annie lobbed the DVD case at the TV the second the hapless guardian angel did his disappearing act. She didn't know why she was putting herself through this, except as a tribute to her mum's Christmas tradition. She had nothing else to do now her Christmas Eve plans had been cancelled.

It hadn't really come as a surprise when a tearful Emma had called to say the cosy pyjama party was no longer an option.

'I'm so sorry, Annie. It's just not fair,' she'd wailed, and Annie had had to suck up her own sense of injustice to console her.

'Honestly, I understand. You've been caught up in the middle of the madness, and your mum's right. We shouldn't see each other anymore.' If David was insisting she was still some kind of weird stalker he hardly knew, she couldn't blame his parents for wanting to protect their daughter from her influence. It would only further a case for neglect against them if they let a woman purported to be a whole loaf short of a picnic stay at their house.

'Did you and David have a falling out? Why is he saying he doesn't know you? I don't understand any of it.' Emma had burst into gut-wrenching sobs on the phone and forced Annie to bite her lip before she joined her. Not only had she lost the love of her life, but also someone she'd come to think of her little sister too.

'Me neither, Em. You'll have to ask him. I don't want to spoil Christmas for you and your family. Maybe we can talk things over in the New Year when things have settled down.'

'Fat chance. They'll be gearing up for the wedding of the year then. That's why we can't have Christmas Eve in our own house. David's forcing us to go to his stupid engagement party instead.'

Annie's legs had turned to jelly with that bombshell. She'd presumed the whole fiancée thing had been an elaborate ruse to get rid of her. If so, David was going to extraordinary lengths to deny he'd ever had any feelings for her.

'An engagement party? That'll be exciting. I'm sure Flame will have lots of celebrity friends there.'

'I don't care about any of that,' Emma had wailed, going against everything Annie believed about the fickle youth of today. She hadn't believed that lifestyle was still what David wanted either, but like everything else she'd believed about him, she'd been wrong.

'I'm sure you'll all enjoy it. Go support your big brother.' Annie had tried to smile through the tears as though Emma could see her.

'I don't want to leave you alone on Christmas Eve.'

'I'll be fine. Me and George Bailey will hang up our stockings and wait for Father Christmas as usual.' She'd known that she hadn't convinced Emma with anything she'd said, but at least they'd had the opportunity to speak again, perhaps for the last time.

Now, as predicted, she was alone in her flat on Christmas Eve. At least she'd been able to put on her onesie the second she'd come home from work without fear of judgement. There was one exception to the evening she'd imagined. Instead of wallowing over what she'd lost, she was making plans for her future. Those times acting as a conduit for David had pushed her out of her comfort zone and shown her she could do anything if she put her mind to it. There was a life still waiting for her out there.

Instead of chocolate wrappers and tissues, she was surrounded by copies of her CV for posting out, and university prospectuses. Come the New Year, she was working on furthering her education, and therein, her career choices. She'd already taken the first step by handing in her resignation. Even if she couldn't secure a better-paid position now, anything had to be preferable than working for an almost-ex who denied all knowledge of her existence. She refused to live her life based on the needs and wants of others anymore and was taking control of her own destiny. There'd be no more sitting around crying and feeling sorry for herself, not that she had much choice, with Christmas being her only day off between now and January.

The door buzzer sounded downstairs and she grabbed her purse to pay for the pizza she'd ordered. Crying might be banned, but comfort carbs were still permitted under the special-circumstances clause.

She pulled out the last twenty-pound note from her purse. Usually she wouldn't be so cavalier with money, especially when she didn't know where her next paycheque was coming from. However, it was Christmas and the sizeable tip she was considering parting with would hopefully put a smile on the face of someone who was working later than her tonight.

The buzzer went off again, and she knew the delivery guy was likely having as tough a time as she was lately. "I'm coming!"

The smile died on her lips when she saw who was actually waiting on the other side of the door.

"I think this is where I came in, wasn't it?" David was leaning on the doorjamb, wearing a lopsided smile and another damn tux. Of course she was wearing her favourite, but freshly washed, fleecy all-in-one.

"You weren't welcome then and you're certainly not welcome now." It was her natural reaction to slam the door on him, but it bounced back off the foot he'd jammed over the step. She retreated back upstairs to safety. This wasn't happening again. She was only getting over the last incident.

Her heart was pounding, her temperature rising, and she was regretting her choice of outfit as she dived for cover.

"Annie, wait."

Not a chance. She wasn't letting anyone over her doorstep unless they came with pizza accessories, and all David Reece had was a fiancée and a track record of lying to her.

"No. I'm done waiting on people. Go away." She didn't want to know why he was back, because she wasn't getting drawn back into his shit when she had enough of her own to deal with.

"Annie, please hear me out." His voice was right behind her, and the days spent apart disappeared as though they'd never happened.

She spun around, her temper getting the best of her since she hadn't had anyone to vent at in the interim, for fear of exposing their secret.

"What? You've suddenly regained your memory, or did you magically find yourself on my doorstep against your will again?" She resisted the urge to lob her purse at him, although she longed to hear the satisfying smack as it made contact with him, and tossed it onto the table instead.

"I deserve that, I know, but I swear I'm not asking anything of you other than to hear my explanation."

His excuse, more like, so he could return to his life guilt-free. No doubt Emma had been giving him an earful over the phone, prompting this crisis of conscience.

"Don't you have an engagement party you should be hosting?" Saying the words alone made her sick to the stomach, knowing he'd promised to spend the rest of his life with another woman.

Annie hadn't expected him to propose to her as soon as he'd woken from his coma, but some acknowledgement that she'd meant something, anything, to him would've been nice.

"I was never engaged to Flame. It was a story she made up for the headlines, as you know."

"You never disputed it, and what about the ring, the party and the fact you told people you didn't know who I was? You utter bastard." Okay, so she wasn't managing to keep her cool, but it was proof that for her that what they'd had during their intense time together had been real, her feelings justified.

He had the decency to hang his head, admitting his actions towards her had been shameful. "I know you must hate me."

He clearly had no idea about the strength of her feelings for him if he thought she could switch them off so easily. People said there was a fine line between love and hate, but that made it sound easy to make the switch. If that had been the case, Annie would've punched him in the face a long time ago without regret. It was her loving him that made his betrayal all the more painful, although she wasn't about to let him know he'd made such an impact on her when she hadn't even warranted a public acknowledgement.

"I swear, I thought I was doing the best for you." He cringed as he said it and Annie knew he didn't believe what he was saying any more than she did.

She nodded sagely. "Obviously. The best thing you could do for a woman you've told you love her is to pretend you've never met and announce to the world you're marrying another woman. They should print that shit in Valentine's cards."

Her sarcasm was reaching optimum output in direct relation to the amount of bullshit he was expelling into the atmosphere.

"When I woke up in that hospital room, I picked up where I left off, in that crazy world of fake celebrity and gossip. I didn't want to drag you into it. I thought I was letting you off the hook by snubbing you that way."

"You couldn't have let me make that decision for myself?" She faced him down with her arms folded, but he was smiling despite her obvious anger.

"I've only just figured that out, along with some other things staring me in the face."

"Such as?"

He was walking towards her, and her resolve to make him suffer for what he'd done was waning the closer he got. Apparently, he hadn't come to tell her to back off from his sister and forget any of his family existed, so she had to acknowledge there was another motive for him being here—one she was afraid to believe.

"You're the reason I'm alive, the reason I have my family around me again and the reason I don't need any of that fake celebrity crap in my life. I love you, Annie. If you can find it in your heart to forgive me, I want us to go on that date I promised you." He slid his arm around her waist, and Annie couldn't move. She was a prisoner, trapped by the truth, but it was exactly where she wanted to be.

"What about Flame?" As much as she loved him and wanted this to be real, he'd already rejected her once for the other woman.

"She got her party and her headlines. That's all I promised her. These lips haven't touched anyone else since you."

"Good." Annie only had his word on that, but when his mouth took hers, the hunger in the passionate kiss made his vow believable. His every touch, every caress, convinced her he was real both in existence and intent.

The doorbell buzzed and interrupted their passionate reunion.

"That'll be my pizza."

"Can we share? I was too heartsick to eat anything at the party."

"Sure. Wait. Does this count as a first date then?" Sharing a pizza under her Christmas tree with a sexy man in a tuxedo hadn't been the evening she'd expected, but it had certainly been one she'd dreamed about.

"I think so, and after dinner, I can take you to see my parents. Don't bother to get changed. I think you'll fit right in." He toyed with the zip on her onesie, rasping it up and down until it began to feel like foreplay. The anticipation of him stripping off her fleecy layer brought her whole body to attention.

"Do you think they'd mind if we were a bit late?"

"Hmm?" David was trailing kisses along her neck, refusing to let go of her as they went to collect the pizza at the door. She practically threw the money at the delivery guy in her haste to get rid of him.

"As I was saying before we were so rudely interrupted" — she chucked the pizza onto the table once they'd stumbled back upstairs — "can we take a rain check on that visit to your folks?"

She began to separate him from that damn tux that still haunted her dreams.

"Whatever you want." David covered her lips with his and she backed him towards her bedroom.

She'd made a resolution to do whatever she wanted from now on, and that included Mr. David Reece. Now that all the other obstacles were out of the way, life was too short not to grab happiness where she found it, and she was sure she'd find heaven with him.

Chapter Seventeen

One year and one day later...

"This one's for you, sweetheart." Annie handed over the parcel she'd carefully wrapped in snowflake-embossed paper to the little girl who answered the door to her.

"What do you say?" Her mother appeared by her side just before she ran off, dragging her Christmas present inside the house.

"Thank you," she called back over the sound of ripping paper.

"You didn't have to do that, but thank you."

"You're welcome." The two women stood awkwardly staring at each other in the doorway. Then Annie felt pressure at the small of her back where David rested his hand, reminding her he was there with her. This had to be weird for him too.

"Annie! David! Come in." Thankfully, Sam came to greet them too, putting his arm around his new wife and making the encounter a little less awkward.

"Of course, where are my manners?" The couple stood aside to let Annie and David enter the house.

"Thank you, Fl...Beverley." Annie ducked past, trying not to stare, but it was still difficult to come to terms with the events of the past year, even though they'd attended their wedding only two months ago.

The bright red hair and cosmetic enhancements had been toned down since the woman formerly known as Flame had traded in her fame for a family life with Sam. She looked like any other normal wife and mother these days. Nothing was left of the pouting-pretend-fiancée who'd cared more about publicity when David's life had hung in the balance. Annie had never seen Sam so happy, and there was no way he would've married again if he hadn't believed *Beverley* was the one.

"I'll never get used to it either. It's as though she's a completely different person." David's whisper at her ear sent shivers dancing up and down her neck. Even after all this time together as an actual, physical couple, he had the ability to turn her insides to mush. Every breath she felt, every touch was confirmation that he was real and that what had happened the previous year hadn't all been a dream.

"Honestly, she does seem to be." They watched as she fussed around in the kitchen, taking freshly made cookies from the oven and wearing a flour-dusted apron over her rather ordinary outfit. The dark green knit dress was perfectly lovely, but it was plain compared to the skimpy, in-your-face clothes Flame had favoured. She only wore a little makeup these days, but it was clear she was a natural beauty who'd never needed the extensive enhancements she'd undertaken in the name of celebrity.

"Everything worked out for the best in the end." David slid his arms around Annie's waist from behind and kissed that ticklish spot at the nape of her neck. If she hadn't vowed to spend Christmas Day visiting everyone important in their lives, she would've been tempted to drag him back to bed instead. He was wearing the soft red sweater she'd bought him, and smelled of spicy citrus and cloves. David was Christmas all wrapped up in one handsome package that only she got to open.

They couldn't get enough of each other, making sure they didn't waste a moment together, but this was an important time of the year for them. Previous experiences had taught them to value those who were close to them. Since Sam was her friend, Beverley and Selena were part of the package deal.

"I guess so," she said as Sam whispered something into his new wife's ear and made her blush. "They look happy."

"As are we."

For Sam's sake, they were all making the effort and trying to put the past behind them. Plus, Serena was a joy to be around. She was such a happy child. She was a real credit to her mother, and it showed that Beverley had shielded her from the horrors of that celebrity lifestyle she'd got caught up in herself.

"Thank you, Auntie Annie and Uncle David. I love him!" The little girl in question came charging into the kitchen and launched herself at Annie, making her the filling in a hug sandwich.

"You're...welcome," she managed to gasp.

When David ceased laughing at her sudden discomfort, he released his hold so she only had one admirer left wrapped around her midriff.

"Selena? Why are you trying to squeeze the life out of my friend?" A concerned-looking Sam walked across the kitchen floor to prise his stepdaughter away, letting Annie breathe again.

"Look what I got!" She tugged Sam's hand, pulling him into the lounge, and the rest of the adults were compelled to follow. After all, Christmas was for excited children, not just lonely people who'd been through a paranormal, life-changing event.

"Oh my goodness!" Beverley dropped to the floor with her daughter and her husband to marvel at the contents of her gift, which took up half the living room floor.

"Well, we've noticed she has a thing for pandas and thought she might like this one too." It had been David's idea to get the four-foot-high plush toy. He had a soft spot for children and toys, and Annie knew he'd make a great father one day—not that they'd talked about having kids. They were still in the honeymoon stage of their romance, but she hoped it was for keeps. Someday, maybe, they could extend this dysfunctional family they'd drawn together.

"I think it's a hit." Sam laughed as Selena hugged the giant panda so tightly that they both toppled over onto the floor.

"Thank you," Beverley mouthed at them, and Annie felt a twinge of guilt at doubting for a second that this match with Sam was anything other than genuine, when she looked as happy as her daughter this morning.

"Are you staying for Christmas dinner? We've got all the trimmings and Beverley is in charge of the pavlova for dessert." It was Sam who extended the last-minute invitation to eat with them, but Beverley jumped to her feet, seemingly on board with the idea of having guests too.

"There's plenty of food to go around. You know what Sam's like. He cooks more than we can possibly ever eat. It's no problem to set an extra two places."

"I would honestly love to. I'm sure it's all delicious, but we promised David's family we'd go there for something to eat. We were just stopping by on our way over." At any other time, she would've jumped at the chance to sample Sam's cooking. Dinner could be a bit hit and miss when she frequently failed to navigate all the fancy gadgets David had installed in their new kitchen. As for him? Well, he was trying, but his culinary skills were limited when he was used to eating in the best London restaurants. She was contemplating asking Sam for some couples' cooking lessons.

"Speaking of which, we should head out before Emma explodes with excitement waiting for us. Thanks for the hospitality. We'll have to return the favour sometime. You know where we live." David shook Sam's hand and dropped a kiss on Beverley's cheek.

"Oh yes, it's that lovely new house out in the country. Sam showed me photographs. It's gorgeous." Beverley was addressing her now, without a hint of the jealousy she'd once displayed towards Annie. Only admiration.

"We like it." It hadn't taken much coaxing for her to leave her flat when David had suggested moving into his place, but by then even he had begun to tire of the ostentatious showhome he'd bought to display his financial success. He'd sold it and purchased a lovely place far away from the city traffic and noise. It was still spacious and more than she'd ever dreamed of, but it had more of a homely feel, with the open fireplace and soft furnishings they'd picked out.

"It's the perfect place to raise a family."

"We, uh, haven't—" Annie knew she wasn't trying to stir up trouble between her and David when there hadn't been any clue Beverley might still hold a candle for her ex. The truth was that she and David hadn't had a discussion about the future of their relationship. After his childhood trauma, she didn't even know if he wanted kids of his own. She did. Emma, Melanie and Nicholas had reminded her what it was to have family around and she was desperate for one of her own someday. That talk seemed a long way off when they hadn't made any long-term commitment to each other, save for moving in together.

"Sam, we'll be over at the café later tonight if you need a hand setting up for the Christmas crowd?" Ignoring the direction Beverley had taken the conversation and confirming Annie's fear that he wasn't interested in starting a family with her or anyone else, David was already on his way to the door.

"That would be great, thanks. I'm so glad you two came up with the idea of dishing up the café's leftover food to the homeless. Nothing gets wasted now and we're doing our bit for those who aren't fortunate enough to have anywhere to go at Christmas—or any other night." Sam followed them to the door, and after a quick dash to the kitchen, so did Beverley.

"Here are a few cookies for you and Emma to share. Bring her with you next time you're over. I'm sure she and Selena would get on like a house on fire." She handed over a paper bag, the smell of the still-warm cookies making Annie want to snack before the much-anticipated Christmas dinner.

"Thank you. Will do." Annie waved her goodbyes and clutched the cookies to keep her hands warm on the short walk back to the car in the cold.

As they drove away in his new, more practical and less-flashy vehicle than his sports car, David tooted the horn at the family standing on the doorstep waving them off.

"One visit down, one to go." Annie sank back into the passenger seat, content to let David drive so she could take it easy after being up half the night wrapping presents.

"If you'd rather stay at home, I'll phone and make our excuses. I'm sure you don't want to spend the whole day running around the country."

"Are you kidding? I've been looking forward to this all year." She grinned back at David, his worried frown evening out as she stopped him fretting about ruining her Christmas.

"Thank goodness. I didn't really fancy having to tell Emma we were cancelling." He clutched his chest, the very thought of disappointing his little sister clearly paining him.

Annie wouldn't have done that to either of them, even if she hadn't been like a child herself waiting for them all to get together and open their presents. Although they'd spent a good part of Christmas together the previous year, they'd had more time to prepare, to anticipate this particular family gathering. She wouldn't have missed it for the world when the Reeces went out of their way to make sure she felt at home and part of the family, something she'd thought she'd never experience again. The same was likely true for David and, to some extent, Emma, who had her big brother back in her life—a reason for them all to celebrate.

* * * *

"Presents before or after lunch?" His mother added the gifts they'd brought to the pile already balanced precariously around the tree.

"What do *you* usually do?" Despite his wanting to be here, he hovered uncertainly on the periphery of the merriment.

Annie and Emma were already in deep discussion about the day's itinerary and hadn't made it in from the hallway since their arrival. He'd been left here with his parents on his own, unsure of the usual schedule. It wasn't his intent to stir up old animosity or make things awkward, but sometimes he was uncertain about his place in this family dynamic.

"Sit down, son. Emma will probably have Annie captured for ages telling her what she has planned for everyone." His father walked into the lounge and handed him a glass of mulled wine before taking up his favourite chair by the fire.

"Thanks." He accepted it gratefully and sat down, placing the glass on the side table next to him. Perched on the end of the couch, he was every inch the anxious teenager at his girlfriend's house, waiting for her to come in and rescue him from small talk with her parents.

It was ridiculous really. They'd had many shared dinners and visits, giving them an opportunity to get to know one another again. Certainly, his time spent with

Emma had been easier. She'd even stayed with him and Annie on occasion. They'd enjoyed trips to the cinema, to the zoo and even nights in watching TV and eating junk food. Their relationship came naturally now that they were seeing each other regularly.

It was the one with his new and improved parents he was having difficulty coming to terms with, not least because he usually had Annie and Emma to act as a buffer and prevent any lull in the conversation...like this one. Those two never appeared to be short of something to say.

"Normally, Emma is awake at the crack of dawn, tearing into her presents before we can stop her. Patience isn't her strong point." His mother was kneeling on the floor, sorting the gifts into more manageable piles than the avalanche waiting to happen beneath the tree.

"She wanted to wait for you and Annie to arrive this morning before we started." His father rolled his eyes, but the smile on his lips made it clear he would do whatever his daughter wanted.

"I'm honoured." David swallowed any bitterness that rose inside him when the attention and love directed at his sibling had been unknown to him for so long. Since finding Annie, he'd been blessed with that gift himself. He never doubted his love or place in her life when she told him every day how much he meant to her.

In the beginning, it had been hard for him to verbalise his feelings in the same way — not because he didn't reciprocate the sentiment, but because in doing so, he exposed his heart to her forever. He was determined to fix that today and truly make it a day to remember for them both. She deserved all of him when she'd given him back his life, his family and his compassion. Best of all, she'd given him her love. It was all he'd ever needed.

Emma bounced into the room trailing Annie in by the hand. "We've decided. Presents first, lunch, a walk, charades and maybe some TV."

"*You've* decided," Annie laughed, and came to sit beside David. He put his arm around her and immediately relaxed back into his seat. She was his happy place.

"Details, details." The subtle but crucial difference in their stories was dismissed with a wave of Emma's hand as she took her place by the tree.

"This one is from your dad and me. The rest are from Father Christmas." His mother directed her towards the largest pile of gifts spilling halfway across the room. It wasn't clear if Emma still believed in the magic of the season or that her presents had been delivered by a fat guy in a red suit via his reindeer-powered sleigh. She still ripped off the wrapping paper with the same glee as David had longed to do on Christmas morning as a child.

"I love it. That's cool. I really wanted this." There was so much for Emma to open that she barely had a chance to glance at each item before she tossed it onto a pile and ripped open the next. There was no doubt she was spoiled, but this was one day of the year every child deserved to be indulged a little. He didn't begrudge her the same excitement as all the other eager youngsters up and down the country This was what a normal family Christmas was supposed to be.

"Aww, that's so cute."

"Have you seen this?"

Annie and his mum were picking up the casualties of Emma's over-exuberant unwrapping and seeming to have as much fun investigating her gifts as she was. He couldn't help but smile to see Annie enjoying herself. She deserved it. It was such a contrast to her attitude towards the season the first time they'd met, and just made her all the more adorable in his eyes.

"Oh, this one is from David and Annie." Emma stopped her ripping frenzy long enough to bring the gift over and curl up on the couch beside him.

She took her time opening this one, careful not to rip the cute reindeer paper Annie had chosen as she peeled off the tape. Hopefully, this one meant something special to her, the same way the handmade stockings last year had touched his heart.

As she unfurled the white furry fabric, the black jewellery box containing his gift fell out onto the sofa.

"It's a unicorn onesie. See?" Annie showed her the hood with the rainbow-coloured horn that completed the ensemble.

"That's so cool." Emma's grin matched Annie's. She had definitely met a kindred spirit who was willing to indulge her continuing unicorn obsession and mad fashion sense.

"I'm so glad you like it. I didn't know if you would wear one." She'd agonised over the decision for days before she'd gone back and bought it. David had never had such doubts when they were both as dorky and loveable as each other.

"She bought me a gingerbread man one," he confided, although only he and Annie were in on the joke. It matched the one she'd worn when they'd first met. They'd worn them last night, watching her favourite Christmas movies, like a normal couple and not two lonely souls who'd simply been thrown together in a weird twist of fate.

"They're very comfy, aren't they, David?" Annie perched on the arm of his chair seeking his endorsement, though it wasn't needed.

"Very." When Emma was pre-occupied showing off her present to their parents, he leaned in to whisper to Annie. "Although, if I recall, I wasn't wearing it for very long."

She blushed furiously as she elbowed him in the ribs. "David!"

"What? You weren't complaining last night...or this morning." He nuzzled into her neck, the erotic memories of stripping off those onesies and what they'd done next enough for him to want to forego the rest of the visit in favour of a repeat.

She shivered under his touch and gave a little giggle, only fuelling his desire. "Not here. Later. At home."

He liked the sound of that for more than the obvious reason. They had made a home together, and that was more important to him than any business success or materialistic possession. It was priceless having someone to come home to at the end of the day, someone unashamed of showing how much she loved him and who made him feel loved every day.

With the promise of picking up where they'd left off later, and Emma coming back to join him, David stopped snuggling into Annie and put some space between them.

"David picked this one for you." Annie handed her the black box that had fallen out of the wrapping.

Emma's eyes lit up as she opened the jewellery case and traced her finger over the silver 'Sister' necklace he'd chosen for her. Without a word, she flung her arms around his neck. The room was suddenly devoid of all the earlier noise and chatter, and as he looked at the other faces around him, he could see they were all watching with tears in their eyes. The significance of the moment, or the gesture, hadn't gone unnoticed by anyone. He was accepting Emma and his family back into his life.

"Are there presents for anyone else under there, or are they all for Emma?" David covered his own emotions with a joke, lifting the atmosphere and taking the focus away from him again.

"There are presents for you and Annie too." Emma released her hold on him, taking this as her cue to play Christmas elf and pass out the gifts.

It was stupid at his age, but as she handed him the small, wrapped box, his heart fluttered with the anticipation of opening it. Although it didn't matter to him what was inside, it was the thought that counted. That feeling that he was part of a family again and someone had taken the trouble to get him a gift was all he needed.

"That one's from us, son." His father shifted forward in his seat, watching him intently and taking more interest in this exchange than he had throughout Emma's stockpiling event.

"There's one for you too, Annie, from us." It was his mother who slid the larger box, decorated with gold bows and red, coiled ribbon across the floor.

"You really shouldn't have," she protested, as she tore into the perfectly wrapped gift with gusto, showing she was just as excited as David and Emma.

He cracked open the leather box he'd uncovered to find a gent's wristwatch nestled inside. It was expensive and fashionable, but it was the inscription he saw when he slid it over his hand that made him really appreciate it.

To our beloved son,
Love, Mum and Dad xx

"Thanks." He could barely speak past the ball suddenly lodged in his throat, so he got up, kissed his mother and gave his old man a half-hug, half-slap on the back to show his gratitude. This was the kind of Christmas he should've had every year.

"Oh, my goodness! Thank you. Look, David. It's a new sewing machine." Thankfully, Annie's excitement soon took over from his sentimentality, showing off her pastel-pink hunk of plastic and metal as though it were made of solid gold.

"We thought it might be useful for your course. I've never used one myself. I hope it's the right one."

"It's perfect, Melanie, and will be so much easier to use than that old one I have at home."

"Good. I'm in awe of your sewing skills. I wish I could do something practical like that."

"I could teach you a few basics if you want?"

"I'd love that, Annie."

As his mother and girlfriend bonded, David opened the parcel from Emma labelled for him and Annie. Inside was a photograph of the three of them laughing on a day out at the beach. She'd made the frame herself, decorating the mount with shells and bits of blue and green sea glass they'd collected along the shore. The presents had all been surprisingly thoughtful and worth more to him and Annie than any price paid.

His parents were similarly grateful for the token gifts he'd brought for them — a silver charm bracelet for his mother complete with 'Mum' charm, and monogrammed cufflinks for his dad.

"What about your present for Annie? You said she got you a gingerbread man onesie, so what did you get her?" It was Emma who upset the party mood and had everyone staring at him with high expectations.

"We opened our presents last night, too excited to wait until this morning. Now, do you want me to give you a hand to clear away all this rubbish, Melanie?" Annie set to work collecting the discarded paper, not meeting David's eye. Although she'd never say it, he could see she was disappointed in the offerings she'd received in return. They'd agreed not to spend a fortune buying each other needless things, so he'd bought her inexpensive items he thought she'd appreciate.

At the time she'd been thrilled to receive a DVD copy of *It's A Wonderful Life*, guinea-pig-shaped slippers and a 'Bedford Falls' mug to put her hot chocolate and marshmallows in. Perhaps compared to today's gifts, they'd fallen short of her expectations. What she didn't know was that he had something special for her, if only he could find the right time to give it to her and could be sure it would be welcome.

* * * *

The lunch spread over the table was a feast capable of feeding way more than four adults and one young girl. Turkey, ham, stuffing, colourful dishes of mixed veg and three types of potatoes. It was an impressive display of food, yet Annie knew it wasn't about showing off. It was an attempt to make this the perfect day for the family.

The sight of the traditional fare, the sounds of the chatter around the table and the delicious smells reminded her of past Christmases – long ago, when she'd had both parents and had taken this for granted, something she knew neither she nor David would do again.

It wasn't within their power to travel back in time and alter history. At least, she didn't think it was. Last year's paranormal adventures were a one-off, as far as she was aware. No, the best they could do was make the most of the present and plan for the future. Some day, she hoped they'd be able to do this with their own family. Yet he hadn't mentioned any desire to have children of his own or even if he saw her in his future at all.

"Help yourself," Melanie encouraged every five minutes, even though Annie was sure she'd burst if she ate any more.

She smiled across the table at David as he pulled a cracker with Emma. Of course, he let her win and didn't complain when she perched a silver paper crown on his head. He would make a good dad, she mused, knowing not to repeat his parents' mistakes, and he'd make the most of every second he had with family.

"Who hides in a bakery at Christmas?" Emma unfolded the joke that spilled out of the cracker, along with a set of mini screwdrivers.

"I don't know, Em… Who hides in a bakery at Christmas?" David dutifully played along with the joke whilst swapping the pink plastic ring he'd won for her screwdrivers.

"A mince spy!"

They all groaned, except for Emma, who laughed as though it was the funniest thing she'd ever heard.

"Why was the turkey allowed in the band?"

"Emma, no more, thank you. Eat your food." Nicholas tapped her plate with his knife, trying to end the cheesy comedy routine…without success.

"Because he was the only one with drumsticks. What do you call a snowman —"

"No more." Her giggling was finally stifled as David lifted a turkey leg from the platter and shoved it into her mouth.

"Children, behave." As adult and child were scolded by their mother, albeit with a smile, Annie couldn't help but wonder what it would have been like to have had a brother or sister. At least David and Emma were going to find out now.

That family she kept picturing in her head was growing. She'd have two children at least, no more lonely childhoods or taking sole responsibility for sick parents. She'd make sure her offspring had each other, no matter what else happened in their lives.

"Is it time for games yet?" Emma scraped the pile of food left on her plate to one side and set down her cutlery. There was so much left on the table that Annie couldn't help but feel the crushing weight of guilt at the waste, but if she ate any more, she'd not only burst at the seams, but she'd also be making a pig of herself. David, who seemed to relish everything life had to offer since his time spent in limbo, had practically licked his plate clean and gone back for seconds.

"There's still dessert to come."

"Can we give it a while before the next course, Mum? While we're at it, can we wrap up these leftovers and take them to Fletchers later? We're volunteering at a food kitchen for the homeless tonight." Before his mother even agreed, David was re-covering the half-full dishes and setting them to one side.

Annie was glad his conscience was in tune with hers, proving she'd been right the previous year in trusting her instincts and believing he was a changed man. The David Reece who'd turned up in her flat, wearing a tux and treating her like a servant, wouldn't have thought twice about throwing all this food in the bin.

"Of course. That's such a lovely thing to do, isn't it, Nicholas?"

"Very noble, son. Now, shall we retire to the lounge so I can stretch out?" After acknowledging his son's altruism, David's father led the exodus from the dining room, patting his full stomach.

"What about the dishes?" Although there was nothing more Annie wanted to do in that moment than open the top button on her trousers and slob out on the couch as she usually did on Christmas Day, it didn't seem fair to walk away from the detritus from their meal.

"Oh, don't worry about that. I'll sort it later."

"Annie's right, Mum. You've done all the hard work today. Go and put your feet up for a while. We've got this."

"But...you're guests." She kept up the protest until David fixed her with a steely stare. "Okay, son. Thanks."

It was a subtle but important stand for him to make and Annie understood it as well as Melanie. He didn't want to be seen as a visitor or anything other than family in this house anymore.

They let the others go ahead, then she and David began clearing the table, carrying dirty dishes out into the kitchen.

"Is there something wrong, Annie?" As soon as they were alone, David took the pile of stacked plates from her hands and set them down on the worktop.

She wound her arms around his neck, thankful for some alone time with him. Goodness knew why they were wasting it talking. "No. Why?"

He took a step back and stilled her hands with his. It wasn't the passionate encounter she'd imagined he'd been orchestrating by volunteering for clean-up duty. "It's just... I don't know... Were you disappointed with the gifts I got you?"

"Of course not. I loved them." She kissed him full on the lips, hoping to distract him so he'd stop scrutinising her with that soul-searching, brown-eyed gaze, afraid he might see that she wasn't being one hundred percent truthful.

The previous year, Christmas together had been a rushed affair on the back of everything that had happened. Only the night before he'd been celebrating an engagement to Flame—albeit a fake and short-lived one. Presents hadn't seemed necessary then, when they'd just discovered each other and the love that had kept them in bed throughout most of the festive period.

This year, though, she'd hoped for something special. It didn't have to be expensive. Though she knew he'd chosen the gifts specially for her, she had hoped for something more—a commitment of some sort beyond sharing his bed.

* * * *

David wasn't stupid. He could see there was something wrong between them. She'd hardly spoken to him since they'd opened the presents his family had given them, and she hadn't been able to make eye contact when she'd told him everything was fine. Yet here she was laughing and joking around with his sister again. The problem was clearly with him.

"Okay. It's a film." Charades was his idea of hell and clearly his father's, when he'd resorted to feigning sleep to get out of playing.

"And a book," Emma shouted, interpreting Annie's expert mime.

"Umm." She stood with her hands on her hips seemingly trying to figure out where to go next before checking the scrap piece of paper she'd picked from Emma's selection. It wasn't in his best interests to suggest his sister was cheating when she knew all the answers, lest he and his mother were the only ones left playing.

"Okay. Right."

"Hey! No talking allowed."

She stuck out her tongue at him then launched into her animated description of Emma's chosen subject.

"A cat."

"Sounds like cat? Bat? Rat?"

He was laughing so hard at her antics as she rushed around like a mad thing, that he thought he might pass out. Since Emma's favourite films were limited to cartoons, and ones they'd been forced to watch repeatedly when she stayed over, he'd guessed the answer straightaway. He'd been having too much fun to bring it to a premature end. By the time his mother shouted the answer with such glee that anyone would have thought she'd answered a question on *University Challenge*, Annie was exhausted.

"You did that for badness, didn't you?" She swatted his knee when she collapsed beside him.

"Me? Never," he protested, but couldn't stop the grin spreading across his face.

"Hmm-m." Annie eyed him with suspicion, but once he kissed her in apology, she stopped pretending she was mad at him.

God, I love this woman. Whatever was wrong between them, whatever had happened in the past—or they'd yet to face in the future—he wanted her to know that beyond doubt. There was never going to be a perfect moment and he didn't want to wait forever to tell her. He was running out of time.

"It's your turn, David." Emma handed over his mother's crystal bowl containing the scraps of paper she'd torn up after dinner.

"Do I have to?"

"Yes."

"David, David, David…" Annie started the chanting until they all joined in, including his suddenly lively father, leaving him no option but to pick out a piece of paper and take centre stage.

"Right." He coughed, gearing up to do this.

"No talking," Annie reminded him, getting some of her own back for the earlier humiliation she'd been put through.

This was going to be a challenge.

"Four words…first word…"

He tugged on his ear.

"Sounds like…" they chorused.

He mimed stabbing someone with a pretend knife, much to his mother's apparent horror.

"That's a bit gruesome, David. Do you have to?"

"*Psycho.*"

"Dagger."

The girls were laughing as they shouted at him and he knew he'd be here all day if he didn't get the others to join in guessing. He dropped to the ground with his tongue hanging out, faking his own death.

"Sleeping."

"Heart attack."

"Really bad acting."

He lifted his head up briefly to glare at Annie then repeated the whole scene again.

"Killing. Kill. Sounds like kill?" He could have kissed his father, but instead clapped his hands and confirmed the correct guess. Sweat was beading on his skin now that all eyes were on him and he was in danger of making a real fool of himself.

They seemed to go through the whole alphabet before Emma shouted, "Will."

He pointed at Annie.

"Annie."

"Me?"

"You?"

He clapped again.

"Will you…" Annie repeated the correct answers.

David took a deep breath, pulled the small box he'd been carrying around all day in his trouser pocket and dropped onto one knee. "Marry me?"

Silence descended over the room, apart from the sound of his heart pounding in his ears. He was contemplating repeating the question in case she hadn't realised he was proposing, then Emma squealed and a smile formed on Annie's lips. His mother gasped and covered her mouth with her hand.

"Yes! Yes, I'll marry you." Annie launched herself at him in a hug, almost knocking the ring out of his hand. She was kissing him, not caring who saw. "I didn't think you wanted to make that sort of commitment again."

"So that's what's been bothering you?" He slid the ring onto her finger, the princess-cut diamond bringing as much sparkle into the room as Annie did. "I was afraid I'd waited too long to ask you."

It hadn't been his plan to do this in front of an audience, but in that moment, watching her messing around, he'd never loved her more.

"I thought, that after Linda… You know… Marriage was off the cards."

"I never loved her as much as I love you, Annie Marlowe. Do you hear that? I love her!" he yelled up at the sky.

Only Annie would understand the significance of his outburst, his family looking at him as though he'd lost his mind.

"It's just so we're not forced to go through the whole wandering spirit bollocks again," he whispered into her ear.

"I got it. We found each other, discovered love and we became part of a family again. I think we can call that mission accomplished."

As his family swamped them in hugs and congratulations, he knew that Annie, Clarence and George Bailey were right. His really was a wonderful life.

Want to see more like this?
Here's a taster for you to enjoy!

Love Repaired
Deana Birch

Excerpt

I parked the loaner SUV in line next to the other shiny overpriced automobiles, did a final check for personal belongings in the seat next to me — no need to learn the same lesson twice, my cell phone had spent the day in my car — and headed into the office. With the sun set, the cool evening air hit my cheeks and I perked up as I walked. My Cayenne sat in front of the large metal garage doors, a sparkle reflecting its recent wash. At least luxury came with attention to detail.

When I reached the glass door, I tugged it toward me only to find it locked. *Jesus.* I'd even failed at picking up my car. I stood on my tiptoes and rapped my knuckles against the glass. On the other side, the room was dark and the half-circular reception desk was abandoned, a black office chair pushed into its place. But from the hall behind it, a light peeked out — my ray of hope.

I knocked again and pressed my lips together while readjusting my shoulder bag. I shifted my body weight from side to side and banged louder.

Florescent beams flooded the showroom and I blinked. My skin flushed, and my mouth went dry. A legal aide at the firm had once said something about man candy, but I thought that was like a unicorn—not real, a legend in a forest I would never visit. But Man Candy had a warm smile, combed-back dirty blond hair and a build that screamed heaven through a tight, black, untucked work shirt. The last few buttons were open and matching pants hung low on his waist. He was also headed right toward me, tapping a wrench in his hand.

With dimples in his smile, he slipped the tool into his back pocket and unlocked the door. His sea-blue eyes must have been designed for skinny dipping.

"Mrs. Benton, I presume." The low, scratchy voice matched the light stubble on his cheeks. His dimples deepened, and the warm showroom air hit my already-heated body.

"Ms." I couldn't resist the urge to brush against him, and as I did, the perfect blend of motor oil and earthy spice came with me.

Testosterone, how I've missed thee.

I walked over to reception and placed the key fob on the desk.

He followed and squinted down at the neat paper piles next to the flat computer screen and keyboard. He picked up my keys from the tail of the stuffed squirrel that held them and dangled it like a time piece.

"Nice keychain." After a quick arch of his eyebrow, the damn dimples reappeared with his tight-lipped smile.

"Thanks"—I glanced at his chest—"Ben." I took the stuffed animal from his grease-stained hands and slid the other key toward him.

"Did you fill it up?" he asked.

"Uh…no." Add one more failure to my day.

Ben shook his head and grabbed the fob before popping it into a drawer. "No one ever fills it up. You know it costs double, right?" He peered up with one eye closed.

"Well, it was either fill it up or make you wait longer."

"Either way, it's my time. I'll have to do it Monday." He rubbed his face with both hands and a tattoo poked out from the tight sleeve around his bicep. His very full bicep.

I cringed and lifted a shoulder. "Sorry. Anyway, I only drove it to my office and back."

Ben walked out from behind the desk and over to the door. Holding it open for me again, he motioned for me to leave.

I'm too young to suffer hot flashes, right? And I was not dreaming of ways to sabotage my brakes or engine. That would be silly—and a further inconvenience that my schedule would not allow.

"You had a failed fuel pump. It's a pretty common problem. That was what was causing the stalling."

Note to self— Get another failed fuel pump.

When we stood in front of my car, he pulled up on the handle, swung the door open, and I froze. A big white pastry box sat on the passenger seat.

"Fuck me."

"Pardon?" he asked with an airy chuckle.

I brought my hands to my face and pulled them down slowly, probably ruining the effects of the anti-aging cream I'd put on that morning. "Fuck. Fuck. Fuck."

"Are you okay?" Ben leaned in closer.

"I forgot the fucking cupcakes. Fuck me. Fuck." I let my bag fall off my shoulder and dragged my feet over to the steel garage. My back met the cool wall and I slid down to the rough concrete. I stomped my sensible beige heel before slumping into a ball and whimpering into my hands. My entire day, week, month… They had all been colossal fails.

The motor oil and musk were back, now touching my wrist and seated on the ground next to me.

"Shitty day?" He draped his defined forearms over his knees with his fingers interlaced.

"I wish I could say it was the shittiest, but it just seems to be par for the course. *Fuck*." I stomped again.

"You have quite the potty mouth for a lady."

"Did you just call me a lady? Oh my God, now I'm really going to cry." Forgetting Shae's cupcakes was the cherry on top of my botched-Mom sundae. But being one step away from a 'ma'am' was the rainbow sprinkles. Asshole-expensive face cream… It obviously wasn't working. And I wasn't even forty.

"You wanna talk about it? I'm a pretty good listener."

If that were true, then Man Candy truly was a unicorn and I was in an enchanted forest. But the words flew out before I could stop them.

"My client lied to me and made me look like a fool in a deposition. I forgot my phone in the car this morning, which means my older daughter has probably called it three hundred times. And because I was behind closed doors with said lying client, I couldn't call her.

"It was my little one's last day at dance camp and I was supposed to bring the cupcakes. Which, as you can see, I did not do. Oh, and their father is in prison for vehicular manslaughter. Sorry you asked?"

He frowned and shook his head. "Where are they now? Your girls?"

"My sister takes care of them so I can keep working."
I wrapped the hem of my skirt around my legs.

"Who takes care of you?" The smile and dimples were gone, but the warmth stayed in his eyes.

"Me, I guess." I shrugged and tried to recall any moment my ex, Pete, had ever really taken care of me, and I drew a blank.

He narrowed his blue eyes. "Is that enough?"

The beautiful stranger next to me had gotten as far as my walls would let him. Although, I had to admit, someone being concerned about me might have made a tiny crack.

"That and the half-bottle of Chardonnay waiting in the door of my fridge."

"That's depressing," he said, getting up. He offered me his strong, rough hand and I clasped it. With a gentle yank, I was on my feet. "You ready for me to add insult to injury then?" He wet his lips and tilted his head.

"Oh, God. I don't even care about the bill. Just tell them to send it to me." I smoothed the front of my skirt and dusted off my rear.

"It's not that." Ben cleared his throat.

I scanned my car for a scratch or dent.

He continued, "I'm really sorry, but I ate one of the cupcakes."

I darted my eyes back to him and he hunched as if waiting to be smacked.

"You eat cupcakes?" I leaned back a little. Whatever moment sugar had spent on his lips, it was not spending a lifetime on his hips. Bastard.

"It's my cheat day. And those damn things were next to me in the car all day. Staring at me. Taunting me. Like, *'Ben, you know you want me.'*" He wiggled his fingers. "Then you were late, and, well…I made some kind of weird justification that I could have one. I'm really sorry."

"You ate one of my daughter's pink frosted cupcakes?" I planted my hands on my hips.

Ben nodded with a clenched jaw.

"You're a fucking unicorn." I picked up my bag, tossed it in the back and climbed into the car.

With the seat belt fastened, I reached for the door, but he held on to it stopping me from closing.

He blinked hard. "Did you and your potty mouth just call me a unicorn?"

"We did." I smiled at the mythical man candy creature, shut the door and drove out of the enchanted forest.

Home of Erotic Romance

Sign up for our newsletter and find out about all our romance book releases, eBook sales and promotions, sneak peeks and FREE romance books!

About the Author

Karin lives in Northern Ireland with her husband, two sons and mad dogs. When she's not writing she can be found reading, or thinking about writing.

Excels in procrastination and tea-drinking. Not so hot at housework or being tidy.

Loves chocolate, romance and Christmas. Where possible she will fit them all into a story.

Karin loves to hear from readers. You can find her contact information, website details and author profile page at https://www.totallybound.com